I0599032

PRAISE FOR *GODDESS CHOSEN*

"Hartlove fashions a riveting blend of history, religion, and horror in this briskly paced series opener. The author balances his ferocious imagination with historical passion. A masterful historical fantasy that informs as well as enthralls."

Kirkus Reviews

"Jay Hartlove has fused several genres in a driving narrative sparkling with historical exotica. I recommend you buy this crazy novel."

John Shirley, author of *Bleak History* and winner of the Bram Stoker Award

PRAISE FOR *GODDESS DAUGHTER*

Hartlove delivers on the tension in *Goddess Daughter*. Fans of his first novel will be pleased to find that the narrative runs through a rampage of deceit, double-crossing and the darker side of human motivation all in the same fashion as *Goddess Chosen*.

J. Malcolm Stewart, author of *The Eyes of the Stars*

"Writing which in its depth invokes past masters like Crichton, Benchley, and Straub."

Critics Studio Magazine

"Hartlove is a master of spellbinding suspense, mystical mayhem, and spiritual surrender."

Library at The End of The Universe

GODDESS RISING

*Book Three
of the
"Goddess Rising"
Series*

JAY HARTLOVE

Cover design copyright © 2020 by Niki Lenhart
nikilen-designs.com

Author photo copyright © S. N. Jacobson

Published by Paper Angel Press
paperangelpress.com

ISBN 978-1-949139-68-6 (Trade Paperback)

FIRST EDITION

10 9 8 7 6 5 4 3 2 1

DEDICATION

To Doselle and Janine Young,
I could not ask for closer friends and heartier support,
ever since this crazy story came to me 35 years ago.
This is fun, right? Because fun is important.

PROLOGUE

"WHAT KIND OF TREACHERY IS THIS?"

Osiris' impossibly low voice echoed through the endless maze of caverns. The eight-foot-tall Egyptian god regarded the leather water bag he held, then turned his solid black eyes with greater distain down at his captive, and only companion, the Hebrew archdemon Sammael.

"I cannot make life from nothing; that's your talent." The bearded man in studded black leather armor and white linen robes waved his hand dismissively. "That water is authentic. Make of it what you will."

Osiris sipped the water again. "It is from a living river. Show me this wall, Deceiver."

"This way," Sammael said as he started off. "You know, after nearly nine years down here with you, I'd like to set the record straight about that whole 'Deceiver' label."

The ebony-skinned god's beaded jewelry and skirts swayed as he ambled in his gold sandals to let the shorter man lead the way. "The demon who tricked Eve into getting herself and Adam thrown out of Yahweh's Paradise, not a liar? You are commonly called the Prince of Liars."

"That's just the problem. I did not lie to Eve. I told her exactly what would happen, and it did. I did not lie to Ramses when I told him Moses had no more magic than what was in the Egyptian temple. I did not lie to Jesus when I told him he could have worldly power. I actually don't lie."

"You deceive. Same thing"

"I inform people of their real choices. I open their eyes to the possibilities. God gave mankind free will. I make sure man makes informed decisions."

"Fine, not a liar. Trickster. Corruptor. Tempter. Leader away from Good. Those names more to your liking?"

The demon nodded. "Those will do. We're here."

"I don't see anything."

Sammael pointed to a space between two slabs of rock in the wall. "The water is trickling down that gap." He then pointed up. "If you trace it, it's coming from that crack in the ceiling. I think we are beneath your Underworld Nile."

Osiris put his finger in the crack and withdrew a drop. "There is life in this water. How are you doing this?"

"I told you. I can't create life. That's you."

"If I pull these stones down, and the river is up there, it will flood these caverns, which will drain the river."

"You'll have some repairs to make. Just don't pull down the whole ceiling," Sammael suggested.

"You will remain my prisoner."

"Breaking open that wall will not break this bracelet," he said, holding up his right wrist to show the silver hieroglyph-etched cuff that Silas Alverado created to hold him in this prison.

The towering god regarded the bracelet, then wordlessly turned around and pointed at the walls that formed the entrance to the cavern alcove. He flung lightning from his fingers and the rocks exploded. Sammael dove for cover behind a rock outcropping. The rubble tumbled down and partially blocked the way out. The sound was deafening, and Sammael held his hands over his ears. Osiris smirked at the demon's retreat. He struck again, and much larger boulders fell into place. One last blast sealed the room. Then he turned to the source of the water far up the wall. Another bolt of lightning loosened the stones, and the crack in the ceiling widened. Water pushed the rocks open and poured down.

Osiris watched the water fill the chamber, making sure his seal held. The water's steady rise proved its containment. The two treaded water as it carried them up to the ceiling. Once the chamber was full, the water stopped rushing in through the hole, and the two swam out.

When they broke the surface, they were indeed on the Underworld Nile. Osiris' jet-black face lit up with joy.

Sammael swam for shore.

As the god triumphantly walked up onto the beach, throngs of souls poured in from the fields to witness the return of their long-lost lord. Osiris reveled in the colors and sounds and smells of life all around him. As they bowed down before him, he looked up to see Sammael wander into the crowd and disappear.

I'll catch up with him later, the god told himself.

Sammael felt the bracelet and, for the first time, it was not freezing cold.

Had his gambit worked? Was the bracelet linked to Osiris, or the cavern Silas had chosen?

He held it with his left hand and it indeed warmed up. He smiled. He looked back toward Osiris and could no longer see the god for the distance and the crowd.

He transformed himself into a crow. The bracelet shrank and moved to his right leg. It wasn't letting go. He took flight and turned toward where he knew, from previous visits, began the path out.

1

ALEC DOOGAN SWITCHED OFF HIS FLASHLIGHT and turned on his night-vision goggles. After two hours searching and cataloging the tile-faced crypts beneath Notre Dame church in Bordeaux, France, he finally found the family crest he sought. What he was really looking for he could not see with the unaided eye. He slipped the flashlight into his shoulder slung satchel and withdrew a spray bottle and a taser.

He sprayed the carved stone crest with a compound that smelled strongly of flowers and applied the modified low-amperage, high-voltage oscillating current. His specially tuned goggles picked up trace discharges, but nowhere near the reaction he wanted. He shrugged his red eyebrows behind his goggles and let out a disappointed breath. He checked the flagstone floor to be sure it was dry and not creating any conductivity problems. He was glad for the dryness for more than one reason. He had explored wet tombs where the smell of decay was unbearable.

He stepped back and realized the tiles, bricks, and stone blocks of this tomb did not form a typical bone box. The contours were right, but the seams were all wrong. What should have been the burial lid was a set of three interlocking panels, with no clear way to open them. He set the bottle and taser down and took out a stethoscope and a small rock hammer. He tapped and listened and indeed the chamber within was far too small.

He started spraying and testing the seams, hoping to pick up any leaking energies. A faint flare caught his eye and lead him to a panel below the false lid. He squatted his tall, solid frame down and continued testing. One seam in particular glowed promisingly. He rummaged through his bag and pulled out a wide steel chisel. Tapping with the hammer, he gently pried out an edge of the facing tile. He sprayed it and shocked it again, and this time it flared with a bright green glow. He pulled the tile away, reached into the space behind, and found overlapping — no, locking stone edges. A latch? He wedged the chisel in between and leaned his considerable weight into the joint, twisting it apart. The false lid above popped open.

Alec lifted his goggles onto his freckled forehead and peered under the lid with his flashlight. He lifted it gently and saw something less than a foot long wrapped in cloth. He fished it out. It was heavy and hard. He cradled his flashlight in the crook of his neck, a practiced move, and unpeeled the cloth to reveal a dagger.

The dry, dusty air suddenly smelled of ozone. He pulled his goggles off and checked them for a short, but found none. Then he recognized the stinging, putrid smell for what it really was. He slipped his goggles back on, switching them on, and grabbed his spray bottle. He set the dagger on the floor, sprayed it and shocked it. The green flare was almost blinding.

He picked it up and turned it around until he found a hallmark stamp. This wasn't a dagger; it was a carving knife from a service set. Moreover, the hallmark wasn't a smith's mark, but a family monogram.

Suddenly, he felt a pressure on his wrist, squeezing it and pushing the blade towards his chest. He was easily strong enough to resist it, but he was driven to find its source. He grabbed the bottle and sprayed all around the air that should contain his assailant. He dropped the bottle and snatched up the taser, raking its charge through the cloud of mist.

The ghostly image of a man in sixteenth-century attire looked shocked at being revealed. The ghost grabbed Alec's arm with both hands and pushed harder.

Alec fleetingly realized he was several hundred feet down twisting, soundproof tunnels, and no one was actually standing by waiting for him at the entrance to the catacombs.

He moved the taser up into the ghost's face to get a better look. He did not recognize the man. The ghost snarled menacingly. Alec tripped the goggles camera.

Just as Alec started to worry how long this struggle would last, the arm of another ghost slipped out of the darkness, into the glowing cloud, and around the attacking ghost's neck. Alec's attacker looked even more surprised than Alec. More surprisingly, the first ghost then started pulling Alec's wrist, trying to stab the second ghost with the knife.

Alec looked down and, in the glow, he saw blood on the blade. He got a glimpse of the new ghost and knew what he must do. He started to let the first ghost control his arm, feigning a lunge at the new ghost. Just as he felt his assailant take the bait, he slashed down across his attacker's chest. The blade ripped through his ghostly flesh, tearing it open and spilling forth a brilliantly glowing green lava flow. The ghost let go of Alec's arm and clutched at his wound as he fell to the floor and dissipated.

Alec looked up at the second ghost, who was dressed in a white cassock and miter hat. Alec noticed an unmistakable knife wound in his chest. The ghost bowed in thanks, crossed himself, raised his hand to Alec in blessing, and faded away.

Alec found the ornate brass gate back into the church sanctuary locked. "*Allo! S'cuse moi! Monsignor* Raban?"

The thin bald priest in his long, straight black robes looked taller than Alec until he stepped up to the gate. At six-two, Alec still had an inch on him, and sixty pounds. "Ah, *Monsieur* Doogan. Did you have any luck?" he unlocked the gate and swung it open.

Alec brushed the dust from his short curly red hair as he stepped out. "Indeed, I did. Better than I hoped for. I have the murder weapon used to kill Abbot Jacque Sullielle." He pulled the cloth package from his bag and unwrapped the knife. "Even better, it is from a carving set that belonged to a family whose name started with the letter H." He showed the stamp to the priest. I found it in what was supposed to be the tomb of Hubert Niccioli. It is a false tomb used as a hiding place for this murder weapon."

Monsignor Raban frowned and shook his head. "This is truly fascinating, but what does it all mean?"

"It means my theory is right: Anna Niccioli, Hubert's wife, was having an affair with Francois Hurriner, the Mayor of Bordeaux. This affair is well documented. Her husband Hubert was a pillar of the community, and it was expected he would be buried in the church crypts. Only when he died shortly after the Abbot was murdered, she didn't bury her husband here. She probably had him buried at their estate outside of town. Instead, she used his tomb as an untouchable hiding place for this piece of insurance. She found the murder weapon and hid it where her lover, the murderer, could never get to it. No doubt she assured her family's continued prosperity holding this evidence over the mayor for years to come."

"*Sacre bleu!* This really is the missing piece of this three hundred-year old puzzle. I must admit, when you first approached us with this tale of forbidden love and murder, I was skeptical. There is nothing showing Madame Niccioli had anything to do with the Abbot."

"That's because she kept her connection a secret, and for good reason."

"*C'est magnifique!* Bordeaux can finally close the books on this infamous crime. How can we repay you? We never finalized an arrangement."

"That's true. I felt funny agreeing to a fee when I really wasn't sure what I would find. I'll tell you what. After all the photographs have been taken, and this whole solution is documented, may I take this knife as my payment?"

"You want to keep the knife?"

"Yes. I collect odd bits of crime memorabilia. Oh, I want you to test it and record everything about it. I'm pretty sure you're going to find blood stain DNA on the blade. The Abbot's blood. Then when you're done with it …?"

"I will tell the criminal authorities this is our arrangement."

Alec rewrapped the blade and handed it him. He held out his hand and the priest shook it. "It's a deal."

2

As Desiree Macklin turned the corner off Essex Street West onto Cow's Lane, she spotted just what she needed. Any place called the Gutter Book Shop would certainly have a better map of old town Dublin than the tourist sightseeing map she had exhausted in her week here. As much as she was enjoying walking the Temple Bar district on her own, she didn't want to miss anything.

She stepped inside and unwrapped the fluffy, green knit scarf she had bundled against the chilly September evening. She pulled her shoulder-length auburn hair out of her plaid coat collar. She was taken immediately with the joyous energy of a big thriving independent bookstore, the kind she loved back in Georgetown, Virginia — until they started disappearing in the shadow of big chain stores. She could easily see herself browsing for hours through the white bookshelf-lined alcoves. A banner over the counter explained he store's name with a quote from Oscar Wilde. "We are all in the gutter, but some of us are looking at the stars."

Before she could ask about maps, she was distracted by the crowd gathered in the back of the store. A nearby poster on an easel announced, "Book Launch. Local Dublin author and researcher Alec Doogan. 'The Magic Around Us.'" She assessed the late twenties, freckled redhead smiling broadly in the author photo and thought he looked a bit pudgy for her taste. She wondered if such a young man would have anything new to say on her favorite subject — a subject she had spent the last four years researching exhaustively.

The presentation was already underway, and all the seats were taken, so Desiree stood off to the side and leaned against a bookshelf.

The author, seated behind a table, was holding up a knife. "This is the blade I recovered from the false tomb. The family initials were enough to solve the crime. Police can believe in hard evidence like murder weapons. What I did not share with the priests or the police is this." He clicked on a laptop and a slide projected onto the screen behind him. The crowd gasped at the sight of a green, glowing, ghost-like face scowling past what looked like a hand holding an electric razor. "I did not recognize him at the time, but this is Francois Hurriner, the Mayor of Bordeaux, the lover of Madame Niccioli, and the murderer of Abbot Jacque Sullielle. That device I am holding is a modified taser. It emits a very low wattage, but high voltage, current. It took me years of trial and error to figure out the oscillation frequency that reacts best with the condenser fluid.

"I appreciate how paranormal research is generally doubted so much that actual facts uncovered using these techniques are doubted as well. If I had told the police I had grappled with Monsieur Hurriner and took his picture, they would not have believed anything else I said, they would have discounted the knife itself, and the murder would remain officially unsolved. On the other hand, I know you want to hear about the ghostbuster stuff.

"The Niccioli story is not in the book. I was in Bordeaux three months ago and the book was already in production. There are lots of other stories like it in the book. I also draw some very basic conclusions about what I have found. I try to be as scientific and skeptical as possible. I do not try to present some great cosmological theory about how spirits and magic exist in the world. I try to stick to the facts. I leave it to you, the readers, to draw your own religious implications. I don't go there. I do show there are things — factual things — that reveal a world of forces for which science has no explanations, yet.

"I am by no means the first to discover this world. People have been working with these forces since ancient times. People have been accessing these forces with rituals and ceremonies with varying degrees of success. I hope the tools I have developed can shine light on what's really going on.

"In the meantime, while I am working toward acceptance by the scientific and religious communities, I present my findings to you, even if only for entertainment. Because these really are some thrilling stories."

He paused, so Desiree raised her hand.

"Yes, you have a question?"

"Does it hurt?"

"Ah, hurt? Which?"

"Your electrical device. Your technique detects the presence of spirits and magic. Have you tested living things for these energies and compared them to the spirits?"

"Yes, absolutely. The spirit energy I have found in haunted objects is the same as the energies you find in living things."

"So does it hurt?"

"Well, I have tested it on myself, and it stings a little. It has very low current, but the high voltage goes right through skin. So it does sting a bit."

A man in the chairs raised his hand. "Is this akin to the Kirlian photos taken back in the '70s?"

"Seymon Kirlian's photographs were shown to be patterns of electrical conductivity due to moisture. Upon rigorous examination, there proved to be no evidence of life energy. By the way, he did his work in the 1930s and '40s. It was just made popular in the '70s. The electrical discharge in my technique only works because of the condenser fluid. The fluid does the actual work of finding and interacting with the spirit energy in a way that shows up in the physical world. The shock just makes that interaction visible."

Desiree glanced around the audience, and caught someone looking at her instead of Alec. The balding, middle-aged man in a grey suit and silver sunglasses looked away as soon as she spotted him, but there was no mistaking where he had been looking. She didn't think much of it. She had asked kind of an odd question.

An old woman in the front row asked, "What about graveyards?"

"As I describe in the book, I have tested quite a few graves. I am confident when I say that, barring some significant spiritual event, people really do go away when they die. I don't pretend to know where they go, but graveyards are just that, yards with graves. No ghosts, no magic.

"On the other hand, some of the haunted houses I have tested showed significant life energy activity. Why these energies are hanging around," he turned and pointed at the green ghost on the screen, "you'll have to ask them."

Desiree raised her hand again. "I have not read your book yet, so I'm sorry if you already covered this. You're talking about spirits that are already stuck here. Have you ever tested something that someone has summoned?"

Alec blinked and had no answer for a long, telling moment. "Oh yes, you mean in séances. I have tested séances, and had mixed results."

"Actually, no. I meant like Pentecostals speaking in tongues, or Voodouns mounted by *loas*."

Alec broke into a face-filling grin. "No ... I haven't. I would love to!"

The audience chuckled, some at Alec's surprise and some nervously at Desiree's question.

"I like how you think," he admitted. "Maybe we can talk after."

She smiled her crooked dimpled smile and nodded. Several of the audience were looking at her, but none more intensely than the guy in the sunglasses. She stared back at him until he looked away. *Creep.*

A shop employee stepped up alongside Alec. "Speaking of after, that's all the time we have. Let's everyone queue up here. We've got a stack of books here for Alec to sign for you. Let's have a nice round of applause for Alec Doogan."

Everyone clapped. About half the crowd left and the other half lined up. As Desiree got into line, she looked around to see whether the guy in the sunglasses had left. He was right behind her.

"I apologize for staring earlier." He spoke precisely, with no discernible accent, which sounded strange to her after spending the week getting used to the Irish accent instead of the Baltimore/DC accent she had grown up with. "I was sure I recognized you. I've always thought I never forget a face, but clearly I mistook you for someone else. I hope I did not make you uncomfortable."

"No, not at all. Thank you for clearing that up. I'm quite sure I've never met you." She considered introducing herself. In fact, he looked as if he was waiting for her to do so. She decided to keep it polite but anonymous. "So you're interested in Mr. Doogan's work?"

His glasses were only partially silvered and she could see him blink at her changing the subject. "Yes, he has some interesting theories. I look forward to reading his book."

"Me too." She turned to face front, hoping she wasn't crossing the line to rude. He seemed harmless enough. She just didn't want to talk to him.

When she got to the front of the line, she noticed the guy had left.

Doogan got up behind his table and extended his hand to her. He was taller and wider than she expected, standing six foot two and easily 250 pounds. "Alec Doogan."

She shook his rather meaty hand. "Desiree Macklin."

"Here, let me sign a book for you, and then I want to chat about your questions." He grabbed a book off the stack, signed it, then turned around and pulled up a chair behind the table for her.

She smiled coyly, batted her bright blue eyes and sat down, commenting, "That's very gallant."

"Macklin. That's a good Irish name, but you have an American accent."

"I'm here on vacation after graduation, getting in touch with my roots."

He signed another book for a customer. He straightened the stack of remaining books.

"I'm actually having more fun than I expected. I just came from the National Leprechaun Museum north of the river."

"So, let me guess. You have a degree in comparative religions?'

"Art history. I study religions on my own."

"You think I should use my detection equipment on people who are in the midst of having religious experiences?"

"Yes. I think you're missing a bet if you just look at things that have been acted upon. People bring spirit energy into the world. Catch them in the act."

He signed another book. She noticed that again he straightened the rest of the books in the stack.

"You are brave, lass. Or a born troublemaker. I have purposely avoided religious experience until I could get some solid evidence and numbers behind my technique. I'm trying to figure this stuff out without stepping on anybody's toes. I have focused on things that people already accept as weird and outside science. Even the séances I have tested did not have a religious context. Once you add in religion, people get very defensive. I agree that catching people, 'in the act', as you put it, would bridge the gap between faith and spirits. It would be a huge contribution."

"Oh, but there are lots of bridges like that. It's not just folks in religious ecstasy. It's also martial arts masters who move *chi* energy around in their bodies. There's a whole world of connections out there."

Alec smiled and frowned at her at the same time. "You're talking big, unified field stuff."

"One test at a time." She nodded in emphasis. "Keep it scientific. Don't jump to any conclusions, but think outside the box, be inclusive. Nothing should be out of bounds."

Alec signed one last book and turned in his chair to face her. "You're talking about *chi* theoretically? I mean, do you understand how these people do these things?"

"Actually, yes. I've seen a lot of it myself."

"Really? I don't mean to doubt you, but you're talking about the whole field of paranormal phenomena all over the world."

"I've had some pretty freaky things happen to me. My interest in religions isn't just a curiosity."

He laughed the kind of chuckle only big men can. "Oh, you can't drop a line like that without letting me have a chance to hear the rest of the story. Are you here alone? Can I buy you dinner in trade for some of this 'freaky' history?"

"Yes, I am travelling alone, and yes, you can buy me dinner."

3

STANDING IN THE MIDDLE OF THEIR APARTMENT LIVING ROOM, Sanantha Mauwad could feel her emotions getting the better of her. "Honestly, Simon, this wasn't supposed to be another of our non-conversations about your unsigned divorce papers."

Simon Carrera, the debonair Mexican fellow psychiatrist, her lover and companion for the last five years, met her gaze from the couch where he leaned back, casual in his confidence. He stroked his salt and pepper goatee, a gesture she used to find cute, but now only irritated her. "Then don't bring it up again."

The fifty-year old Haitian black woman stared at him in disbelief. She struggled to keep this on track, to move ahead. She felt a sweat break out over her scalp under her high-wound turban. "So that's your final word on the subject — don't bring it up?"

"Yes. I've told you, I will finalize it when I am ready."

Sanantha was speechless, dumbstruck with a rising surge of anger, disappointment, and sadness. Worst of all, she felt something she never wanted to feel again. Through all she wanted to say, past all the feelings that clambered for expression, she still felt that tiniest cracking sensation in her heart. The deep dimples of her usual easy, broad smile were slack with her disbelief. It was at that point she realized there was nothing more to say.

For years he sidestepped the question of why he had never finalized his divorce. Eventually Sanantha got him to admit that he feared such a final break would make his memories of his life with his ex-wife irrelevant.

Irrelevant. She had never expected to that word would apply to her.

She had to go. She had nowhere to go, but she had to go. She had given up her apartment on the north side of Kuala Lumpur two years before and moved in with Simon on the admittedly nicer south side, clinging to the hope that a happy complete life together would be enough to let him move ahead, to move on with her. Before she had the chance to say something more, something that would just embarrass herself, she gathered herself up straight with her turban pointing regally behind her, grabbed her purse off the coffee table and walked out.

Her forced composure got her as far as her car. She leaned her forearms on the roof of her late-model Fiat coupe and hung her head. Had he really decided she didn't matter anymore? Had her dream of a life together only been hers all along? Was there no other way to make him see what was at stake? She sniffed back the tears and shook her head. No, she had tried from every angle, given him every chance.

She looked around the apartment parking garage at all the empty cars. All their owners were home. Home. How many of these cars were waiting to carry away a broken heart? "Just you and me, babe," she said to her car as she opened the door.

She refused to believe she was out of options. She gripped the steering wheel in front of her as if there was some new direction she had yet to explore. She didn't even have friends she could talk to. She had fallen out of touch over the years with all her old friends back in D.C. She could hole up in her office for a few days until she sorted out her next steps.

No, that was defeatist thinking. She needed to bring new resources to this problem. What would she tell a patient? Find a source of comfort and strength. Go there and recharge, regain perspective, then tackle the problem fresh.

She laughed at herself, practicing self-therapy. "I spend all of my time and energy helping other people, even Simon, but I can't help myself. Oh, wait a minute, girl, not self-pity. Maybe I should take more of my own advice."

She smiled a tiny, weak smile, barely big enough to crease the edges of her eyes. She knew what she had to do. She looked up reflexively, as if eyeing the apartment above her. All her stuff was still up there. Stuff could be bought. Even if it meant facing the living nightmare of Kuala Lumpur traffic. She started the car.

•   •   •

Sanantha closed the door behind her as she stepped out onto the roof of her apartment building, a small paper bag in one hand and a wine bottle in the other. Although the bag was brightly colored with the name of a toy store, she set the bottle down and fished out a corkscrew and a clear plastic cup. She wasted no time opening the bottle and pouring herself some of the Australian Shiraz she had come to love since moving here back in '05. She glanced at the bottle and noted it didn't even have a vintage date. She shrugged and took a sip. Kind of sour, kind of flat. After the second glass she wouldn't be able to tell the difference anyway.

She wiped the tear streaks off her face before she withdrew the last of the bag's prizes, a box of children's colored chalk. She took another sip and surveyed the flat expanse of roof tar paper for a suitable space. There in front of the giant swamp cooler evaporator box should do nicely. She looked down and was pleased she had worn her skinny jeans that day. She stepped out of her three-inch heels and went to work.

She pulled out the red and white chalk. The red was rather pale, almost pink. That would actually do nicely. She lightly sketched out an enormous outline first. She thought about what she was doing and had to admit she really didn't think this would do any good. She had to try anyway. As she checked the proportions, she found herself humming a tune from her childhood. She recognized it as, "I Got Peace Like a River in My Soul", a chant she learned in Haiti, chalk drawing religious *veve* icons in the dirt peristile receiving yard at church.

21

Mwen gen pè kon yon rivyè
Mwen gen pè kon yon rivyè nan nanm mwen
Mwen gen lanmou kon yon lanmè
Mwen gen lanmou kon yon lanmè nan nanm mwen
Mwen gen jwa kon yon fontèn
Mwen gen jwa kon yon fontèn nan nanm mwen

She smiled. It had been thirty-five years since she sang that tune. She recited it a few times as she continued to draw, remembering more of the melody with each round. She had it fully recovered and sang it with abandon by the time she got down on her hands and knees and started filling in details.

She noticed she had stopped crying. She let her mind wander to the happy times she had growing up in rural Haiti, the simplicity of village life, the certainly of the *loa*'s protection. She recalled these through the innocent eyes of a child, no doubt. Still, it made her smile.

With each set of curlicue strokes, she made herself recall a happy memory of her times with Simon. Their dinners when they were dating. His taking her sailing on his boat. Him letting her redecorate his apartment. She remembered why she loved him. His wit, his warmth, his intelligence, his generosity, and his caring for her.

She remembered how her life in Washington, D.C. had been turned upside down after poor Charles Redmond's death. She shuddered despite the warm sun at the thought of that fateful battle with the demon Sammael. She tried for two years to make sense of her life after seeing what she had seen. How glad she had been to leave that all behind when Simon invited her to join him on his getaway island in the South Pacific. The last five years really had been wonderful.

Even when she got drawn into the Desiree Macklin cloning mystery — with its snakes, guns, poisons, and black magic martial arts — through all that danger Simon had solidly backed her up.

She stopped herself, sure that thinking fondly of him would just bring her back down. Yet it didn't. She felt buoyed. Maybe there was hope of getting him back.

When she had filled in all but the center of the design, she got up and stepped back. The chalk was gone down to nubbins. The design was all filled in and looked like a painting, white on pink. Eight feet wide and six feet high, the chalk heart looked like a design for a wrought iron artist to build into a gate. She knew it was stronger than any iron, that it could open a gate to the spirit realm. It would if she got the next part right.

She held up the bottle and, pleased to see she had not finished it yet, poured one last glass and set it in the middle of the design. Kneeling down at the base point, she placed her hands at the edge. "Grand *Matriesse*, Mother of Mercy, You Who Weep for the Ills of the World, Wellspring of Dreams, Great Goddess of Love, Erzulie I call upon you as one of your lifelong devoted. Please take my offering of your symbol on Earth. I have always thanked you for every blessing and lauded your name as the author of every good thing that has ever happened to me. You have been my rock and my inspiration, you who are the heart of compassion for the universe.

"Now I have put my own heart at risk. I thanked you for bringing Simon into my life. He truly has been a blessing. Now I fear I am losing him. I fear I have pushed him too hard, and he is backing away. All I want to do is love him, to be his strength, his companion. Yet he clings to his past, to his memories of happy times with a woman who does not love him anymore. I love him. I cannot get him to see how I am his future. I need your help. You who are the source of love and understanding, can you please help make him see? I know he loves me. Is it too selfish to ask that he let go of his past and love only me? Please help me."

She didn't expect any kind of sign or answer. She did have more hope after drawing the *veve* than she had expected to have. When no sign came, she smiled and nodded. Erzulie had heard her.

She looked around at the other rooftops nearby and was pleased no one was watching her. The September spring breeze and sunshine had been kind to her up here.

She checked her cell phone: 5:30PM, no messages. Simon had a meeting at six, so she could collect her things in a few minutes without him there. No doubt he would have something to say if she saw him. It wouldn't be what she needed to hear.

She got up and collected the empty bottle, the chalk, the bag, and her shoes. She was headed for the door when her phone rang.

"Hello, this is Doctor Mauwad."

"Hello, am I speaking to Sanantha Mauwad, MD?

"Yes. Who is this?"

"Ma'am," the woman's voice came through with a solid Southern accent. Sanantha guessed South Carolina. "I need to first verify that I am speaking with the right person. Did you move from Washington D.C. to Kuala Lumpur in December 2003?"

"Yes. If you don't tell me who you are, I am going to hang up."

"Oh, I wouldn't do that if I were you, ma'am. I am Special Agent Jill Bitterman of the United States Federal Bureau of Investigation. I need to ask you some questions about the death of a patient of yours — a Mister Charles Redmond, in April, 2001. Do you have a few minutes to answer my questions, ma'am?"

"Oh for pity's sake. You're dredging up Charles' death eight and half years later?"

"We have uncovered additional evidence concerning the circumstances of Mr. Redmond's death, and we need you to clarify some details." Sanantha didn't like how the woman's accent gave a lilt to the word death. "Would now be a good time for you?"

She considered the three glasses of wine and her fragile emotional state before answering. "I doubt I can add much to what I told you back in D.C. I worked with the police for weeks after the incident."

"I appreciate that, ma'am, and the Bureau thanks you for your cooperation at that time. I am hoping you can continue in that same spirit of cooperation now."

"Well, I would rather not answer your questions in a cursory, off-the-cuff way. I may have to collect my thoughts to give you any kind of detail. May I ask what new evidence you have found?'

"No, Doctor, I am not at liberty to share any evidence we have. First of all, I need to know, during the incident, did you have any interaction with the perpetrators?"

"Do you mean the gunmen who were firing at the crowd?"

"Yes. Did you have any interaction with the gunmen?"

"I was one of the crowd. I was being fired on like everyone else."

"Mr. Redmond did not die of a gunshot. He died of internal bleeding from a crushing blow."

"Yes. I explained that at the time. Charles and I were overrun by the crowd trying to escape the gunmen. There was a stampede of people and Charles was trampled."

"So are you saying that was the extent of your interaction with the gunmen?"

"Yes, I am. It sounds like you're doubting me. Should I get a lawyer?"

"You are free to retain counsel if that is your desire. Is there anything else you would like to add to your recollection of the events of that day?"

"Not off-hand. I could address your concerns a lot better if I knew what has prompted you to doubt my testimony."

"I will be calling you again with more specific questions. Is this the best phone number to reach you?"

"Yes, this is my cell number."

"Please keep it available. In the meantime, I suggest you go over the events of that day to refresh your memory."

"Okay, I can do that. Do you suspect additional foul play?"

"I cannot share any information about our investigation at this time. Thank you for your continued cooperation."

"You're welcome."

"Goodbye, Doctor."

She stood there stunned. How could they possibly know? Everyone on the plaza was hypnotized by Sammael, so no one could have seen her working with Joseph. *Merde.* Working with one demon to defeat another. More to the point, what could the FBI have dug up almost nine years later? Probably not anyone's testimony. Pictures of footprints? It rained afterwards. Her head reeled.

"*Merde!* Papa Legba, give me strength. After all this time, the police!"

4

D ESIREE SMILED, AMUSED AT HERSELF, and the dimple in her left cheek creased up making more of a smirk than she intended.

Sitting next to her, driving the 1966 Austen-Healey 3000, Alec caught the look and grinned his open broad smile. "I only met you three days ago, and already I've come to know that impish grin of yours. What are you up to?"

She continued looking out across the Irish countryside of green hills and sheep. Everywhere sheep. "I am amused at how my vacation has suddenly turned into a ghost hunt. Here I was looking for local color in the pubs of old Dublin, and now I'm taking a ride in the country with a dashing self-made Indiana Jones in a hot vintage racing green convertible. And what are we doing? We're driving into Northern Ireland to test the grave of Saint Patrick for ectoplasm. This really does go with the rest of my crazy life."

"Indiana Jones, eh?" he said, puffing himself up. "Actually, do you mind if I get serious for a moment? I've been thinking about some of the things you said the other night after my book party. I have some questions, if you don't mind."

She shifted herself in the worn black leather seat as best she could in the cramped space to face him better. Alec's broad shoulders took up more than half the width of the interior. She knew where this was going.

"To tell the truth, I wasn't sure how much of my story I wanted to share. I mean, it is rather unbelievable. I'm glad you showed me you are open-minded over dinner. So, fire away."

"Okay. You said your interest in the paranormal comes from having your own soul tampered with in a cloning experiment?"

"Yes, I wasn't me for about four months, and I may have died when my dad brought me back."

"Right, you said your dad is this big-time geneticist. If you weren't you, then who were you? Were you cloned into somebody else?"

"That's where things get weird. My genes were forced to change me into a copy of my mother."

"Your dad did that?"

"Oh lord no. It was my dad's business partner, who had been having an affair with my mom. My mom was bitten by a snake and went into an irretrievable coma. My dad's partner stole my dad's cloning formula and turned me into a clone of my mom, his lover."

"What did that do to you? Didn't that wipe out your identity?"

"That's right, I was a completely different person. My memories were offline, and I have no access to any memories that happened while I wasn't there. Sanantha Mauwad, who was my father's shrink, and then mine too, she says I'm probably much better off not remembering. It would leave me with all kinds of identity issues."

"Did this guy know the procedure was going to replace you?"

"Oh, yeah. He was crazy obsessed with my mom. He was willing to sacrifice me to get her back."

Alec looked at her slack-jawed. "That's got to be the most evil thing I've ever heard." He took a breath before continuing. "You said you might have died in the transition back. Obviously he revived you. People die for a moment during medical procedures all the time. I've done a lot of research on near-death experiences."

"Well, my brush with death was a little different. There was a whole series of awful things — some were accidental, and some were done with evil intent. There were snake bites, car crashes, kidnappings, carrier viruses, poisonings … and I won't even try to describe the whole sequence. Suffice to say, my identity was killed while the cloning virus kept my body alive. I wasn't dead for a just few minutes. When my father killed the virus to bring me back, there was no me to bring back. I had been gone for over an hour."

Alec paused and looked at her sideways. "But you're here today."

"That's where things get spiritual. I mentioned my psychiatrist, Sanantha Mauwad. Turns out, she is also a Voodou practitioner. When she saw I was gone, she called on her Voodou goddess Erzulie, who granted me mercy, and gave me a spiritual jump start. So as far as I have been able to piece it together — and this really is guesswork — I am walking around with a soul transplant from a god. I know, I know, a lot of people would like to think all our souls are from God. It would seem that I got mine a little more personally.

"Come to think of it, that's terrifically ironic," she interrupted herself. "Young Nae, the guy who wiped me out in the cloning, believed in an old Korean faith that everyone has a piece of the divine in them. That's supposed to make us strive to do better, to live up to our divinity. With him, it only justified his immorality."

Alec slowed down and pulled the car over onto the shoulder. "Let's find out about that soul of yours." Before she could say anything, he got out and opened the rear boot. He pulled out a spray bottle, his taser, and what looked like the screen of a laptop computer.

She was somewhat incredulous. "You want to do this right here and now?"

"Why not? It'll only take a minute. You said you've been wondering what really happened for the last four years." He got in, turned on the screen and set it on her lap. Then he sprayed his right hand. The cockpit of the car inside the cloth roof immediately filled with a riot of flower smells.

"Wow. That's some strong stuff."

"Hold that up and flat." He placed his hand, fingers outstretched, onto the screen, and shocked himself in the back of the hand. He flinched and covered with a grin. "See, only stings a little." He picked up his hand and there was a dark handprint with bright pointy discharges all around the outline extending about an inch away. "So that's our baseline. Normal human." He pulled out a roll of paper towels from under his seat and thoroughly wiped his hands and the screen. "Now we test you."

She shrugged and grinned. "Sure." He reset the screen. She took the spray bottle and squirted her whole hand. "How wet does it have to be?"

"Not that much. You can shake off the excess. Out the window, please. It just has to be wet enough to conduct the spark from the back around to the front."

She shook off her hand, out the window, placed it on the screen, and winced up in anticipation of the sting. The shock wasn't so bad after all.

"Let's see what we got," he said eagerly. The screen showed her handprint in dark silhouette, same as his, but the rest of the screen was a solid color with no discharge flares.

"Did it work?" she asked, looking down at it. "Should we do it again?"

He frowned at the screen for a long moment. He pushed some buttons on its side and frowned some more. "No, it worked. I just need to figure out what this means." He pushed some more buttons, the screen shifted and her handprint appeared much smaller in the center. He gasped.

"What is it?"

He turned the screen up to show her. With her handprint shrunk to a tiny outline, the screen finally showed the edge of the discharge corona, all the way out at the edge of the screen. Given the proportions, her discharge reached over two feet from the edge of her hand.

She screwed up her mouth to one side and blinked several times. "Oops."

"Whatever your friend Sanantha did to bring you back, it supercharged you. You have the life energy of six people, maybe more."

"Well, I haven't been sick a day in the last four years."

"Your theory about what happened suddenly isn't so far-fetched."

She didn't want to talk about the implications of that day. "I guess I should stay back when you're testing things. My aura is going to interfere with your readings."

He nodded. "That's true." He kept staring at the screen.

She got the impression he was staring at the screen because he really wanted to stare at her. Sitting shoulder to shoulder with someone who blows up his pet theories must be disconcerting, if not frightening. "I hope my being a soul freak doesn't mean we can't still be friends."

He snapped out of his reverie. "Of my goodness, of course not. You're still the same girl who was sitting here ten minutes ago. Sorry if I kind of went off into my own little world there. Let me put this stuff away." He got out and went around the back.

Clearly he was nervous about this discovery. She would have to act as normal as possible to put him at ease. How do you act normal? She would definitely have to call Sanantha and tell her about this.

He got back in and started the car.

"So tell me why we need to go give Saint Patty a poke."

"Right, our destination. By the way, if you're going to shorten it, it's Saint Paddy, short for Padraig. And it's not just Saint Patrick, it's also Saint Brigid and Saint Columba. There was a prophecy that all three saints would be buried in the same place. In the 12th century, John DeCourcy, the Norman conqueror of Ulster, took it upon himself to have all three unearthed from their original resting places and moved to Down Cathedral, to fulfill the prophecy. Anytime you move a buried person, you create opportunities for spirit activity. I figure moving three people, each with a huge amount of spiritual energy, well, that's bound to create something worth measuring."

"Are there stories about the site being haunted?"

"Not haunted, but people have claimed healing miracles there."

Desiree chose to not worry Alec further with the story of how she revived a sparrow that her father had pronounced dead. "Great. It's also a place a lot of people know. So when you write about it in your next book, folks will identify with it."

•   •   •

Malcolm Dunn, the groundskeeper of the Anglican Cathedral Church of the Holy Trinity at Downpatrick, was not budging. "I don't care what your solution is made from, no one is going to deface the grave marker, and that includes spraying it with anything."

Alec could see there was no hint of faltering in the man's narrow-set gray-blue eyes. He was pretty sure the man's eyes appeared lighter blue the more upset be became. Determined to keep his own calm, he tried again. "The Dean of the church, Reverend Hull approved this procedure," he said holding out the printed sheet, "including this list of ingredients. It's for the monument's own good. I am testing whether air pollution from Belfast is degrading the granite. That stone is a national treasure. I'm here to preserve it, not deface it."

"Belfast is forty kilometers from here. We don't get the city's air pollution out here."

"Reverend Hull ..."

"The Very Reverend Henry Hull is not here today," Dunn huffed, which made his large pear-shaped body bounce menacingly. The buttons on his khaki shirt were holding on with all they had. Even though Alec had five inches on him, the older man cleared outweighed him. "Unless you have written permission from him, I am not letting you near that stone."

Alec held his smile as best he could. He appreciated the man's duty, but he was not listening to reason. "I do not have a printout of his email approving the visit. I expected him to be here. At the very least, I did not expect this part of the country to have zero cell phone reception. If I could get my phone to connect, I would show you his message. Is there anyone at the church office who could open his email on this end? They could get you a copy of what he sent."

"Reverend Hull does not keep an office here. He works from home on account of him taking care of his missus. So he wouldn't have sent you an email from here anyway."

Desiree, who had been quietly watching, stepped up. "Alec, can I see your phone for a minute?"

"Sure. Look. Zero ticks."

She held it up above eye level while looking at the screen and started walking around the paved paths of the park-like grounds.

Alec tried a different tact. "Mr. Dunn, we drove all the way up from Dublin. Do you think we would have made such a trip if I didn't think this was all settled ahead of time?"

The groundskeeper raised a condescending eyebrow. "You should have printed out your permission before you left Dublin."

Desiree came back and handed the phone to Alec. "Is this what you need?"

The screen had Reverend Hull's email up, complete with the Anglican cross in his signature block. Moreover, the phone was registering full reception bars. Alec stared at her and wasn't sure what to say. So he turned to Dunn and handed him the phone instead. "My assistant got through after all."

He read the letter, nodded, and handed back the phone. "Good enough," he declared. "You may proceed." As Alec and Desiree stepped past him, he commented to her, plenty loud enough for Alec to hear, "Well done, lassie."

Alec still wasn't sure what to make of it, but he certainly wasn't going to question what she had done in front of Dunn.

As soon as they were out of earshot, Desiree commented, "Nice cover story: testing for decay."

"It's worked several times before. How did you get the phone to connect?"

"I don't know. I just walked around and it found reception. I swear I did not bewitch your phone. I'm glad he didn't think we were scam artists. Maybe it was that luck thing we talked about."

"Maybe. It made all the difference. I had run out of angles to try. Thank you."

"You're welcome." She looked around the clear blue sky as they walked to the cemetery side of the church. "Beautiful day to go ghost hunting."

"I'm concerned all this sunshine is going to attract tourists."

"Can I see that list of ingredients, assuming it's not a fraud?"

He handed it to her. They were both wearing backpacks full of gear, but their hands were free. "Yes, it is an accurate list. It is not the recipe instructions for how to make the fluid."

"So all these flower extracts and spices combine to make the secret sauce that can bridge the spirit plane and this world?"

"That's right."

"Where in the world did you find this?'

"I pieced it together from several ancient descriptions. Each of the texts were incomplete or had errors. Between the lot of them, I figured it out."

"Ancient texts? What culture?"

"Ah, that's right. You're history, art, and religion. They were all from the Middle East. It is possible some of them date back to ancient Egypt. Here is our objective."

They walked around the massive stone slab sitting in its own paved platform and found a large bronze plate cast with a description of how the three saints had been brought here.

Desiree noted, "It says here, 'according to tradition'. Does that mean they don't know for sure if Saint Patrick is really here?"

"We're about to find out." He unslung his backpack, and Desiree followed. He knelt down and pulled out a few preliminary tools including the rock hammer, stethoscope, litmus paper, and a UV light. He glanced over to see how Desiree was doing. She was looking dubiously at a coil of rubber tubing and a turkey baster. "I brought the whole kit," he explained. "I had no idea what we might find here. Be sure to put everything you don't use back in the pack where you found it."

She frowned at him for making such a big deal of it. "Okay." She looked in her backpack again and brightened. "Here we go," she announced as she pulled out a camcorder. "Since I can't be near the stone while you're testing it, I can sit back there on that hill and film you."

"Great idea. That will also give you vantage to keep an eye out for Dunn or any tourists. Take the extra battery pack with you."

Alec assessed the stone. It was a roughly rectangular slab of grey granite, twelve feet long, eight feet wide, and two feet thick. It had large chunks broken off — one of which removed the last couple of letters of the carved name Patric below a Celtic cross.

As Desiree was turning to take her position, he told her, "This is a memorial stone, not the actual grave. De Courcy originally buried the three saints under the altar inside the church back in 1185. The church was destroyed soon after and it lay in ruins for centuries. When restoration began in 1790, they discovered the stone coffins, and they were moved out here into the cemetery. Unfortunately, the marker was vandalized and the location was lost. This stone was placed here in 1900. So my first job will be to locate the burial site. I'll start here and sniff it out."

"Why start with the stone if it's so modern?"

"Remember, I'm tracking psychic energy. This is where people have been coming and revering Patrick for the last hundred years. I'm hoping that will give me a starting place to pick up his spiritual scent. So be ready to follow me if I take off out into the graveyard."

Alec began tapping the stone and listening with the stethoscope. It rang solid all the way around to the side with the largest missing piece. There he heard a dull hollowness that told him there was a flaw. He took out the bottle of condenser fluid and dribbled some down the broken edge, then sprayed all around it. He turned on the sensor screen and laid it across the wet stone face down. He shocked the stone with the taser. He looked back to see if Desiree, some twenty feet away, was catching the action. She gave him a thumbs up from behind the camera.

He picked up the screen and it showed a swirled mass of curled fractals. He had seen this kind of pattern before on haunted objects. He zoomed in on the lines and found a distinct pattern repeated over and over. He called out to Desiree. "I've found a definite signature."

He pulled out a cable and connected the screen to his goggles. He further described for the film. "I'm tuning the goggles to detect this specific pattern." When he had done so, he put them on and took up the spray bottle and taser.

He tested the ground around the stone, but found no reaction. Next, he sprayed and shocked the air, trying all different directions. "I'm afraid, even with the right signature, this might be like looking for the proverbial needle in a haystack."

"That cemetery looks pretty crowded," Desiree observed. "It's less than an acre, all inside that hedge wall, and there's hardly any space between the graves. If they buried three stone coffins side by side in there two hundred years ago, you'd think someone would have come across them digging all those other graves since then."

"You think I should look somewhere else?"

"I'm thinking up closer to the church, under one of those lawns. I mean, these are three saints, right?"

"Why not? Keep an eye out for Dunn. My excuse doesn't apply to the lawn." He walked up onto the grass in front of the church and continued spraying and testing.

Desiree had to move away from the church to keep her distance from Alec. As he moved around, she ended up next to the memorial stone.

Suddenly Alec saw a reaction near the church entrance. It came on all at once and he wondered why. He looked back and saw Desiree had sat down on the stone. He started to tell her to not disrespect the site, but stopped himself when he realized she was energizing the signature.

"Stay right there!"

He followed the glow to a specific spot. He sprayed and shocked the spot and the view in his goggles lit up like fire. "Found him! You can get up off the stone now."

He took the goggles off and reset them to default. "Now let's see if Brigid and Columba are here too." He sprayed and shocked the lawn all around Patrick's site and indeed he found two other sites next to his. "This is fantastic. There they are, after all this time."

"I wonder," Desiree commented, "if they've got some kind of radar or x-rays or something to see the stone coffins."

He walked back to the pile of equipment he had left by the stone and retrieved his sensor screen. He took an impression of one of the other saint sites and found a pattern distinct from Patrick's. "That proves it. These are different signatures." He did the same for the last one, but this time the screen showed two repeated patterns, side by side. He reset the screen, took a step further away from Patrick and tried again. This one came up with only one signature. "There seems to be a corrupting signal near Patrick's grave."

After recording the two others, Alec focused on Patrick. He took an impression, expecting it to be the same as on the stone. The stone pattern was there, but so was the pattern that had bled into that first reading of Patrick's neighbor. He zoomed in on the second pattern. It was much more jagged and closed than Patrick's open curls. It was brighter as well.

"You look concerned," Desiree said. "What did you find?'

"There's a second signature on Patrick's grave. It's even stronger than Patrick's."

"A second person?"

"Even if a second person was buried with him, or if they accidentally put these coffins on top of another older grave, a normal person just doesn't emit this amount of energy, or in this complex a pattern. I've got the screen adjusted to same level I used to see your aura. That's the level these saints emit. So does this additional person."

"I don't know that much about Saint Patrick, but wasn't he supposedly visited by angels who guided him on his quest?"

This caught Alec off-guard. "You're right. In fact, he was specifically directed by an angel to come to this county to die. This is the county where he set up his first church. Legend tells he was visited by angels several times."

"Could they have been the same angel? His guardian angel?"

Alec looked at the screen and his mind reeled. Evidence of an actual angel? "Okay, my mind is blown. We can leave now."

"That signature is an angel, isn't it?"

He didn't want to commit to such a huge conclusion, but it seemed inescapable. He nodded.

Desiree spread her arms out and threw back her head. "Wahoo! Alec Doogan, you have outdone yourself!"

He had the screen zoomed in so a single repeat of the pattern filled the screen. As he marveled at what it could mean, he absently traced it with his finger. He felt a rush of power that started in his legs and rose through his loins and up his spine. It was like nothing he had ever felt before. It was warm and electric and arousing and invigorating all at the same time. It only lasted for a moment. He looked and Desiree wasn't reacting to him so it must not have shown. Was it the thrill of possibly cracking one of mankind's greatest mysteries? It felt more like this symbol triggered something within him. It had felt really good. He would have to investigate further. No need to mention it until he knew more.

5

DESIREE CONSIDERED HOW BIG A STEP THIS WAS, letting Alec take her home to his apartment after dinner out. At least she had convinced him to let her pay for her own meal, in the interest of maintaining their working relationship. As much as she enjoyed his company, she did not feel romantic about him, and she wanted to keep him from starting down that road with her. She was greatly relieved while Alec was unlocking the door he said, "I've got a meeting with the college first thing in the morning, so I won't keep you long. I do want to show you those pictures of the angelic script I was telling you about."

He opened the door, flipped on the light, and they were both shocked to find a man in a gray suit standing in the middle of the living room. It was the guy from the bookstore. He was still wearing his creepy silver sunglasses. "Mr. Doogan, I apologize for entering your dwelling without permission, but I could not think of a better way to convey the importance of my advice."

Alec stepped up and swelled his considerable stature. "I don't care what you have to say. You can't just break in here. Get the hell out!"

The man looked entirely unaffected by Alec's attempt to intimidate. "I caused no damage upon entering. You must hear me out, you in particular, Ms. Macklin. You are in grave danger."

"Grave danger," Alec mocked. "Who the hell are you to say we're in danger?"

Desiree interrupted. "I met him at your book signing last week. How do you know my name?"

"Oh great, a crazed fan."

"My name is Joseph. You are dealing with forces you do not understand."

"You don't know bollix about my work. I only publish the cute stories I come across."

"Joseph?" Desiree said quietly to herself. Where had she heard that name before?

"I am not talking about your book. The condenser testing at gravesites is going to uncover dangers you cannot comprehend." He looked intently at Alec. If not for the sunglasses, Desiree thought he squinted. "Or maybe you already have."

"Get out."

"Ms. Macklin, I must insist you break off this line of research. This path has dire consequences, especially for someone of your spiritual makeup."

"All right, that's enough." Alec reached out and grabbed him by the shoulder.

Joseph did not move. "Do not touch me. I did not come here for violence."

"Like I'm worried about a balding fifty-year old in a business suit. Come along, you've delivered your dire warning."

"What did you mean by my 'spiritual makeup'?"

"Oh really?" Alec turned to her, letting his hand drop from Joseph. "Don't engage with him."

"You're too important to be exposed to these kinds of dangers."

"Enough." Alec grabbed him again.

Joseph seized his hand, spun him around and pushed him in the back so hard the big man stumbled to the far wall. Then he stepped up to Desiree. "I did not come here for violence. My warning could not wait."

"Why do you think I'm in danger? Why should that matter to you? I don't know you."

Desiree saw Alec scan the room for a weapon. She also noticed for the first time the room was impeccably tidy. He pulled what looked like a jointed stick off the wall where it had been displayed. She didn't think Alec would actually hit him, so she didn't warn Joseph. She didn't have to.

"You cannot harm me, so do not try," he warned Alec without turning around.

Alec hit him across the neck anyway. Joseph's face lit up in shock as he howled, grabbed his neck, and fell to his knees. Desiree stepped back in horror. She looked up at Alec and he was surprised too.

Joseph struggled to his feet, still clutching the back of his neck. Desiree saw him grimacing so hard he couldn't speak. He stumbled out the door.

"What did you hit him with?"

Alec looked at the painted, segmented stick in his hand. "It's a priest's ceremonial flail from ancient Egypt. It's just what was handy. I didn't even hit him that hard. I thought he was going to grab you."

"I think you broke something," she said as she raced out the door. She caught up with him at the end of the block. He was bent over groaning, but still managing one plodding step to the next. "Are you going to be all right? Shall I call an ambulance?"

"No doctors," he gasped.

"Maybe you should sit down and figure out just how badly you're hurt. If your neck is broken, you shouldn't be trying to walk."

He ignored her and kept moving.

She put her arm around his shoulders to steady him. "Seriously, let me help. Alec didn't mean to hurt you this badly."

He stopped and looked up into her face. "Please don't waste your goddess energy on me. I'm not worthy of it. It's my own fault. I should have seen it coming."

"Now you're talking nonsense. Look, there's a bus bench right up here. Come sit down and let me have a look at you." She guided him to the seat. He seemed to be fading fast. He wasn't even resisting her anymore.

"Can you feel your hands and feet? Does anything not work that you can tell?"

"There is nothing physically wrong with this body."

"What?"

"I have failed you. Do not pity me. I came to protect you and now I cannot."

"You are delirious. I'm calling an ambulance."

"You don't even know who you are." The melancholy in his voice held her deeply.

She looked at him long and hard. She reached up and took off his sunglasses.

He started to avert his eyes, but she held his cheek still.

His yellow irises surprised her, but they weren't as frightening as she expected. "Who are you Joseph? And who am I?"

His voice was weak but earnest. "I am an angel of Ptah. I was given this form by a great magician twelve years ago. He passed from this plane nine years ago, and I have been looking for a purpose ever since.

"You are the avatar of Isis on Earth, a living presence of the goddess."

"Erzulie, actually," she corrected.

"Same deity," he said quietly.

She had no comeback for that one.

"You have the mark of someone who has died and been reborn. Protecting you should have been my mission."

"Alec's flail is ancient Egyptian. Did it break the spell that keeps you in this body?"

"Yes."

Anger and sadness boiled together into determination. She gritted her teeth and a tear rolled down her cheek. "I've been looking for a purpose for the last four years too. I need you here, Joseph. You are my only connection to who I really am."

"I am undone."

"Not good enough."

She looked at her hands, took a deep breath, and wrapped them around the back of his neck. She closed her eyes and forced herself to remember the sparrow in Malaysia. She focused on how it had lain motionless in her hand, how she refused to believe it wasn't going to get up, how she envisioned it moving, and how it finally did. Her hands felt hot and his neck felt cold to her touch. She imagined him strong and vital, she pictured him standing up and stretching with renewed vigor.

She looked down and saw — no, sensed — a pattern of lines running up his back. They stopped at his neck, like they were broken. She stretched her fingers across the gap to the lines in his scalp.

She noticed her heart was racing, and the heat in her hands was flowing from her heart. She felt the heat flow through her hands into him, until she felt the heat no more.

She blinked and let go. She looked again at her hands, half expecting to see smoke or something. They looked normal.

He blinked and turned his head side to side. He took a deep breath, brought his head up and squared his shoulders.

She felt giddy and disbelieving at first. Could she have healed not just a man, but a broken angel?

He got off the bench and down onto his hands and knees before her. "I am forever in your debt. I will do anything to be worthy of this gift. You truly are the embodiment of mercy."

She stood up straight, restrained a nervous giggle, folded her arms proudly, and smiled her most mischievous crooked grin. "You're welcome."

Alec came running up. "I called an ambulance. Is he okay?"

"Yes, he'll be all right. Call off the ambulance."

"Really? It looked bad. Are you okay?"

Joseph slipped his sunglasses back on, stood up, and held out his hand. "It was a terrible misunderstanding. I apologize for frightening you."

Alec hesitated a moment but then shook it. "I'm sorry I hit you. I really didn't mean to hurt you. I'm so glad you're not hurt."

"My warning stands. You are toying with fire."

Desiree jumped in. "But you're going to help us, right? Teach us so we don't get in over our heads?"

Joseph smiled at just the corner of his mouth. Desiree bet that was as much smile as he ever gave. "That is correct. I will be happy to guide you."

Desiree explained before Alec could object. "Joseph is an expert in the paranormal. Take my word for it: we want his counsel."

"So you know him after all?"

"Actually, an old friend of mine told me all about him once. It just took me a moment to recognize him."

Joseph double took at that.

She asked Joseph, "You remember Sanantha Mauwad?"

He was visibly stunned. "You know Doctor Mauwad? How is she?"

"She's fine. Living the good life in the South Pacific. I wonder what she'll say when I tell her I met you."

•   •   •

Sanantha was almost done packing her largest suitcase with her business wardrobe when her cell phone rang. She hoped it wasn't Simon wondering where she was. She knew his schedule well enough to come to their apartment when he was away. She did not want to cross his path. Not yet. "Hello?"

"Sanantha!" came the cheery young female voice.

She couldn't place it.

"It's me, Desiree!"

"Oh my goodness, Desiree! How are you? You have no idea how much I needed to hear a friendly voice."

"Really? Is everything all right?"

"Oh, Simon and I are having issues. Never mind that, what brings you to call? Are you still in DC?"

"No. I'm vacationing in Ireland. Getting in touch with my roots as a Macklin," she said in an overdone Irish accent. "I called because you will never guess in a million years who I met here on the Emerald Isle."

After a moment's silence, Sanantha said, "Okay. Am I supposed to guess?"

"Joseph de Alverado."

Sanantha's eyes swelled wide and her mouth fell open. A cold sweat broke out all down her back and her legs went weak. "No, dear God no," is all she could say.

"No, no, it's all good. He's being a perfect gentleman, friendly and helpful. He's not on any kind of mission. His old master is long gone. He's been wandering the Earth looking for a project. I guess he found me."

"What's he going to do with you?" Sanantha could barely control the shaking in her voice.

"Protect me. He says I am the Avatar of Isis, and it's his duty to guard me."

"Guard you from what?"

"Well, I met a young man named Alec who does paranormal research. You know, ghost hunting and stuff. Joseph says we could get ourselves in real trouble if we aren't careful. So he wants to help."

"Do you understand what he is? He's not like us. He doesn't think like us. He's a demon, mission or not."

"Well, he says he's an angel. Whatever the label, I understand he's different. He teleports and shoots lightning from his eyes. You told me about him years ago. Mostly he lacks a sense of humor. He knows a lot about stuff you and I have talked about. You know, why and how I'm alive. His explanations about Voodou and ancient Egypt make a lot of sense. A lot of things are making sense for the first time."

"I'm sorry, I'm still really worried for you."

"Well, if you still have doubts, I can put him on the phone right now."

"He's there!?"

"Yeah. We're having coffee. Well, I'm having coffee. He doesn't drink anything. Here he is."

"Hello, Doctor Mauwad. I am so glad to hear you are well after all these years."

Her teeth clenched up tight at the sound of his voice. She had to force them open to speak. "If you harm one hair on that girl's head …"

"Sanantha," he said calmly, "I would sooner kill myself than let any harm come to her. She speaks of me as her connection to who she is. In fact, she is my only connection to the world I come from. She is a goddess in human form. I only exist to serve my gods."

"You served Silas without flinching for years."

"My Master is gone. I only serve the gods now. Only a dwindling number of members of our village in Haiti still believe in my gods. Desiree is the genuine article."

"Joseph, you sound sincere, but I have to tell you plainly, I just don't trust you. Desiree is more precious to me that you will ever understand."

"Actually, Doctor, she explained how you revived her with the help of the goddess. I agree with you that she is precious. That is my whole point in wanting to protect her."

"She said something about ghost hunting. Has she gotten herself into something sinister?"

"I think I intervened before she and her companion created any trouble."

"What kind of trouble?"

"The dead are usually dead for a reason. Bringing them back to this plane is at the very least upsetting the order of nature."

"Yes, I recall you have a very orderly view of how things are supposed to be."

"At worst, such contact can bring evil into the world."

Sanantha refrained from saying, "… like Silas did when he conjured you." Instead she said, "Give the phone back to Desiree, please."

"Sanantha?" came her voice.

"Where in Ireland are you staying?"

"Dublin. Why?"

Sanantha did not answer as she gathered her thoughts.

"Are you coming here?" Desiree guessed with some excitement.

"Maybe. Probably. Just don't leave Dublin for a couple of days without telling me where you've gone. I want to hear from you every day to make sure you are still all right."

"Really. You're not my mother."

"No, but as your priestess, I did bring life to you. I am the only friend you have who knows what you're dealing with. Even if you think I'm overreacting, please do not let your guard down around Joseph."

"All right. Fair enough."

"Please say you'll call me tomorrow at this same time."

"Okay, I promise."

"Thank you. I'll call you if I decide to come join you. Goodbye for now."

"Bye bye."

Sanantha hung up and stood there trying to process. She prayed for a sign from Erzulie and she got this? She heard the front door opening.

"Sanantha?" Simon called. "I saw your car downstairs." He came into the bedroom and sized up the suitcase on the bed. "Where are you headed?"

She closed the case, picked it up, and declared, "Ireland."

6

SANANTHA FOUND HER SEAT and stood at it for a moment surveying the view of the Boeing 767-200 interior that was going to be her world for the next eleven hours. She had an aisle seat on the center section of the widebody cabin. Her day had already passed into a dreamlike state during the first eight-hour flight from Kuala Lumpur to Abu Dhabi. This final, longer leg promised to be even more unreal. Movies, music, naps, a potboiler mystery she picked up at a newsstand, none of her options were going to make the flight seem shorter. She sat down.

She had exhausted her ability to fret about Joseph's reappearance on the first flight. Desiree was now twenty-four, a college graduate, a woman coming into her own, and an utter babe in the woods when it came to the horrors she knew came with Joseph. Of course, he was glad to find her. Sanantha spent the last five years monitoring — at a friendly distance — how Desiree lived with a soul given her directly by Erzulie. Erzulie, whom Joseph called Isis.

Sanantha had been reluctant to admit to Desiree, or herself, that the girl had lost her own soul in the cloning disaster. Sanantha felt bad when Desiree had asked her directly if she had died that day in the jungle. She hadn't known for certain — not certainly enough to say. How do you tell someone she probably isn't the same person anymore because she is walking around with a transplanted soul?

Thinking about the last time she saw Joseph, the irony hit her. She managed to save Charles' soul from the Devil, but lost his life. Four years later, she managed to save Desiree's life, but lost her soul.

Now it was five years later, and here she was being drawn into another round of god knows what. Was she on some sort of cycle of contact with the supernatural? She wanted to hide, but she couldn't.

Her musings carried her through the greeting and safety instructions the petite Middle Eastern woman attendant recited in Arabic. She perked up and took notice when a lilting, trilling Irish accent punctuated the English delivery. Sanantha leaned into the aisle to see a tall, thin woman with a bright orange-red pageboy cut at the mic. She wore a green uniform, as opposed to the blue ones everyone else wore. "On behalf of our sister airline, Aer Lingus, welcome to Etihad Airways flight 1049, flying non-stop to Dublin, Ireland. Our time in the air will be about ten hours and fifty minutes, with our arrival at Dublin Airport scheduled for 11:15am local time."

Sanantha felt as if someone was watching her. She turned and saw a man seated one over from her, in the other aisle seat of the three-wide center section. He had wavy black hair, olive skin, and a somewhat practiced-looking smile. *Salesman,* she assumed.

"Sorry to stare," he started in a slight Italian accent. "I was just admiring your headdress. Is it Moroccan?"

"Haitian."

"Very nice pairing with the yellow Dior suit."

Oh good. Eleven hours fending off a flirt. "Thank you,"

"I apologize for being so forward. Fashion has always been a big part of my life."

She assessed his dark gold silk suit and crisp pale pink shirt. Apparently.

He reached across the vacant seat. "I am Benito Nomini."

She shook his manicured hand. "Sanantha."

"Ah, with an 'n.' Makes it your own, I like that. My parents thought enough time had passed that people would forget the last infamous Benito. Alas, it is one of those perfectly good names that will forever carry the taint of history — like Adolf."

Sanantha made the connection. "You know, I hadn't even thought of Mussolini. I think you're safe."

"Ah, maybe in Haiti. I still get the odd look when I am home in Italy."

Okay, so not a flirt — a narcissist. He managed to get her talking about him in the first two minutes. "You're not going to Italy now."

"That is true. I've been finishing up some old business across southern Europe, and now I have business in Dublin. You too?"

"Personal, visiting a friend."

The plane began pulling back out from the terminal.

"I guess this seat will stay empty," he said. "Do you mind if I put my books here? I brought a couple and I always have such a hard time getting my bag out from under my seat once we're buckled in."

"Oh, no, that's fine. I'll probably put some of my stuff there too."

"Perfect," he said as he reached under and pulled out an overnight bag.

Sanantha noticed it was made of Hermes signature fabric. She also caught a whiff of his cologne. It was sweet, but thankfully not too strong.

He took out a hardbound book and a couple of paperbacks, put them on the seat, and replaced his bag.

She glanced at the covers and was taken by the hardcopy, *The Magic Around Us* by Alec Doogan. She had just heard the name Alec somewhere. She pondered for a moment, then remembered Desiree had said she met …

"Benito, may I take a look at this book?"

"Of course. It's new, I just got it from Amazon. The author is a ghost hunter who claims to have scientific evidence. I have always had a keen interest in the paranormal."

"Really?" She turned the book over and was met with the posed smile of a stout, fresh-faced young Irishman in a cable-knit sweater in front of a bookcase.

This must be Desiree's new friend. What a weird coincidence.

"Yes, it's kind of a family tradition for me. My father was a rabbi who was deeply into the kabala, and my mother became obsessed with spirits when her brother died."

Interesting that a Jewish mother would name her child after a fascist dictator. "Oh, so you didn't just get the traditions, but the mysticism too."

"Indeed."

"When you're done reading it, may I take a look?"

"Oh, of course. In fact, you go ahead first. I've got these others, and I will have lots of time to go through it later."

"Are you sure? I don't know how I'd feel about someone reading a new book ahead of me."

"I insist. That way we can talk about it afterwards."

"Well, thank you."

Alarms were going off in the back of her mind. He was full of contradictions and coincidences. The name mismatch was curious. The paranormal interest coming on the heels of Joseph's reappearance was unsettling. *What were the chances of him having Doogan's book on a flight she was taking to see Doogan, even if tangentially?*

So what was she accusing him of? Being at the right place at the right time for her to read Doogan's book before meeting him? That was more like dumb luck.

Maybe she was being paranoid after talking to Joseph. She could do worse than sitting with this handsome, charming, clearly successful man, with whom she would have something to talk about. Of course, the last thing she needed in her life was another handsome, charming, successful man.

She decided to keep her caution at hand, but to try to enjoy this long flight.

•   •   •

Desiree hoped the knock was Sanantha as she peeked through the window in the door of her rented cottage. She swung it open enthusiastically. "Welcome to Ireland!"

"Oh my goodness!" Sanantha took a step back. "You're even more beautiful all grown-up than I remember!"

"You haven't changed a bit, still as regal as ever."

"'Regal'? Now there's a word," she jested as she stepped up and gave Desiree a warm bear hug which Desiree happily returned.

"Come in, please. I was surprised you could come on such short notice."

"Yes, well, I was in the middle of rearranging my calendar when you called."

"Oh, just the one bag?" Desiree asked, bringing it in.

"In fact, I was already packed."

"Oh. Please come in and have a seat."

"Thank you. Actually, I've been sitting for two days."

Desiree slid the suitcase alongside the couch in the small sitting room. "All right. Can I get you something? We're in the Isles, so how 'bout a cuppa tea?"

"That would be lovely."

Desiree led her into the kitchenette, filled the electric kettle, and plugged it in. "Not to pry, but if you were already packed, and not going somewhere else, does that mean you and Simon …?"

"Are taking a break, yes."

"I'm sorry."

"Me too. I'm taking it as an opportunity to take more control of my life."

"That's the spirit."

"I'm also taking Joseph's reappearance as a challenge that I have more important things to do with my life."

Desiree was waiting to see how she would bring up Joseph. "Like I said on the phone, I don't think I need to be defended against him."

"That's fair. I still want to see what he is planning for you. You are the great treasure he has been seeking ever since his master disappeared."

"You really don't trust him."

"Trust is the wrong word. He would have to have an incorruptible moral core to be able to wield such power only for good. His master was willing to kill millions to achieve his laudable goals because he felt the ends justified the means."

"That was Silas, not Joseph."

"I understand. Just consider how hard it is to always do the right thing when you have the power to do anything and get away with it. I sincerely hope he has only good intentions, that he has only your best interests at heart. I just want to be here to make sure."

Desiree could see her struggling with her doubts and fears. "I appreciate your wanting to look out for me. I admit, at first I was a little taken aback by the whole mothering thing. I've had a couple days to think it over and, to be honest, since this is going to be an adventure, I'd rather have you along for it anyway."

The kettle whistled and she unplugged it. She got out cups and the tea. Her cell phone rang. "Hello? Oh hi. Yes, she just arrived. No, that's fine, we're about to have some tea. Okay, great. See you in a bit." She hung up. "Speak of the angel, that was Joseph."

"He's coming here now?" Sanantha used that controlled, flat, masking tone Desiree recognized.

"Too soon? That was why you came all this way, right?"

Sanantha pursed her full lips as her eyes darted around the air above their heads. "Sure. Why not. It would have been nice to enjoy that cup of tea first."

"Oh, there's time for the tea."

"Ah, no, he'll be here in the next five sec—"

She was cut off by the knock at the door.

"That's Joseph. He gets around."

"Right," Desiree remembered as she walked to the door. "How convenient." She peeked through the window and opened the door. "Hello, Joseph. Please come in."

"Good afternoon."

Desiree noticed Sanantha had stayed in the kitchen. "Sanantha, won't you come join us?"

She was pleased to see her friend had taken the moment to compose herself. Sanantha breezed out of the kitchen with a pleasant, if professional, smile on her dimpled face and extended her hand to him. "Joseph. How extraordinary to see you again. You are looking well."

He shook her hand in his usual cordial, but not really smiling, way. "Doctor Mauwad, it is indeed a happy turn of fate that we meet again. You too look as if not a day has passed."

54

"You call this a turn of fate. Was it truly an accident that you found Desiree?" Sanantha got right down to business.

"Yes, it was. I had heard about Alec Doogan's book, and Desiree and I happened to come to his book signing at the same time. I immediately recognized her as carrying the mark of the goddess, but I did not seek her out."

"I need to be straight with you, so I hope you don't mind me getting right to it."

"I understand."

"I know you hold yourself to a very high standard of integrity, so I am not going to doubt what you say. Whether you meant to find her or not, now that you have, I am assuming you have big plans for Desiree. I need you to know that I will not let you drag her into anything that puts her in danger."

"As I told you on the phone, I too am here to protect her."

"That's what I am afraid of. I don't want her put in a position where she needs your protection."

She turned to Desiree. "You went through too much four years ago — enough danger for several lifetimes. I want you to be able to live your life on your terms, as normal and as peaceful and as happy as you want."

She turned back to Joseph. "I believe you mean well, but danger follows you like a shadow. It's part of who you are."

Desiree put her hand on Sanantha's arm. "I love you too, Sanantha, but my life has already moved away from the tranquil path you describe. Alec has shown me that I am something extraordinary. Joseph's explanations are like a breath of fresh air clearing away the fog I've been staggering through for years. I hope this doesn't lead to the danger you worry about, but I can't walk away from this."

"You can walk carefully, and not alone."

"Doctor Mauwad, I don't think you understand the degree of her powers. Desiree healed me from a blow that should have broken my anchor with this body."

Sanantha turned on Joseph. "Yes, that is impressive, but that is also exactly what I'm talking about. Just by being here you are exposing her to supernatural dangers." Then to Desiree, she added, "You told me about the sparrow years ago. I assumed your ability to heal would grow. Can't you see that by standing next to the fire, you're going to be forced to put your powers to the test, whether you want to or not?"

Desiree was glad for the opening. "Yes, I do see that. So guide me. I'll make you the same deal I made Joseph. Stick around and teach me. Help me learn how to use this extra soul whatever to its best purpose."

Her sage friend took a deep breath, glanced at the balding angel, and let it out nodding. "All right. I don't know how much help I'm going to be learning about your abilities, since I'm going to be spending all my time protecting you from the trouble that follows him. I will stick around."

Desiree didn't know Joseph well enough to understand his subtle expressions, but this last dig seemed to hit a nerve. He pursed his lips and looked at the floor in an obvious attempt to control himself. Then he put on a false smile and looked up at Sanantha. "I am glad to have you on board. Now if you ladies will excuse me," he said stepping to the door.

"Oh, okay. Are you sure you won't stay for tea?" Desiree asked.

"No, thank you. I will see you soon. Goodbye." He let himself out.

"All right. Goodbye then." When the door clicked shut, she turned to Sanantha. "I think you hurt his feelings."

Her eyebrows climbed high. "Seriously? I don't care."

"We have an angel, and you don't care if you offend him?"

"If you go through the Bible, every single instance of human to angel contact has led to bad things for the human. Angels are agents of change. They have their own agendas. They're dangerous."

Desiree stepped back into the kitchen and poured the hot water into a teapot.

"You said this friend of yours Alec is a ghost hunter?"

"Yes. He has a fluid that allows him to see spiritual residues."

"Really? He doesn't say anything about that in his book."

"You've read his book?"

"Yes, my seatmate on the plane had a copy."

"That's some coincidence."

"I agree. It was all rather Kismet. So what does Alec think of partnering with an ancient Egyptian archangel?"

Desiree rolled her eyes and tended to the tea. "Well, I haven't told Alec what Joseph is. At least not yet. Alec knows he's an expert on mystical things and an old friend, but I haven't told him about the non-human part."

Sanantha nodded. "That will be a shock when the time comes."

"I will tell him. I want to figure out a few more things first. Actually, there is something I want to run by you." She brought the pot and two cups to the small table.

Sanantha sat down. "Okay," she said skeptically. "This is after talking to Joseph?"

Desiree sat down and poured the tea. "This is after digesting lots of things. Back in Malaysia, Young Nae told everyone that the comatose snake-bite victim he was taking care of was me. That person was, of course, actually my mom, genetically disguised to look like me. So that first snake bit Mom."

"Yes, it took your father and me a while to figure that out."

"That snake set in motion the whole sequence of events that led to Young Nae's turning to evil. So I'm thinking that snake may have played the role of the tempter — like the snake in the Garden of Eden. It gave Young Nae a choice, and he chose evil."

Sanantha did not look like she was taking this very well. She reached over and poured the tea with her face locked in a frown. "You know I met the demon who was that snake from Eden."

"Oh, I know. That's why I have to talk to you about this. So then there was the second snake, that really did bite me. I was a genetic soup teetering between myself and my mother's genome when it bit me. That bite forced you and Dad to tip me back to being me. In the process, though, I would have died if you had not used your Voodou to channel Erzulie into me. Erzulie also manifests as a snake — a white snake. We talked about that four years ago. I think the second snake — the one that bit me — was Erzulie. I don't think it was an accident at all. She saw me as a vessel to get a foothold in this plane of reality."

Sanantha peered into her tea and looked like she was about to cry.

"Don't be sad. I think this is awesome. Joseph says Erzulie is a modern form of his goddess Isis. That means Isis saved me, at your request, but because she has big plans for me."

She blinked and looked up at Desiree. "You're probably right. You know what I said about angels being trouble? Any time a god has big plans for you, run."

7

A LEC DOOGAN SIPPED HIS ESPRESSO as he watched the street through the café's front window. He shifted his weight on the worn pad of his wooden chair and decided not to look at his watch again. After a moment, he sat his laptop on the small oak table and opened it, deciding to re-read the email from Ruth, the manager of the Gutter Book Shop. He was glad he didn't need an internet connection to access his opened mail in the Mindspring inbox.

Dear Alec,

Thank you again for your engaging appearance at the Gutter last week. I'm writing you today to pass on a message. A gentleman named Benito Nomini came in this morning and asked me to tell you of his urgent desire to meet you. He said he greatly regretted missing you read here. He also said he is a student of the paranormal and that he is a man of independent means who regularly supports such research.

He was keenly concerned about your privacy. Not only did he not want your contact information, he didn't want to leave a phone number or email address for fear that he might passively glean yours in any exchange. Instead he offered to meet you in a public place he hoped would be convenient for you. He suggested the Brown Stag coffee shoppe at 10 am tomorrow morning. He seemed sure of his choice. Indeed he did not make an accommodation for you to offer an alternative.

I must say, it was a rather unusual conversation. He appeared genuine, yet odd as to the practical details. You may have a wealthy eccentric fan.

In any event, you always have the option of simply not meeting him. I hope it all works out for the best.

Sincerest regards,

Ruth Shrewsbury

Alec read that last paragraph again. He thought about how his fellowship from the University of Dublin, on which he had lived the last year, was about to run out just as his research was bearing fruit, just as he met Desiree. No, he did not have the option of simply not meeting him. What was this fellow's name? "Benito Nomini," he muttered.

"At your service."

Alec startled to find him standing right next to him. Tall, broad shouldered, dashing black hair, Roman nose, expensive clothes — yeah, this could be him. He stood up and extended his hand, which Benito shook firmly. "Alec Doogan. Glad you could find me."

The Italian flashed a confident smile. "I knew you from your book jacket photo. Thank you for coming to meet with me."

"My pleasure. You gave clear instructions. And I come here all the time."

"There are so many freaks in the world, I wanted to put you in control."

"I appreciate that. Have a seat. Can I get you a coffee?"

"Thank you, no. I already ordered. I should be buying for you, but you already have one," he said pointing. "You're missing a big perk of celebrity," he said with a grin as he sat down, "letting your fans do things for you."

Alec eased back into his chair. "I guess I'm not used to having fans."

"I would like to help you with that. I was already coming to Ireland for another matter, and I read your book on the plane. It resonated with a lot of things I've been thinking about for a long time."

"My book is four hundred pages. How long was your flight?"

"It was long. The Middle East to Ireland is a stretch, but I've done it before. When I found out you were touring it here, I jumped at the chance to meet you. Alas, I missed your reading."

"It must have made quite an impression if you still wanted to reach me."

"It did. For many years I have been funding research into the existence of spirits. None of the other researchers I have worked with had the clarity of vision you showed. I also got the impression you only shared a small part of your work in the book."

Benito's hands were in nearly constant motion as he talked. Alec found it distracting. "Really?"

"Almost like you were only sharing the parts you thought the public would accept. So I need to ask you: have you made discoveries that go beyond what's in those pages — things you aren't ready to share with a wide audience?"

Was this guy for real? Alec had made a point of being internally consistent so no one would question what he had left out. "Authors rarely put all their research down in a book. It would be boring to the casual reader."

"I agree, you are far too fine a writer to data dump on your readers. On the other hand, several of the conclusions you reach tell me you had more evidence than what you shared. The interplay of identity residues with active spirits and how those are perceived by the living, looks to me like you are building a bigger theory, but you haven't nailed it down yet."

"I'll admit, I still have a lot of questions. I don't mean to be coy, but when you know that you don't know, and hard facts elude you, then you're left with conjecture. I'm trying to be seen as an expert. You don't show people you're guessing if you're supposed to be an expert. Science mandates reproducibility. I don't have that, not yet."

"I admire your dedication to the Scientific Method. How much more research would it take to fortify your theory? A year? Two or more?"

"I think I hear an offer coming, so I want to be honest with you. I cannot guarantee anything. On the other hand, I have made some big strides recently — big enough that I have let myself have hope of finding real solutions."

Benito pointed at Alec with a flourish. "That's where you want to be. Still lots of mist on the road," he said waving his hands, "but you can see there is a road. Nobody I've worked with has even found the road yet. They're all still groping at the fog. If you're on to something, then I want to help."

He got up and retrieved his drink from the bar.

Alec took a sip while he considered how to move to the next stage. The familiar taste of coffee helped him center. This kind of negotiation was new to him, and it felt good to hold onto a familiar anchor — even if it was just a cup of coffee. "Well, I won't turn help away. May I ask what you do? I mean, if I'm going to be counting on your help, I'd like to know how stable that help will be."

"Very astute that you should ask. Happy to share. I'm an image consultant. I design corporate branding, I advise celebrities on their public image, I even do damage control for governments. I am very much in demand. You need not worry that I will pull funding due to a downturn in my business."

"If I may ask another personal question: how does a successful image consultant get interested in the paranormal?"

"Lifelong fascination. I was raised with a mix of religious and cultural influences, and I've had a few things happen to me that made me wonder about the afterlife. I saw there was very little commercial gain to be made outside of charlatanism, so corporations and governments were unlikely to support such research. Churches have plenty of money, but they are too biased to do any real truth seeking. I decided to use my wealth to fill that gap.

"My turn," Benito said with a glint in his eye. "What is the most exciting thing you've discovered — the thing that gives you hope of making a breakthrough."

Alec thought for a moment on how to tell him, to lure him in, without giving too much away. Another sip of coffee helped. "The condenser fluid seems to be much more useful than I let on in the book. Yes, it detects spiritual residues which I have used to find hidden burial sites. It also can measure how much spiritual power people have within them."

"Within people?"

"Yes, to see whether a medium really has the ability to contact the spiritual plane. You said you want to avoid charlatans. This technique should unmask fakes right away."

"That is useful. Does it get you closer to an objective proof?"

This was getting further than Alec had planned, but he had this guy hooked. Time to reel him in. "My hope is, I will find out how to use this fluid to manifest will power. If spirits have something to tell us, this could be the ink they can use."

Benito leaned forward, put his elbows on the table, and clasped his restless hands still. "You know, if that works, it could be made to work the other way too."

"I don't follow."

"If this fluid obeys willpower, it could guide spiritual power from the beyond to do our bidding."

Alec leaned back in his chair and tried to find any trace of doubt or joke in the Italian's face. There was none. "You mean magic?"

"Why not?" He freed his hands to fly wide. "You've got to let yourself think big, Alec. Let your findings take you wherever they lead. Don't doubt your limits and only test what you think is likely. You're building a bridge between here and the spirit plane where anything is possible."

Alec took a deep breath. "You're right, the research needs to go where it needs to go. For the record, I take things one step at a time. Hypothesis, test, measure, repeat."

"I wouldn't have it any other way. So if I may ask, has this been full-time or part-time for you?"

"It started out part-time, but the last few months it's taken over my life."

"How have you been supporting yourself?"

"I have an income stream, but it won't last forever."

Benito laughed out loud. "Well it's a good thing I came along. How much will you needed to continue full time for a year?"

"A year?" Alec tried but failed to remain cool. "That's very generous. I'd say thirty thousand, plus travel expenses."

"Thirty thousand pounds is a very reasonable number. Are you an Irish citizen?"

"Yes."

"Better make it forty, with taxes. I like the number forty."

"Oh, sure, of course. Do you have in mind to buy the rights to my work?"

"Yes, but only for the year while I am paying you, and only so you don't publish anything in the meantime. At the end of the year, or if you make a breakthrough before then, you and I agree to re-visit this agreement, allowing me first right to purchase any discoveries you have made for fair market value."

"So you're just buying my time until I find something, and then you want first crack at buying it. That's a remarkable offer. I'm not sure how I could say no."

"I try to make it easy for my partners to say yes. I'll have my accountant draw up a contract. That way you can read it before you agree to anything."

"Do I keep the rights to my work so far?"

"Absolutely. I have no interest in cutting in on your book or anything you've done to date."

Alec ran the conversation back through his head. "All right. I'll pull together my unpublished work and make you a report of where I am at this point. I'll share that with you as soon as we sign. That way you know where I am starting."

"That would be marvelous." He raised his coffee for a toast, and Alec did the same. "To the beginning of great things."

•   •   •

Alec barely noticed the petite Indian library assistant walk up behind him as he pored through computer archive files.

"Mr. Doogan," she said quietly with a lilting accent. "We're closing in half an hour. You've been here most of the afternoon. Do you need any help finding something?"

"Oh no, I've found everything I've looked for. I just need to make up my mind about something."

"Well, I probably can't help you with that," she said with a smile before turning to tend to other visitors.

He smiled back and took the interruption as a chance to stretch. He looked up at the dark barrel-vaulted wood ceiling, two stories up, over the main hall of Trinity College's library. He hadn't just spent a long time here today, but countless hours over the last few years. He loved the way the low late afternoon light streamed in past what seemed like miles of bookshelves, stacked as pillar ribs down the length of the cavernous space. He breathed deep the smell, that smell of thousands of old books that fired his curiosity every time he came here, no matter how many times he had come before.

Despite how much he loved being here, and maybe because he found it so easy to wile away hours here, he uncovered too much information and he had too many options to choose from. He needed a spirit guide — a shining example that he could keep close at hand and close to his heart as he moved into what was sure to be a scary adventure, one that would likely move too fast for him to feel in control. He really wanted to pick one from the traditional Irish Catholic saints, but none of them had faced the kind of sudden success he was afraid of. The icon he kept coming back to was Catherine of Siena, out of the Vatican tradition.

After his meeting with Benito, he had considered going to his family priest for counsel. That would have been a painful conversation that would not have gotten him any closer to the help he needed. Father Corrigan made it very clear how little he thought of Alec's work with spirits. To ask him for advice on how to stay strong while ramping up his ghost hunting would just invite more ridicule. No, he was much better off seeking help from books he loved.

Looking at a painting of her, holding a branch of lilies while looking out from under her white nun's wimple with gentle, but knowing eyes, he wondered if this was the hero he needed in his life. She had stood up for her Pope through an insurrection that, according to the history, was led by demons. She called them out and turned the revolt around, saving the Pope and the Papacy. He nodded. Such courage was exactly what he needed.

He scrolled through a gallery of icon paintings and found the one that resonated with him the most. He sent the image to print.

•　　　•　　　•

Alec flipped on the light and hung his keys on the hook by the door. After setting his laptop case on the desk, he turned his attention to the paper bag tucked under his arm. He carefully unwrapped the print and the wooden frame before setting them down, then took off his coat and hung it on its peg. Moving quickly, but carefully, he took the frame apart, inserted the picture, reassembled it, then placed it on the shelf above his desk, where it overlooked the whole front room.

He sat down and took a deep breath. "Holy Saint Catherine, I need your help. I need your confidence, your righteousness. You faced down demons to defend what you knew was right, and providence proved you the victor. I am facing great uncertainty. I am suddenly faced with the possibility of success far greater than I ever imagined. It scares me. My backer thinks I could become a miracle worker. I am so afraid of overstepping what God has intended for mankind. I am thrilled at the possibilities, at the chance to really help people by unlocking spiritual secrets. At the same time, I know I am venturing into untested waters. Who knows what evil I could attract along the way? I feel like I am at the brink of something wonderful, but at the same time it terrifies me. How did you know, how did you overcome uncertainty and defeat enemies no one else would even face?"

He opened a file drawer in the desk and pulled out a folder. "I found this symbol that I think is the spiritual signature of an angel who guided Saint Patrick." He took out a printout of an enlargement of the jagged curlicue and showed it to the icon. "How wonderful if I could show the world proof of the existence of angels. Think of how many doubters would gleefully turn to God with such assurance. I myself feel great health and vitality just touching this symbol. Did your visions give you these same feelings?

"You know I'm not a strong person. I take medication to be able to face the world full of people. Even with the meds I find myself drawn to things I know are not good for me.

"This symbol," he said unthinkingly stroking it, "this feels right. I cannot find anything in any literature to tell me which angel this was. Believe me, I've looked. How could I feel so good if this wasn't from good? Surely God, Jesus, the Holy Ghost, and all of you Saints have watched over me my whole life. I know I wouldn't have survived some of the crazy things I have put myself through if I wasn't protected. One thing I am confident of is God would not let me get such a positive feeling from this symbol if it wasn't from a source of good."

He put the symbol back in its folder on the desk and looked earnestly up at the icon. "You will be my rock, my inspiration, my guide on this path. Please do not let me be tempted by evil, but help me find the way of righteousness. Amen."

•   •   •

Alec picked up the pen off the café table and held it above the signature line. "I must say I am impressed it only took your accountant one day to put this together."

Benito held up Alec's memory stick. "I'm equally impressed with how you gathered all this research in the same time."

"I keep my files organized as a matter of course," he said as he signed his name next to Benito's signature.

"I'll wire the first round of funds immediately."

"Day before yesterday, you said my research could lead to magic, the bending of reality to the will. I've been thinking about that. Do you believe in God?"

"Oh yes. I know God is real."

"Yet you don't seem bothered that magic imposes a human will on the spirit plane. Isn't that opposing God's will?"

"The Bible tells us that God gave man dominion over the Earth. The bridge your fluid builds between this plane and the next is as natural as swimming in the sea. If God didn't want this fluid to exist, he wouldn't have created it."

"God allows us to make mistakes, and God allows evil."

"Well, before you get too mired in the conundrum of free will, I would point out that you are hardly the first to walk this path. The men who found the parts of your formula in ancient times probably asked themselves the same questions. Some of them were good men, and some were probably not. It's up to us to do the right thing."

Alec searched his face for a sign of jest or sarcasm, but he appeared completely earnest.

"Speaking of those who came before, I promised to share with you the research I have funded to date." Benito reached around and grabbed a messenger satchel hung over the back of his chair. As he brought the case around into his lap, Alec spotted an engraved silver bracelet around his right wrist.

"Are those inscriptions hieroglyphics?" he asked pointing.

Benito followed Alec's finger and realized he was talking about the bracelet. "Oh, yes. Protection prayer. Gift from an old student," he dismissed. He opened the case and handed Alec several sealed clear plastic envelopes containing papyrus fragments. "I am really hoping you can pick up where this fellow stopped."

Alec poured over them for a moment before concluding, "Coptic. I'd say first millennium B.C.E. at the latest. Look like spell books, but they're not about Egyptian magic. There are repeated mentions of Ahriman, the Zoroastrian god of darkness." He looked up at Benito. "Could these be Egyptians translating and copying over older Sumerian text, the way Medieval monks copied over crumbling ancient Greek texts?"

"That's what the previous research concluded too."

"Do you know how old the original text was?"

"No, but probably much older. If these are spell books, do you think your work with the condenser fluid could tell us more about them?"

"I don't know. The fluid finds spirit energy. These ancient magicians tried to achieve magical effects by connecting their subconscious to the spirit plane. Once you are thinking in spirit terms, like being immersed in a foreign language, then you can consciously manipulate spirit energies." He flipped through several of the protected pages. "This one details steps for mental preparation. That's a start."

"How so?"

"These spells appear to describe how the Sumerian priests made that connection to the spirit plane." He looked up and met Benito's fascinated smile. "My fluid could be used to test these."

Benito leaned back in this chair and spread his arms wide. "Now you're singing my tune!"

8

SIMON HERRERA GLANCED AT THE CLOCK on the cable box when the doorbell rang. "Seven in the evening," he muttered to himself. He peeked at the front window curtain and saw a heavy-set woman in a blue business suit and a blonde ponytail standing in the porch light.

He opened the door. "Can I help you?"

"Yes, sir," she started in a distinct Southern accent. "I am looking for Doctor Sanantha Mauwad. Is she at home?"

"No, she's not. May I ask who you are?"

She held up a badge wallet she already had in her hand. "I'm Special Agent Jill Bitterman, from the United States Federal Bureau of Investigation. Are you Doctor Simon Herrera?"

"Why, yes I am. How did you know that?"

She slipped the wallet into her inside jacket pocket. "Your last names are on the apartment mailbox downstairs, sir. When will Doctor Mauwad be returning home?"

"She's traveling at this time, and I actually don't know when she will be back."

"You said traveling, sir. Do you mean out of the country?"

"Yes. She said she was going to Ireland to help a friend."

"When did she leave?"

"Tuesday. Yeah, three days ago."

This seemed to strike a chord in the woman, as her eyebrow twitched. "I see. Did she mention me in any way, that she and I spoke recently?"

"No, she didn't mention you at all. Is she under investigation?"

"I am not at liberty to say, sir. You said she went to see a friend. Do you know where in Ireland she is staying?"

Simon noticed the only thing she carried was a small black leather purse she had slung over one shoulder. His gaze drifted to her blue suit jacket as he thought of the weapon she no doubt had holstered there. Oh, not heavy — bulletproof, with a vest under her blouse. She kept her hands still, lightly clasped in front of her as she spoke. Short trimmed nails with no color. "Yes, Dublin. She did tell me that much."

"Doctor, did her departure seem sudden to you, or was this trip well planned?"

"It was rather sudden. I believe she got some bad news from the friend and thought it best she go right away."

"Have you spoken with her since her departure?"

"No, I have not. But you could call her. She's not doing anything that would prevent her from taking a call."

"I am aware of that option, sir."

"Doesn't the FBI investigate crimes within the U.S.?"

"Crimes that originate in the U.S.," she corrected without criticism.

"Sanantha hasn't been in the U.S. in four years. Does this have anything to do with what happened before she came here?"

"I am not at liberty to discuss the matter, sir."

"I am fully informed of the events from that incident. I would be happy to answer any questions you have if it would help your investigation."

"I appreciate your willingness to help. I also appreciate your interest in deflecting attention from your girlfriend." Simon almost smiled at how her Southern drawl stretched out the word girlfriend. "I have specific questions that can only be answered by Doctor Mauwad."

She really was all business. Only the barest minimum of makeup. The night air drifted in the door passed her and he noticed no hint of perfume. "Can you at least tell me if I am completely off-base?" he tried. "I wouldn't want to waste your time."

She squared her shoulders, reclasped her hands, and did not say a word.

"Well, I'll just throw this out in case it helps. Sanantha only got involved because she took over my practice while I came here to Malaysia on a vacation."

"A vacation? My understanding is you have moved here permanently. Is that correct?"

"Well, yes. Can you at least tell me if this is concerning a patient of mine? I need to make sure my patient's confidentiality remains protected."

"I assure you, Doctor, I have reviewed all the pertinent records and done so under the proper legal authority."

Simon thought about that for a moment. "It's the Patriot Act, isn't it? Since 9/11, you can look at whatever you need if there is terrorism involved." He brightened at the conclusion. "Oh, so this is about the terrorist. Which also explains how an FBI agent is tracking the case around the world."

He first noticed the grey in her blue eyes when she squinted slightly in what he could only characterize as a steely look. "Since I am halfway around the world in the wrong direction, I'm going to go out on a limb here. Do you know if Doctor Mauwad was aware of Mister Redmond's involvement with the terrorists prior to the incident where Mister Redmond was killed?"

"Well, yes. She was trying to help him cope with the stress of his situation. She certainly would have known he was involved in crime."

Agent Bitterman pursed her lips in the briefest moment of reflection. "Nope. Sorry. I still need to ask her."

"Did she not tell the authorities about the terrorists? You know psychiatrists have a duty of privacy to their patients, even after death. Our job is to help people, not get them in trouble with the law. She may have been trying to walk that line to not incriminate her patient."

The eyebrow twitched again. "I understand what you're saying."

Simon pressed again. "All the same, you're after the terrorist and she didn't give you all the details you want."

"You said you have not spoken with her since she left. Is that normal for you two to not speak for three days, even if one of you has taken a long international flight?"

Caught unprepared, Simon took a moment to collect an answer, which he gave cautiously. "We didn't part on the warmest of terms."

"So she might be gone for some time."

"True."

She reached into her jacket and produced a card. "If you speak with her, please have her call me at this number."

Simon looked at the very official-looking card and missed her extended hand. He shook it.

It was firm, exactly as he expected. 'Thank you for your time, Doctor."

9

ALEC TOOK IN THE DAPPLED LIGHT coming in through the trees, the squishing sound of wet leaves underfoot, the aromas of damp earth from under the bushes, and chuckled. "This woodland setting makes me feel like Merlin."

Benito, two steps ahead of him, turned and smiled. "And why not? You wanted secluded and natural. Why not get mythic as a bonus?"

He shifted the weight of his backpack. "Well, a big part of wanting secluded was to save myself the embarrassment of being seen yelling and waving my arms about to no effect. That might break the sense of mythic."

"You sell yourself short, young wizard." He stepped out into a clearing. "I think this is the spot you picked on the map. Rahin Wood, about a quarter mile from the road, and there's the pond up ahead."

Alec looked around. "Fair, 'tis." He unslung the pack and opened it. "You've got the table in yours."

"Really?" Benito set his satchel down and opened it. "Look at that. You really know how to pack." He pulled out the fold-up sawhorse and popped it open. "That's fun. It's like something a stage magician would use."

Alec brought his pack over and started placing bottles and cases on the small table top. "If you're done playing with my stuff, I need a live animal that lives here." He handed him a jar. "It can be anything, even an earthworm."

"I see just the candidate." He walked to a nearby tree and, reaching for what appeared to be just bark, plucked off a large spotted brown moth.

Alec was quietly amazed at Benito's eyesight as he took the offered jar. "Thanks. That's pretty much all I need from you. The video camera is in there too."

Benito fetched it, stepped back and held it up. "Ready when you are."

Alec took an index card out of his shirt pocket and laid it on the table alongside a glass rod, a dagger, a handkerchief, a tall stoppered vial, and a spray bottle. He then poured a shot glass of whiskey and set it next to the captured moth in front of the other items. He uncorked the vial and walked around the table, pouring out salt to form a pentangle in the grass.

He looked over at Benito and stopped cold. "This is not going to work. I'm about to summon a spirit from the Beyond from inside this protective diagram. Meanwhile, you are standing twenty feet away looking like meat hung out for the wolves."

"Don't summon a malevolent spirit."

"Well, not on purpose. Truth be told, I have no idea who I'm going to summon. It's too risky."

Benito held up his right wrist and the light caught the silver bracelet. My student who gave me this said it could restrain even the most powerful of demons. I have, in fact, seen it provide amazing protection. I think I'm covered for any annoyed forest spirit you contact."

"If you're sure. At the first sign of trouble, I want you to stop filming and run as fast and as far as you can to safety."

"Agreed."

Alec had another thought. "God, I hope I don't create any fire. The last thing we need is another forest fire like the ones that swept southern Europe last month. Did you hear about that? Spain, France, Italy, Greece, straight across. Crazy."

"I did hear about those. I heard they were set deliberately."

Alec thought he caught a smirk, but couldn't tell at that distance.

"The one in Marseille was started by a military maneuver gone awry. Brilliant. I think you're safe here in wet, green Ireland."

That's some sense of humor. He checked his notes on the card and picked up the spray. "Okay, here goes nothin'." He took a slow breath. "I call upon Akasha, the light of the universe, to anoint these items to do my bidding." He misted the table top and the air around it. "I stand at the center and claim dominion over the forces present here." He held the rod and the dagger up high. "With this wand I exert my will, and with this dagger I command obedience. I call now into the spheres seeking a kindred spirit, a friend to guide me. I implore any of you here to see me, a loyal son of this land, powerful but naïve. I will give you life in exchange for knowledge. Use the life force of this moth to find a way onto this plane. You and this moth and I all belong here. Come join me in this beautiful glen. Let me breathe life into you, even if for a moment, so you can feel the sun and smell the flowers."

The moth fluttered madly, beating its wings against the glass. Alec wasn't sure if he should let it hurt itself. The spell required a living subject. As he was deciding, the jar bounced on the table. He was surprised the moth could hit the lid that hard. He looked closer and the jar bounced again, higher, and it wasn't due to a blow from the captive.

He held the rod over the jar and said, "See the moth's life. Focus and find your way here. Draw strength from my will."

The jar bounced again, but this time it settled too lightly, like it was being held aloft. Then it lifted off the table and hung in the air, the moth flapping furiously, but clearly not holding the jar in midair.

Alec caught a distortion in the air around the jar. Leaf fragments swept up into the space and filled the shape of the lensing air. He clutched the rod tighter and focused on the quivering he saw. It intensified and took the shape of a hand holding the jar.

"That's it. You can do this," he encouraged, holding his own apprehension in check. The hand grew into an arm, the arm grew into a body, and the body grew a head. It was like looking through shimmering water, as if the air had thickened, with leaf bits trapped in the shape. He couldn't make out any details, but he was definitely looking at a tall, broad shouldered man standing in front of him holding the moth.

"Welcome, friend, and thank you for joining me." He caught himself and remembered the spell's insistence that he remain in command of the spirit. "I hold you safely here, under my protection and my authority. What do you call yourself?"

The spirit made a sound like rushing water mixed with rustling leaves and howling wind. He caught a couple of consonant sounds, but that was all. "Please say that again, but faster this time."

"Cu Chulainn."

Alec was stunned. He could not have hoped for better. "Welcome, Hound of Ulster, Son of Lugh, hero of Táin Bó Cúailnge! *Sláinte a cairde!*"

The head shape distorted and Alec saw it as a broad smile. It spoke. "*Sláinte a cairde!*"

"Bravest of all the heroes, I thank you for stepping forward to assist me. I am seeking a spirit guide who can teach me the ways of the natural order. I need a mentor to show me how to command nature."

"That will be a big step for you, young master. You called me brave. You too are brave. I approve! It is better to live one day for glory than a hundred lifetimes in meek obscurity."

Alec smiled at how this was exactly what he expected from such a legendary risk-taker. "Are you able to teach me the secrets I desire? Would you be my partner in this adventure?"

"I am all about adventure. Where is your weapon?"

"My weapon? Do you mean this dagger?"

"Well, it ain't much, but I guess it's a starting place. The real art of combat is to master a sword."

"Oh, goodness no. I don't want to master combat. I wish to master magic."

"Magic? Well, why didn't you say so? I'm a great teacher when it comes to combat, and I have wielded magical weapons in my time, but I'm no magician. For that you'll need a sprite or an elemental god."

"Do you know any such being that could help me?"

"Ay, you're standing right in the home of one of the most beautiful and generous goddesses, one I have known through many adventures." The shimmering form turned around and pointed. "That pond shares its water with the Boyne River, which runs just passed those trees, which is the home of the goddess Boann. Come down to the water's edge with me and I will introduce you."

"I should not leave my pentagram. Within this boundary I am the ultimate power."

"Fair enough. Let me see if she'll come to you." The distortion handed Alec the jar with the moth, then ambled down to the pond. He lingered a moment, then ambled back.

Alec looked over at Benito, who gave him a thumbs-up without looking up from the video camera.

"The Goddess Boann is intrigued by you. She says she will grant you protection and honor your will and command if you come visit her."

Alec appraised Cu Chulainn sternly. "And you?"

"Oh, you summoned me. I am under your command regardless of where you stand."

Alec stepped out from behind his table of implements, looked down at the salt line in the grass, and, clutching the dagger and wand firmly in each hand, stepped across. Nothing happened. Cu Chulainn remained. Alec let out his breath and smiled. "Let's go talk to the goddess."

He reached back and grabbed the shot glass of whiskey.

As he stepped up to the pond, he noticed it was absolutely still. The surface was mirror smooth. The reflection was not of the sky and his surroundings, but of a stone temple. He couldn't help but look up to see what the image reflected. He felt foolish when he found only sky. He peered again and saw a throne at the top of stairs, and on the throne sat a woman with long flowing blonde hair. A light radiated from her skin that calmed Alec, it washed away his fears. Her white gown was wrapped about her oddly, as if hiding one of her arms and one of her legs. She also wore a scarf in her hair that covered one eye.

Alec didn't want to appear weak, but felt like he was being honored as a guest. He bowed slightly while keeping his eyes on her. "Thank you, Goddess, for agreeing to see me."

"Welcome Alec of Clan Doogan. You visit me with some very ancient tools. Clearly you have learned much. What do you hope to learn from me?"

"Mastery over water. And if such mastery is not directly possible, I hope to strike a bargain for you to exert your power over water on my behalf."

"You speak of a bargain. What do you bring to me?"

"I offer my services as your agent on Earth. Once you have taught me the magic, I will be able to carry out your wishes in the world."

"Tempting. But I actually meant what have you brought me today?"

"Oh, today I bring you the finest Irish whiskey." He knelt down and poured the glass into the edge of the water. "The best mankind can make from your water and the grain that grows in it."

"Tasty. A fitting tribute. I will tell you this much. You will not need me there every time you want water to obey you. You will need to learn to act as I did when I created the Boyne."

"Your Holiness challenged the Well of Segais."

"I did. I coaxed it into a frenzy, drove it to spill over and form my beloved river. Drove it mad, I did, until the waters ran all the way around Erin and down to the sea."

"How do I duplicate that, Your Holiness? You're a god."

She leaned forward and waved her free hand about in a circle. "It's the frenzy, lad. Ye have to dance, and it must be widdershins!"

Alec noticed Cu Chulainn standing by, nodding.

"Do you know what she means?" Alec asked the hero.

"Aye. Reach out to the water with your will, and dare it to follow you. Then spin around and force it to do your bidding."

Alec looked at the wand which guided his willpower and the dagger which gave force to his commands. He turned back to Boann. "May I try it here and now, with your guidance, on this pond?"

"Oh yes!"

Alec was happy for the support, but it did not escape him that he had gotten a nature goddess excited. He knew lots of tales were men drown when a god got excited and careless.

He held his implements out above the water and imagined seizing it. He wanted to move it away, so he imagined pushing. When he had that image firm in his mind, he started to spin around with a little hop step, to the left, counterclockwise. He pictured himself teasing the water, dragging it with his motion.

As he turned, he caught Benito and the camera, and realized this was exactly what he had feared, film of him flailing about making a fool of himself.

Then he felt a tug. His right hand with the dagger pulled against something, even though he saw nothing. Then he heard a slushing in the water. He pulled against the resistance and watched the water on his next turn. It was rippling as if someone were mixing it with an oar.

"You've got it," Boann said. "Now push harder."

He could hardly believe it. He pulled harder and spun faster. The edge of the water lifted up and rolled back. It looked like some great wind were blowing it, but the air was still. He pulled again and turned even faster, dancing now with joy. The water pulled back several feet, exposing the pond floor.

Alec couldn't resist, and he danced down onto the mud, pushing the waters back further and further. He got several paces out and saw he had created a U-shaped parting several yards wide and deep. The three-foot high wall of water he was holding at bay gave him pause, and he started dancing back to the shore. He didn't want to get stuck in the soft mud, so he kept his steps rapid. Back on dry ground, he slowed his step and let loose his pull on the connection. The water relaxed and flowed back to fill the space.

Cu Chulainn let out a whooping cheer that startled Alec. He was already giddy from his success, and the outcry left him laughing and shaking his head.

•   •   •

Alec had just finished toweling off after a shower when his cell phone rang. "Hello?"

"Alec, it's Sanantha Mauwad."

"Hi, Sanantha."

"Are you at home?"

"Yeah. What's up?"

"Do you have your computer handy?"

"Sure."

"I just emailed you a link to a YouTube video I think you'll want to see."

"Really? All right. Give me a minute."

"I was Googling your research and this came up."

He pulled on a pair of shorts and went to his desktop. "Okay, I'm here. Right, got your message. So what am I opening?"

"Just open it and then we'll talk."

The site came up and the frame filled with a clip titled, "Alec Doogan, Paranormal Researcher is the real deal." It showed Alec standing by the pond spinning his dance with the water pushing away. "Saint Christopher protect us! What in hell's name is this doing online?" The clip continued until he walked out advancing the wall of water.

"I was going to ask you that same question. Your research has taken quite a turn, I'd say."

"Well, yes. I've been busy."

"So you didn't know this was going to be posted for the public?"

"Absolutely not." Fury was clear in his voice. "I'm going to wring Benito's neck."

"Benito?"

"Yeah, he's my new backer."

"What's his last name?"

"Nomini."

There was a long silence on the phone.

"Why? Do you know him?"

After another pause, she finally said quietly, "Yes. I met him on the plane to Ireland. He had your book. He let me read it."

"Yeah, he sought me out from the book. He's been paying for paranormal research for a long time, and he thought I could use some help. He actually came at a really good time for me. Now I see he's a loose cannon on deck. Taking this public is going too far."

"You know, Joseph warned you about getting in over your head."

"He's been really helpful. He brought me some old scrolls, and that's what we were checking out. He just wasn't supposed to take anything public yet."

"You should read the comments below the clip. A lot of people are taking this very seriously," she said.

"These people are asking to be my apprentices. Damn, these folks are serious. Man, I've got to have Benito take this down right away."

"That would be prudent. If Benito could find you, these folks can too. Did Benito tell you where he got these scrolls?"

"He said another researcher he funded found them, but the other guy didn't have my formulas to make them work."

"So he had a spell for controlling water?"

"No, the spell was for summoning a spirit. That's what my formula does: it bridges the gap to contact spirits. The spirits showed me how to move the water."

"Alec, I don't mean to be an alarmist, but this is exactly what Joseph warned you about. Spirits are unpredictable and have their own agendas."

"I get that. Joseph has his expertise, and that's great. He's more interested in shielding Desiree from harm than anything I'm doing."

"I may not like Joseph personally, but I trust his expertise implicitly in these matters. You should too."

"I've been contacting spirits for the last two years. It's just always been me visiting them haunting somewhere. These spells let me call out to them, summon them to me, and they obey me. That's the amazing part. I'm not going to walk away from that."

"All right, I hear you. I can't counsel you beyond being a good friend of a friend. On the other hand, I do know a lot about spirits and how people interact with them."

"Yeah, Desiree mentioned that you practice Voodou," he said.

"That's correct. We contact spirits through ceremony. It's the ceremony that gives us control over the contact. I've seen the kinds of things you're seeing now for the first time. It's really easy to let yourself think you have power and are in control. I just want to caution you to take it slow, one step at a time, using controls, like you discussed in your book."

Alec looked up from his computer at the framed picture of Saint Catherine of Siena. "I appreciate that."

"May I ask you a question? Which spirit showed you how to move the water?"

"That was the old Celtic goddess Boann. And yes, I've done my homework."

"I'm sure you have. I'll get off your back. Please go tell Benito to take that video down."

"Absolutely."

He hung up the phone and looked up again at the icon. "Saint Catherine, now is when I need your strength and your example. Please do not let me get in over my head."

•   •   •

Alec was glad for the sunlight in his usual window seat at the Brown Stag café as he poured over crumbling papyrus fragments held safe between plastic sheets. He switched between the magnifying glass and the legal pad, translating and annotating as he went. It was slow work, and very little seemed to fit together. Each sentence he made out just raised more questions. Yet his preliminary work had yielded such amazing results. The treasures he could unlock in here were worth being patient.

Hearing his name spoken snapped him out of his concentration. A tall, massive man in a suit was asking after him at the bar. The bartender pointed the man to Alec. Maybe telling bartenders to keep his identity a secret was one of those fame precautions Benito mentioned.

The man was bigger up close than Alec expected. He also did not hold out a hand as Alec thought, but rather held up a badge. Alec recognized the gate logo before the man identified it. "Mr. Doogan. I apologize for dropping in on you like this. I am Revenue Commissioner Michael Archibald. If you have a moment, I'd like to ask you a few questions." His direct manner really was not blunted by his otherwise soothing thick Irish brogue.

"Should I hire a solicitor?"

He smirked without actually smiling. "That depends on how you answer my questions. Probably not at this time. I only want to fill in some facts we need to make sure you are not being defrauded."

"So you're looking out for me?"

"We like to think that's what we do." He said this with a straight face, in spite of the Treasury Department being universally loathed. "May I sit down?"

"Yes, of course."

"Thank you. A large sum was recently wired to your bank account from a bank in Italy. We noticed some irregularities in the originating account, and we're concerned you may have been pulled into a money laundering scheme."

"No, that money is a legitimate payment for services. How do you know what payments I get? And how did you find me here?"

"Banks have to tell us about large sum movements, especially across international borders. As to finding you here, you come here almost every morning. Repeat payments are also something we keep an eye on."

Alec studied his cold, pale blue eyes, aging skin and gray-streaked wavy blond hair. If he wasn't the genuine article, he certainly knew how to project an air of authority. "You said you saw 'irregularities' in the Italian sender's account. Do you think he's a criminal?"

"All I can say is we've been watching him and we will continue to watch him." He slipped Alec a card on the table. "Here's my number. If you see anything suspicious, I'd appreciate a call."

"You act like I need protection. This may look like trouble, but how do you know I'm not a criminal in league with this guy?"

"We know more about you than I am at liberty to say. We know you're not a criminal. We'd know right away if that changed."

Alec picked up the card. Michael Archibald. *Should be Michael Wreckingball.*

"Sure, I can call if I smell a rat. By the way, I'm going to be getting more of those payments from Italy, probably every month."

"Thank you for your cooperation." He got up and offered his hand. It was enormous.

"Glad to be a dutiful citizen." Alec's attempt at sarcasm fell flat.

"Good day."

Out on the street, Joseph was enjoying a brisk walk to meet Alec for coffee. Even though he didn't have to walk anywhere, he enjoyed walking. Beaches were his favorite, but quaint towns were nice too. As he approached the café, he noticed a large, well-dressed man get into a very sleek, pearlescent white sports car. Joseph's love of fast cars had served him well ever since Silas brought him into this world a decade ago. He did not recognize this one, so he took a closer look. Broad stance, low center of gravity, very aerodynamic. As it roared to life and pulled into traffic, he caught the model, BMW 666i. He had not seen that one before.

10

A S ALEC WATCHED COMMISSIONER ARCHIBALD LEAVE, his vision blurred for a moment and he felt dizzy. He closed his eyes to let it pass, and saw a mountainside. He popped his eyes open in shock despite the wooziness. Very cautiously, he closed his eyes again and once again he was standing in front of a mountain. He looked up its flat face and saw a huge crevice of a cave, a crack that curved and formed a symbol. He tried to turn his head to look around, but the dizziness made him move slowly. He gripped the café table in front of him with both hands while turning his head cautiously, exploring this virtual world he had tapped into. The landscape was barren, blasted clean with wind and ice. He didn't know what any of it meant, but he hoped the vision would last long enough for him to make sense of it. He was alone, just him and the triangular face of this scared mountain.

He caught a flash of movement, something fast wriggling down out of the cave toward him. He could only catch glimpses as it darted between boulders and down ravines. He lost it for a long, tense moment. Far closer than he expected, a dragon popped up onto a rock next to him, not thirty feet away. His heart leapt and he flushed with sweat. In that moment he forgot he was actually still safe in a café in Dublin. The monster was huge, at least forty feet long, jade green with enormous frills and jagged edges everywhere. He froze and waited. Running seemed pointless. As terrifying as it was, it clearly had come to him for a reason. It regarded him for what seemed an eternity, then slithered slowly off the rock and up to Alec. It reared its front ten feet up into what looked like a formal pose, then brought around a claw and presented him with a ball. No not a ball, a pearl, a gigantic pearl, four inches across. It glowed with a rainbow of refracted pearlescence.

He pried his eyes up from it and looked the dragon in its brilliant red eyes. "Is this for me?"

He heard a voice say, "Oh yes," but it wasn't the dragon. "Take it and remember," the familiar male voice said. The vision broke up, and faded. He grasped at the pearl and it was gone.

He opened his eyes and Joseph was sitting across from him with an enormous grin on his face. "I know that look. You had a vision."

"Were you sitting here the whole time? Did you do this to me?"

"I walked in while you were under. I recognized what you were going through and sat here to wait it out. You're covered in sweat. It must have been intense."

"'Intense' barely touches it." He looked around the café, still not entirely sure what was real or not. "I was there. I could feel the wind and taste the cold and feel the stony ground under my feet. I've never had such a hallucination before."

"That was not just in your mind. I'm telling you, these visions are much more. Where were you, and what was being offered to you?"

"Did you say, 'Take it and remember?'"

"Yes, getting what was offered and remembering what happened are critical."

"I was facing a huge, flat-faced mountain, with a curved slash of a cave in it, and a Chinese dragon came out and offered me a pearl the size of my fist. What the hell does that mean? I've been working with Celtic spirits and Mesopotamian spells. Where did China come in?"

Even though he was still wearing his mirrored sunglasses as always, Joseph looked at him with a frightening intensity, as if he was drilling into him. "I don't know. We must find out. This is too real and too important to brush off. Something is sending you a message that we cannot ignore. I need to get to the ladies' apartment and use the Internet to find your sacred mountain." He got up to leave.

"Hold up, I'll come with you."

By the time Alec was on his feet, Joseph was at the door. "Catch up," Joseph called back.

When Alec got to the door, Joseph was nowhere to be seen.

Joseph knocked on the cottage door and, when no one answered, he considered teleporting inside. He looked around for bystanders and found none. He decided to knock again in case he hadn't been heard.

Sanantha answered, breathless. "Oh, Joseph. I'm glad it's you. Desiree is having some kind of massive hallucination." She walked back still talking, leading Joseph in. "It's not a seizure. I'm not sure what it is. It's like she's having a nightmare while she's still awake."

They got to the bedroom and Desiree was on the bed on her belly writhing around wild-eyed.

"It almost looks like she's being mounted by a *loa*."

Desiree squirmed up on all fours and looked at them in the door. She blinked furiously and shook her head, then collapsed flat.

Joseph rolled her over onto her back and checked her eyes while Sanantha took her pulse.

She startled awake, looked at the two of them, and curled up crying. "Oh my fucking god, what was that?"

"That was a vision. Were you in China?"

Sanantha shot him a stare.

He held up a finger for her to wait.

"Yes," Desiree answered weakly.

"Did you think you were a dragon?"

She looked at him in shock. "Yes. It was amazing and horrible at the same time. I didn't know I could move like that. I was fast and powerful, but," she clutched her body, "I was a giant lizard!"

Sanantha looked like she was about to burst with questions.

"Was there a pearl?"

Desiree looked up at him wide-eyed. "Yes. It was beautiful. It was my most precious possession. But I needed to give it to someone. I desperately needed to give it away."

"Do you know to whom you needed to give it? Was it Alec?"

"I don't know. Alec wasn't there. I was alone, crawling around in my cave, furious and sad, and so many emotions I could hardly make sense."

Joseph stood up and crossed his arms over his chest and sighed deeply. "Well, that seals it."

Sanantha could not hold on any longer. "Seals what?"

The doorbell rang.

"That will be Alec," Joseph said coolly.

Sanantha was not going to be interrupted. She yelled to the front, "It's open, come on in!" Turning back to Joseph, she pressed, "What is going on?"

Joseph took his turn yelling to the front. "Alec, get in here! You're going to want to hear this."

Alec stepped in looking bewildered. "How did you get here so fast?"

"Never mind that. Desiree just had a vision just like yours, with one small difference. She was the dragon."

Alec looked like he stepped on a tack. "Holy Mother of God! How is that possible?"

Sanantha cut in. "You had a vision of being in China, and saw a dragon?"

"Oh yeah. Right there in the café. Scared the Christ out of me. And the dragon gave me a pearl the size of my fist. Most beautiful thing I ever saw."

Sanantha turned to Joseph. "I smell intervention."

He grinned back at her. "Indeed." Then to the two confused young people, "It appears Isis has had her way with you two. The Celestial Dragon is a godhead. Gods easily slip on the robes of other gods. In this case, Isis — that's you Desiree — wants to give something extremely precious to you, Alec. It's so important she put you both in the same vision, playing the two roles, giver and recipient."

"In China?" Sanantha wondered.

"I was in a cave," Desiree supplied.

"And I was at the foot of the mountain looking up at the cave," Alec added.

"So you saw the outside of the mountain?" Desiree asked.

"Yeah, the face of it was really flat, and triangular, and your cave was the shape of a big curved slash across the face. It almost looked like a symbol."

Joseph asked, "Can you draw the symbol? It might show us what Isis is trying to give you."

"Sure."

Sanantha handed him a note pad. He had his own pen. He drew the shape and showed it around.

Sanantha blinked recognition. "You said the face of the mountain was triangular, like the whole mountain would be a pyramid shape?"

"Yeah, like that."

She rubbed her eyes. "Joseph, I think you're interpreting this too abstractly. Isis doesn't want to give Alec 'something' valuable. She is showing us something specific. That symbol is the name Vishnu in Sanskrit. And that mountain is a real place, called Kailash, in Nepal."

Joseph rolled with her. "So if the dragon is Desiree, and the place is real, does that mean the pearl is real?"

She swallowed hard. "It's called *Om Mani Padme Hum*, the Jewel that Grants All Wishes."

Alec found his ground. "The Celestial Pearl is ubiquitous in Asian art. Do we know what it's supposed to do?"

Sanantha shrugged. "Other than the name, no."

Alec concluded, "So here we have a god not only revealing that an age-old myth is in fact real, but that god wants to deliver it, to me?"

Desiree answered. "She must think you need it — and badly enough to intervene at this level, with matching visions."

Alec looked from face to face around the room. "So what am I supposed to do, go to Nepal and look for a dragon?"

"No, I'm the dragon," Desiree said. "I'm supposed to give it to you. So I go to Nepal and retrieve it."

"You're going to need some help," Joseph said.

"Oh, I absolutely want your talents with me."

"I'll stay here and research Kailash and the myths surrounding the pearl," offered Sanantha. "I'll call you with my findings."

Desiree looked at Joseph. "How quickly can you get us to Nepal?"

"With all the connections and flight time, we could be there by tomorrow night."

He could see how disappointed she was.

He raised his eyebrows and leaned in. "I've never been to Nepal."

She nodded slowly. "Oh. Right."

•   •   •

Sanantha settled in at Alec's desk. "Thank you for letting me use your computer. Your fast Internet connection is going to make this a lot easier."

"My pleasure. Whatever we can do to support Desiree on her trip."

Sanantha couldn't help but notice the icon painting of a woman holding lilies sitting on the shelf above the desk. She had assumed Alec was Catholic, and this confirmed it. She also noticed how clean and tidy everything was.

"If you don't mind, Benito is coming over to show me some scrolls he wants me to analyze. You said you two met on the plane, right?"

"Yes."

"If you don't mind my saying so, you sounded rather put out when I told you he was backing my research."

"I was a bit taken at the coincidence."

"It's a good coincidence, I hope?"

"Oh, yes. He was quite charming on the long flight. I'm actually glad I had a chance to meet him casually first."

"I'm glad to hear that. It's important to me for everyone to get along."

She turned back to the keyboard. "I think I'll start with the pearl itself."

"You said it 'grants all wishes.' That's a big promise but with no context."

"We do know the Celestial Dragon is seen universally across Asia as the benevolence of nature. I'm bookmarking articles here, if you don't mind."

"No, that's fine."

"I'm seeing Japanese myths about *naga* mermaids, Chinese myths about swallowing the moon, art scholars talking about lightning coming out of the sphere. This is going to take a while. Oh wait, here's something on the name. Oh, now that's interesting."

Alec stepped up behind her. "What did you find?"

The phrase translates as the 'Jewel that grants all desires', but it is taught by Buddhists to school children all across the continent as a mantra to mean the wisdom of the Buddha is the jewel." She turned in the chair to look up at him. "That would make sense as a teaching tool, but it doesn't tell us why Isis wants you to have it. The wisdom of Buddha is in dozens of sutras and stories. We're talking volumes of material."

"So what are Desiree and Joseph looking for, I mean physically? Is there an object at all?"

A knock at the door came. "That will be Benito."

Sanantha got up as Alec went to the door.

"Benito, please come in."

He stepped in passed Alec and lit up at seeing Sanantha. "*Come molto fortunato!* Dr. Mauwad, what a delightful surprise!"

She offered her hand, but when he took it he also stepped in and kissed her on the cheek. "It's good to see you as well, Mr. Nomini."

"Benito, please. But how are you here?" He looked back and forth between her and Alec. "On the plane I showed you Alec's book, and now you are in his house. I am confused."

Alec stepped up. "It's my fault. I apologize. Sanantha came to Ireland to see her friend Desiree. I don't think you've met her yet, but she and I did some field work and we've become friends. When Sanantha told me she met you on the plane, I should have filled you in."

"Well, better late than never. I love it when life gives us such signs."

"I thought it was a quite the coincidence," Sanantha agreed.

"Such a boon cannot be due to chance alone. Things don't just line up like this by themselves. When destiny speaks, we have to listen," he said with a flourish of his hands.

Sanantha allowed herself a small grin. "You could have mentioned you were coming to see the author of that book you let me read."

"You could have told me your friend, Deirdre ..."

"Desiree."

"*Grazie.* Desiree was working with the author of that book. But if we had, it would have taken all the fun out of this discovery, no?"

Sanantha's dimples deepened with her widening smile. "Alec tells me you not only fund his research, but you bring him fragments to work on."

"Yes, the projects I have funded over the years have netted me lots of interesting puzzle pieces. Alec here turns out to be good at fitting them together."

She turned to Alec. "Are you making sense of things?"

"Yes. Things that I would have thought were just random similarities have turned out to be related."

"Causation?" she asked warily.

"Yes, I think so," Alec said with wide eyes.

Benito jumped in enthusiastically. "How often do you get to use that word when you're talking about the supernatural?"

•   •   •

The rust-covered jinty shuddered into motion and backfired as it left Desiree and Joseph standing at the top of the main street of Purang, Nepal. The steady breeze, which smelled slightly of hay, was chilly, but warmer than she expected. The several locals who also got off the bus carried laden bags over their shoulders as they walked into the town of whitewashed mud brick buildings. Desiree saw a gathering of people at the end of the street. Joseph must have noticed her staring.

"Barley harvest market. Last commerce this place will see with the snows coming next month."

"Not much of a crowd for such an important time."

Joseph looked around. "This used to be the capitol of a wealthy empire. The palaces have all been turned into monasteries. The cycle of rise and decline has come full circle."

"The guidebook didn't talk about that."

"I'm just telling you what I see."

"Do you see where we should start? I don't see Kailash."

"I caught a glimpse of it as we landed. It's north of here, over those mountains."

Desiree brightened but then caught herself. "So you know where … it is?"

Joseph cracked a crooked grin. "Yes, I can take us there."

She felt sweat break out across her back. She had joked with him about teleporting to Tibet, but when suddenly faced with actually making a jump, she was having serious second thoughts. "Have you ever?"

"Travelled with someone? Yes. I travelled with my Master a couple of times, and he never voiced any concerns."

"Silas was a master magician. He knew what to expect."

"I even transported him once by himself, over a great distance. I can only assume he landed safely, since he then won a huge battle."

"Can only assume? Didn't you ask him later?"

"There was no later. I never saw him again after that. But I know he was victorious, so he couldn't have arrived injured."

"You are not making me feel any safer."

"I appreciate I am generally not very comforting. I can only say I have been doing this for thousands of years. It is as natural for me as breathing."

"Okay. Do I hug you or what?"

"Clasping hands is sufficient," he said offering his.

She noticed how wet her palms were when she took hold. "Sorry. Do I clench up or relax or what?"

"Makes no difference. I'm just opening the way so we stop being here and start being there. Everything you are stays the same."

She frowned trying to grasp how that worked. She looked around to see that no one was nearby watching. She took a breath and held it, and closed her eyes tight. "Okay, do it."

She was suddenly surrounded by a loud roar of wind, even though she felt no air movement. It surprised her and she squeezed out a yelp. When the sound stopped, she opened her eyes and saw them standing on a snow-covered hillside that overlooked a lake and miles of open space. The wind was much colder here, and it cut through her parka.

Joseph was looking at her with a frown she took for concern.

"I assume that squeak came from me."

He smiled. "Yes, it did. Welcome to Kailash."

She let go her iron grip on his hands, turned, and gasped. "Oh my God! It really is a pyramid." She grasped her hair with both hands and rocked her head back to take in its towering height. "It's so big!" She ran around the corner they faced and pointed up at the curved gash across its face. "There's the Vishnu cave. It doesn't really look like a cave in person. Joseph, this is a huge mountain. How are we supposed to find something the size of a baseball? What do you see?"

He stepped up beside her and pointed down to the base. "I see we are not alone."

A solitary man was on his knees praying, holding a string of beads. After a moment, he got up, shifted his makeshift cardboard mat over a few feet, then knelt down and prayed again. They watched him do this half a dozen times.

"He's not going all the way around the mountain like that, is he?"

"Looks like it."

She sized up the distance. "He won't make it in a day."

"No. He'll sleep when he needs to. Should take him about a week."

She watched for a long moment. "Why?"

"I can see why. Sometimes seeing the truth is not pleasant."

Desiree was impressed at how Joseph wanted to protect her. "I have to understand."

"His children were killed in a flood and he blames himself. He bears the scars of several suicide attempts. He has turned to atonement instead. This pilgrimage will purge him of his ego. He will probably join the priesthood. I've seen this before. Often when people cannot make sense of fate, they surrender themselves to a higher life of piety."

The story got to her and she fought back a tear. "Four straight sides, lakes on each side, rivers extending out to the compass points, just like the book said. 'The Center of the Universe'. This place is holier than I thought." She looked at Joseph. "We can't just hold a scavenger hunt here. We need to know a lot more about this place if we expect it to give up its secrets to us."

"I see Kailash gets its power because it is the reflection in the real world of a much holier place."

"I don't understand."

"Places are holy because they are only a thin shade away from a source of real power. These hidden places are where magic and deities live."

"Mirror realities, with magic and gods?"

"Yes, same place, but in the Spirit Plane."

"You are an angel of the Opener of the Ways. Can you travel to one of these Spirit Plane versions?"

"Yes, but, as you said, this is holy ground. Even I would not dare tread there without knowledge and reverence."

"You said there were monasteries back in town. We'll start there."

•   •   •

As Alec returned from seeing Benito out, Sanantha, seated again at the computer, said, "You two seem to have made up after the videotape posting. You were furious."

"I was, and I had words with him. He then explained that since my condenser fluid focuses willpower, he wants to see if having lots of people focusing their attention will make it easier to achieve results."

"You mean followers? Focusing the power of faith in your work?"

"Exactly. I thought it was far-fetched, so I plan on testing his theory. All those folks who responded to his post will be invited to watch me conduct a spell on a live feed."

"Like a video conference?"

"No, just a broadcast. Benito says he'll show me how to do it. I don't need their actual feedback during the show. I'll be able to tell if their added willpower makes the spell work better."

Sanantha chose her words carefully. "I hope you see what a big step it is going from connecting the dots of Benito's previous sponsorships to gathering followers and asking them to believe in your abilities to perform miracles."

"I do. It is a big step, but I see it as a logical progression. What allows me to connect those dots is the fluid. I researched the formula from the ancients. It lets me reach passed physics into the spirit realm. If Aleister Crowley was right, and willpower is the coin of the universe, then why not see if we can increase our spending power?"

"May I make a personal suggestion?"

"Sure."

"As a trained psychiatrist who has seen the power of faith, and who has seen magic performed, I only caution that you explore this fluid and what it can do in as objective a way as you can. It is really easy to start believing in your own natural abilities, that you have a gift or a knack. I have seen such belief turn into justification for the abuse of power."

"You're worried wielding this power could go to my head?"

"I wouldn't insult you like that. You seem pretty level-headed, so I'm not really worried. I think what you're doing is amazing and wonderful. You could unlock mysteries that mankind has chased for ages. I hope you will grow to trust me enough to let me stick around and counsel you. This can turn into a slippery slope. It doesn't have to."

"You've seen real magic?"

"Yes. Joseph and I met when he was working for a magician who thought his power gave him the right to decide life or death. He had some pretty lofty goals, but his abilities had seduced him into feeling the ends justified any means."

"Joseph worked for this guy?"

"With Joseph, still waters run very deep."

"Desiree certainly trusts him. I get the impression you don't."

"I believe in him. You're right, that's not really the same as trusting him. He tends to gather trouble around himself. I guess it's an occupational hazard of working with magic. Which is why I am cautioning you. This stuff is very seductive."

"Thank you for the warning."

●　　　●　　　●

"It looks like we've got two monasteries to chose from: this one and the one at the other end of town," Desiree said with a wave of her hand. "We've watched monks come and go from both of them. Are you getting any vibe from either one?"

Joseph turned from the ironclad wooden door to give Desiree a disapproving look. "I do not get 'vibes'. I see the truth of things as they are. Both temples have scholars who could help us. This one, Khorchag Gonpa, houses a large historic silver statue of a Bodhisattva. The monks we saw walking out just now believe strongly in the Bodhisattva ideal of bringing back wisdom from the spiritual plane. The monks at the other temple, called Gongphur, believe they are entrusted to keep great teachings safe. I think we will find more openness and helpfulness at this one."

"Joseph, that's a vibe."

Behind his ever-present semi-silvered sunglasses, he rolled his eyes before he knocked on the door.

A young bald monk in a simple grey robe answered.

"*Tashi delek,*" Joseph began. "*Chog mchan skad cha bshad bla ma?*"

Desiree was surprised that Joseph spoke Tibetan, until she realized how obvious that should have been.

"*Ga re byas nas?*" the monk asked.

"*Jo-O Jampal Dorjee.*"

"*Nges pa?*"

"*Om Mani Padme Hum.*"

She recognized that phrase. Joseph's lack of subtlety was once again on full display.

He must have impressed the young man, because he bowed and opened the door for them. The monk led them through a courtyard that clearly was used by the carriages of dignitaries when this building had been a royal palace. A couple of other monks who were walking through the courtyard saw them and stopped to watch.

A large carved double door led to a reception hall. The young man said something to Joseph, bowed, and trotted off.

"He's getting an abbot."

"You came right out and told him what we're after?"

"Yes. I saw no sense in subversion."

"Why did you think they wouldn't reject us as fools?"

"I told him we were sent here by their patron saint."

She started to object but he answered her preemptively with a devilish grin at the corner of his mouth.

Wow. Angels are not above lying.

A moment later, a middle-aged monk approached, again bald, but in a saffron robe. "*Dga bsu zhu Khorchag Gonpa,*" he said with a small bow.

Desiree was tired of being left out of the conversation. "Pardon me, but do you speak English?"

He smiled. "Yes, I do."

"Thank you," she said, extending her hand. "I'm Desiree Macklin, and this is Joseph de Alverado."

He hesitated at her hand before politely shaking it. He then placed his palms together in front of his heart and said, "I am Renpo Kashiligan Samsuri. I am one of the abbots here. You told my acolyte that you seek the Jewel that Grants All Wishes."

Desiree shot Joseph a sideways look. "Yes, I had a vision, and we're pretty sure it was divine guidance."

"From Bodhisattva Manjushiri?"

She took a breath. "Not exactly. We think it was from the Egyptian goddess Isis."

He thought about this for a moment, but not as long as Desiree expected. "She told you we have the Pearl?"

"She said the Pearl is on Kailash. We visited the mountain, but it is far too sacred a place for us to trample looking for a hidden treasure. We are hoping you can guide us with your knowledge and wisdom. I was told to find the Pearl, but I do not want to desecrate the holy mountain."

"I appreciate your reverence. Why should I believe the goddess of an ancient civilization compelled you to come here?"

Desiree and Joseph traded a resigned look. "Because Joseph here is an angel from that ancient religion."

"And Desiree here is an avatar vessel of that ancient goddess," Joseph added.

Renpo looked thoughtful but not shocked.

"We know how outrageous this sounds," she conceded. "We have no reason to lie to you. We barely know what we're looking for. We need your help."

"I don't doubt you are who you say. I would test you if I did. I question the information your goddess gave you. The myths surrounding the Pearl are not connected to Kailash. The Pearl is said to rest in Khyi Tor, the cave of the lost dog. Khyi Tor is lost in one of the many mountains of southern Tibet. The cave entrance is supposed to be blocked by ice in the winter and by floods in the summer. There is no such cave on Kailash. It is also said the cave only opens once every twelve years, in the Year of the Dog. This year, 2009, is the Year of the Ox. You may be mistaken."

Desiree tightened down her courage. "Doesn't your faith teach the Jewel that Grants All Wishes is actually Buddha's teachings?"

"Yes, that's correct."

"And isn't Kailash the center of the Buddhist universe?"

"Kailash is the physical form of Mount Semeru, which is the spiritual center of the universe."

"What if I told you one of Joseph's abilities is to travel to the spirit plane counterparts of holy places? The lost dog cave may not exist on Kailash. It might not exist on any mountain on Earth. It might exist on Mount Semeru. What better place to keep the symbol of Buddha's wisdom?"

Renpo raised an eyebrow and stared at Desiree. She always had difficulty reading that classic Oriental poker face.

Then he looked at Joseph and something connected. His eyes widened.

Joseph read it right. "I can take you there."

Desiree saw his eyes glisten up before he blinked back tears. "I would not believe a word of your amazing, nearly profane claims, except I have had my own visions. When Daki came and got me, I told myself to not bring my hopes and expectations, to simply hear you out."

Desiree spotted a mosaic of the Celestial Dragon with the Pearl on a far wall. She pointed eagerly. "Did your vision involve that dragon?"

"No. I saw the Third Turning of the Wheel will come in my lifetime, and that the fifth Buddha, the Bodhisattva Maitreya will return and teach the true dharma. His teachings will free mankind from greed and oppression. You seeking the Pearl means the Buddha's teachings will be brought out into the open and will be made manifest. I did not want to believe you. The Buddha said, 'The mind that perceives the limitation is the limitation.' You two messengers from a lost civilization might be the ones to usher in a new age."

Joseph nodded. "When can we leave?"

"Kailash is more than half a day's journey. We will have to leave in the morning."

Desiree shot Joseph a look while holding up two fingers at waist height.

He nodded.

She turned to Renpo. "Not the way we travel. We can go now, if you're ready."

"Oh?" He regarded Joseph. "Indeed. Allow me to get my coat."

Desiree noticed his sandals. "And some boots. It's really cold up on that mountain."

The monk smiled dismissively.

Joseph corrected her. "When we get to Semeru, he'll be walking on that most hallowed ground in bare feet."

Renpo placed his palms together and bowed to Joseph, who returned the gesture.

•   •   •

Sanantha looked up from the computer screen and rubbed her eyes. "This is fascinating stuff, but I've got to take a break."

"You've been at it for over four hours," Alec agreed from the back of the house.

"My head is throbbing. Do you have any wine?"

"No, sorry. I finished it off last night," he said without coming out from the bedroom.

She pouted. "Do you have any over-the-counter pain meds?"

"Sure. Check the cabinet in the WC."

"Thanks." She got up and did so, while asking, "What are you doing back there?"

"Sorting laundry."

His bathroom, like the rest of his house, was impeccably tidy. She had no problem finding a bottle of naproxen. She also spied a prescription bottle of Celexa. She knew this well and didn't even have to pick it up. Citalopram, SSRI for OCD. That made sense.

"What did you find?" Alec asked from around the corner.

She grabbed the naproxen and closed the cabinet. "Pardon?"

Alec stepped up behind her in the hallway. "In your research."

"Oh, right. If the Pearl is a real object, it must be a talisman of truth. Buddha's ministry was all about seeing things as they really are, without the filters of ego and expectation. Remarkably, this is a topic Joseph is well versed in, even though he is not a Buddhist. Maybe that will help them find it. I can't find anything describing what it might do, because no one ever talks about it being a real object, but the inference is it would let you see things clearly."

"Objective truth?"

"Yes, I know. To strip away all dogmatic prejudice, all preconceptions, that would be amazing."

"That would be incredibly useful in my work. So much of what I am discovering is guesswork and interpretation. To see if I am getting real results or not would be huge. You should call Desiree and let her know what to look for."

"They'll be on a plane over Eastern Europe at this point. I'll leave her a voice message."

•   •   •

Abbot Renpo Sensuri returned wearing an overrobe Desiree thought looked like he had wrapped himself up in his entire bed's worth of blankets. She smiled when she spied he had put on socks under his sandals.

"I am ready," he said quietly.

Desiree held up a hand to Joseph while facing the monk. "Father? Um, do I call you 'Father'?"

"Brother Renpo will do."

"Brother Renpo, are you really all right with this? I mean, a couple of strangers walk in here and offer to magically take you to the spiritual center of the universe, and you just say, "I am ready?" It's taken me weeks to ease into this stuff, and it still doesn't feel normal."

"A cornerstone of my faith is to see things as they really are, not colored by my anticipations and fears. Yes, this is an extraordinary turn of events, but it is happening, whether I am ready or not. My job as a practitioner is to be ready and to act on the truth." He smiled. "My heart is racing, and my head is spinning, but I am ready."

Joseph and Desiree clasped hands and extended two for Renpo. "It's really simple," Desiree assured him. "Joseph does all the work. We're just along for the ride, and it only takes an instant."

He stepped into the circle and took their hands. Desiree noted how he did not grip tightly like a frightened person. Desiree decided to keep her eyes open this time, both to look less frightened herself, and out of curiosity.

He looked to Joseph. "I am in your hands, literally."

Joseph bowed very slightly to him, and the room went black. Black and still despite the startlingly loud rush of air around them. Then it was light. She noticed black wisps of smoke drift away from them once they landed. The bracing cold air surprised her, she had been so focused on the teleport.

Renpo was all eyes as he slowly and completely took in where they were. The sheer joy on his face made Desiree grin.

"Can I let go now?" he asked.

"Of course," Joseph said as he stepped back. "But stay close by. You will have to physically follow me through the break onto Semeru." He took his glasses off and studied the ground around them.

Renpo did not seem surprised at Joseph's yellow eyes.

"Here. This looks right," he said at an entirely unremarkable spot. He launched into what looked like a *tai chi* routine, pinwheeling his arms around, pushing to the left and right, kicking upward. It looked too fast for *tai chi*. Was it *kung fu*? She looked at Renpo and he seemed familiar with this dance. Maybe it was *kung fu*.

Desiree was watching intently when he pulled up flat, with his arms uplifted, body and legs akimbo all in a plane. He made one last chopping springing motion, and the air itself split into an actual gap. She looked over and Renpo was just as amazed.

"Follow right in behind me."

Renpo was closest, and Desiree squeezed up close behind him. She pushed through and the edges of the gap felt slippery.

She stepped out the other side, and it was a beautiful sunny day. The mountain was smooth with rolling fields of grass, dotted with wildflowers. In fact, it was weirdly smooth, and with straight edges. "It's an actual pyramid." She oriented herself to the corner they faced. "The big slash cave with the Sanskrit name is gone off this one." She spun around to take in the countryside. "The rivers run straight out to the four corners of the Earth."

Renpo was grinning like a kid in a candy store. "It is the Center." He knelt down gently, placed both hands on the grass, and kissed the ground. He rocked back onto his legs and advised, "Be cautious to not speak carelessly here. This is a place of great power, and your words and sounds can conjure magical results."

"Do you think we might see the Celestial Dragon here?"

Renpo raised his eyebrows and shrugged.

Joseph was scanning the mountain. "I'm not seeing any sign of the Khyi Tor cave."

"It will be at one of the rivers. The waters seal the entrance in winter with ice and with flooding in summer. It's Fall now, so it should be open." He reached into his robes and pulled out a small metal bowl and a carved stick. He held the bowl in one palm and struck it. It rang louder than Desiree expected. Renpo listened intently until the ringing died away. He struck it again. An echoing ring came back from one of the faces of the mountain. They started walking that way.

"Is that bowl meteorite iron?" Joseph asked him.

"Yes, I was hoping the holy properties of sky iron would help us here."

"We used sky iron back in Egypt when we wanted to add spirit to a task."

"It is good to see certain truths in action."

Desiree wasn't sure what to make of this exchange, but she was happy to see them getting along so well. "Joseph, did you use *kung fu* to open the gap?"

"*Chi gong* is a more accurate term."

"What's up with that? You're Egyptian."

"I had to summon energy and move it into my hands and feet. Human *kung fu* masters use the motions to move their *chi* life force."

"I recall Sanantha say the man who changed my genetics had almost magical powers moving his *chi* around."

"You would do well to learn how to do it so you can move your power at will. Maybe Brother Renpo here can teach you some basic *kung fu* to get you started."

Renpo smiled and nodded. "I would be happy to." He rung the bell bowl again and the echo was close by, near the river they approached, as he had predicted.

As they walked, Desiree noticed how every breath she took reinvigorated her. She wasn't sure if it was the smell or the cleanliness of the air. Walking across the slope of the mountain wasn't much exertion, but she felt as though she could run forever here and never get tired. Instead of running, though, she slowed her step and just enjoyed being here. She watched the wildflowers sway in the gentle breeze. She listened to the babble of the river up ahead. She unzipped her parka, threw back the hood, and let her shoulder length auburn hair shake loose. They were in no hurry to find the cave. Besides, Renpo had already found the right direction with his cute little bell bowl.

She noticed she had stopped walking, and considered maybe sitting down to better take in how glorious this place was. She saw Joseph and Renpo coming back to her. They looked concerned. She didn't know what they could be concerned about. Everything was just as it should be.

"Desiree, snap out of it," Joseph bent down to talk to her. Then she realized she had already sat down. "This place is making you euphoric. You've got to concentrate on why we are here."

Renpo agreed. "I am finding I must concentrate very hard to stay focused. This place naturally draws us away into bliss. Thankfully it does not seem to have the same effect on Joseph."

Joseph took her by the forearm and helped her to her feet. She still didn't recall sitting down. "Come on. You can stick with us. We're here for the Pearl. Keep reminding yourself of the Pearl."

"The Pearl. Got to find the Pearl." She looked him in the yellow eyes. "Isn't this place awesome?"

"It will be more awesome when we get the Pearl home."

The river had steep, rocky banks. Being near the base of the mountain, the water was rushing noisily. Renpo rang the bell again, and the echo came from up the river on the near bank, under a rock outcropping. They hiked up and then picked their way down the rocks to the river's edge.

Up under the overhang they saw a large glassy boulder. Desiree touched it. "It's ice."

Joseph stepped up next to her. "I see something inside."

'You're right. It's not a block. It's a wall."

Renpo peered intently, shifting side to side to see passed the distortions. "The Khyi Tor. I see an altar." He tapped on the surface. "This is many inches thick. We won't be able to chip through it. The myth says the cave is blocked by ice in the winter."

"Well, here is the reality of it. Both of you should step back," Joseph advised. "Way back, behind me."

"Please remember what I said about magic in this place."

"I'll go slow." Joseph took a step back himself, before firing a thin stream of brilliant white light from his eyes. It refracted through the ice and shot rainbows across the riverbed.

The beam crackled quietly but Desiree smelled something acrid and hot.

Ozone? Was he using lightning?

Sanantha had told her Joseph could do this, but seeing it in person was altogether more awesome. She noticed Renpo was openly amazed as well.

The ice cracked noisily under the attack, and Joseph moved his beam around, chasing the crack across the surface, opening it up with successive ringing snaps. He carved a split across the height of the wall and it buckled. He chased a crack across to an edge and one whole half of the wall fell out in huge chunks.

All three of them looked cautiously around the riverbed to see if anything else had been triggered. All appeared calm.

Renpo wasted no time climbing into the cave. Desiree followed into a small hollow behind. The altar Renpo had seen was in the center of the space. Intriguingly, a bouquet of flowers, long since dried and crumbling, had been laid in front of the wooden cabinet. "Any stories about who brought these?" she asked.

"None that I know." He opened the two grill doors and found a pale gray ball sitting in a cup.

She started to reach for it, and Renpo stopped her. "One step at a time. Mister Joseph, you said you can see the objective truth in things. Is this the Pearl?"

Joseph leaned in and took a long look. "No. It's a trap. Contact poison, I think."

He frowned. "Check around the back."

Desiree found a panel that could be shifted slightly. "My dad had a couple of puzzle boxes he let me play with when I was little. I remember they usually had a key part that slid away and let you undo the rest of the pieces." She felt and pushed around the edges as she spoke. "Oh, here, found one." She slid a framing piece up and out, which allowed a side panel to lift out, which finally let the back panel slide away. The compartment it revealed contained a green porcelain bottle shaped like a sitting Buddha. Desiree and Renpo looked to Joseph.

"Not poison. In fact, maybe an antidote?" He pursed his lips. "Not antidote. I'm seeing a cleaner, or clarifier." He picked up the bottle, upstopped it, and sniffed it. "Not poison."

Renpo took the bottle and smiled. "It's the Buddha. The Buddha's teachings clear away the illusions of ego and reveal the objective truth." He turned it to show them the shape. "We pour it over the Pearl, and strip away the poison of delusion."

"Do symbols like that really work?" she asked.

Renpo smiled broadly. "They do here. Symbols here create reality back on Earth." He walked around to the front and lifted off the top lid, which was no longer held down with all the other pieces removed. He poured the liquid over the Pearl. The dull gray coating dissolved to show the gleaming white sphere. "There it is. *Om Mani Padme Hum.*"

Joseph broke their amazed silence. "In your vision, Isis cast you as the Celestial Dragon. The Pearl is yours, so take it."

She took a breath. Renpo nodded to her. She put her fingers around it, not sure what she would feel. It felt cold and hard, just like a great big pearl should. She took a second to check if she felt any different, but noted no change. She picked it up and hefted its weight. "I don't feel anything." She handed it to Renpo. "Here, you try."

He took it in both hands and looked around the cave. "You're right. I don't feel any different."

"Sanantha left us a phone message about her research that we picked up when we stopped in New Delhi. She said she thought it might give someone the ability to see the truth. Kind of like what Joseph does naturally."

"Apparently nothing is hidden or a lie here," Renpo concluded. Then he noticed the dried flowers on the ground. He knelt down and, holding the Pearl in one hand, touched the flowers. "Bodhisattva Manjushiri."

"Your patron?" Joseph asked.

"Yes. He must have found this shrine and decided not to take the Pearl, and left this token instead. He must have known that whoever took the Pearl …"

"… and didn't die trying," Desiree interjected.

"Whoever successfully took the Pearl, would see that it was him who left the flowers. It was his gift to the future."

"You know," Joseph commented, "when I look at those flowers, I don't see who left them. Only you can see that when you hold the Pearl. It doesn't just show you the truth, it shows you the whole story. That is powerful."

Renpo had stopped and was staring at Joseph and Desiree.

"What is it?" she asked.

"I believed you when you said you were creatures of spirit. Clearly we would not be here if that was not true."

"But it's something else to see it for yourself, isn't it?" Joseph said.

"Indeed," Renpo sighed. "The two of you are glowing."

"Now that it's in our hands, we should leave," Joseph concluded. "I don't want to take any chances that we have set anything new into motion."

Renpo started to hand it back to Desiree.

"No, that's all right," she said. "You hang on to it. You understand how important the unwashed truth is." He pocketed it in his robes.

They were interrupted by the sound of rocks crashing outside. "A landslide?" Renpo wondered.

When they rushed to the mouth of the cave, Desiree froze when she looked across the river at the far bank. The stones of the slope now made up the unmistakable shape of an angry dragon's face. The rocks were moving. As they ground together, they created a terrifying guttural growl. "We've been found out."

"Time to go," Joseph said calmly as he stepped onto the riverbank and whipped his arms around to gather the magic.

The rock dragon pulled free of the far shore and coiled its fifty-foot length to strike.

"Now Joseph!"

"Yes now!" he said as he cleaved open a rift.

The thousands of stones that made up their adversary jumped across the river, the leap sounding like an extended thunderclap, claws and fangs extended, just as they slipped through and away.

The freezing cold wind that blew off Kailash took them by surprise. Desiree pulled her parka closed and zipped it up as quickly as she could. She laughed and raised her voice above the wind. "As blissed out as I was over there, and as cold as it is here, it's really good to be back."

11

SANANTHA CLOSED THE WINDOW ON ALEC'S COMPUTER that showed the pondside YouTube video, noting the clip had been viewed over 6,000 times. In its place, she brought up the administration page of the new website Benito set up for today's live viewing. He posted the new site's address on the YouTube site for anyone who wanted to help with the next round of magical experiments. The ploy seemed to work, as she watched the counter of current logged-in viewers climb passed 20,000.

She picked up the phone, which was already connected. "Benito, if everything is ready on your end, we've got over 20,000 viewers waiting online."

"Sounds good. Alec is ready. We're about a minute early. We can't be late even by a few seconds. Online audiences lose interest almost instantly. Let's do this."

The viewscreen on the website popped open with a view of the fountain in St. Stephen's Green in central Dublin. Alec was standing by the fountain wall with a little table of bottles and implements. Benito's voice narrated from off-camera. "Welcome back friends to the next demonstration of Alec Doogan's amazing feats of magic. Magic, yes, real magic. No tricks, no gimmicks — just raw, pure command of the elements using nothing more than willpower and knowledge. Today we are live, and we need your help. You've seen that Alec can move water with his mind. Pushing back the edge of that pond was about all he could manage using only his own willpower. That's where you come in. With you contributing your wishes, your hopes, your will, Alec will pick that up and add it to his power over the water in this fountain."

The jiggling hand-held camera made the viewing more accessible and immediate. Sanantha had to hand it to Benito, he knew how to draw attention. She also noticed Benito himself never appeared on camera.

"Now we did not get a permit from the police to do anything to this fountain, so we're going to move quickly in case trouble comes along.

"Alec, are you ready?"

"Yes, I am."

"What Alec is going to attempt is actually very dangerous. Water is extremely heavy and capable of great destructive power. So although we are asking for your assistance, we do not want you trying this on your own at home. I'm going to turn the sound down so you can't hear Alec's incantations. You'll be able to follow the visuals with no problem."

The video went silent and Alec started waving his wand and lifting various implements off the table. He sprayed a few things with a small atomizer and pointed meaningfully at the 30-foot diameter round fountain with his dagger. He then stepped away from the table and started a hopping, spinning dance. He frowned intently and appeared to be speaking the whole time.

The water that was spraying up from the floral decoration in the center of the pond stopped, and a section of the water rose up out of the basin. It appeared as a hillock poking up above the fountain wall. It was spinning in time with Alec's dance. He thrust his wand and dagger at the water as he turned, and the bulge climbed taller and taller. It narrowed as it grew, becoming a column of swirling clear blue water as the rest of the fountain pool lowered.

As he turned, he hesitated each time he faced the camera and motioned encouragingly with his wand hand.

The sound clicked back on again and Benito said, "Now is when we need you at home to really pour your wishes out to Alec. He really needs your help right now. Go on, reach out with your willpower and hold that water up!"

Two more turns around, and Alec stepped up to the fountain. He suddenly stopped spinning and jabbed his dagger into the column of water. In less time than seemed possible, in the blink of an eye, with a shattering crack the microphone picked up, the column froze solid.

The handful of onlookers who had gathered burst into cheers and shrieks of surprise.

Alec stepped back and marveled at his creation. Ten feet high and three feet wide, the spiral shaped column gleamed in the morning sun.

The onlookers cautiously approached the ice. After only a few seconds, one brave young man leaned over the wall and touched it. "It's solid ice!" Others gathered around Alec and congratulated him.

Alec stepped up to the camera and addressed his viewers. "These folks here think this was stage magic. I'm not going to try to explain to them what really happened. You know what happened. You helped me make it happen. I could feel your willpower feed into my spell. It was like getting onto a pony and having it take off like a broncing bull. Thank you very much for your support. We need to close up shop right now, before the authorities see what I've done to this beautiful fountain. It will thaw, but it's going to take hours, if not days. Thank you again! Stay tuned to this website for more announcements."

The screen went black. Sanantha sighed and leaned back. She heard Benito calling to her on the phone that was still off the hook. "Sorry, I completely forgot we had this line open."

"Wasn't that spectacular? How many viewers did we have at the height of the spell?"

"25,000. Benito, I'm really concerned about Alec."

"How so? He seems fine."

"I'm worried this power is too seductive. He mustn't start thinking all this power is derived from himself. These forces are coming from spirits and channeled willpower."

"You think this is going to go to his head?"

"How could it not? He just did the impossible with a handful of bottles and a video camera. If he starts thinking he deserves this power, it's going to affect his judgment."

"Let me get this straight," Benito interjected. "If he thinks this power is all his, then he might what, think he can use it however he pleases? Alec is an honest, conscientious man."

"I know that. I just want to keep him that way. I've seen this kind of power seduce men into thinking the ends justify the means. If you can make miracles, why let morals get in your way of changing the world? Am I making sense?"

"You are. If this fell into the wrong hands, you would be absolutely right. But Alec is a good man. I don't think he is going to become a threat to anyone, even with magic."

"I think he'll need guidance. I want to guide him. Can I count on you to guide him too, to keep away from that slippery slope?"

"*Multo bene!* Of course. Doctor Sanantha, you are a good counselor, and a good friend. But you worry too much!"

•   •   •

Sanantha sat on the low round wall of the St. Stephen's Green fountain watching the now liquid water spraying up from the floral display center. She had picked her hair out in a fluffy afro and was enjoying the cool fall air. When she saw Alec crossing the plaza, she stood up to greet him. "Hello. Thank you for coming."

He looked around jokingly. "Returned to the scene of the crime. I wonder if they're watching for me."

She sat back down and he joined her. "It's been two days and the police never came knocking, so I think you're in the clear."

"A clean getaway. Coppers don't know how to use the Internet. Hey, I don't think I've ever seen you without a turban. It looks nice."

"Thank you. I take it down once in a while. I've been thinking a lot since your demonstration, and I've done some research I want to run by you. You said the spirit who helps you with moving water is the Celtic goddess Boann."

"That's right."

"This whole adventure started when you and Desiree discovered an angelic trace on Saint Patrick's grave. So we have a pretty good case that Patrick had divine help in his mission. His mission was to replace the old Celtic religion with Catholicism."

"That's true." He looked around, distracted. "Can we get away from here? This place is suddenly giving me a bad feeling."

Sanantha looked around, including into the water, to see if anything was amiss, and saw nothing. "Sure. You want to go get some tea or coffee?"

"Coffee would be lovely. I know a place not far from here on the other side of Grafton Street."

"Lead on." Sanantha continued as they walked. "Can I ask you about the legend of Saint Patrick?"

"Sure, every Irish boy is happy to talk about our great saint."

She was glad to see him back at ease, walking through the park grounds talking about something familiar. They passed a bronze bust of a handsome man looking down at them, as if interested in their conversation. Thomas M. Kettle. "I wanted your take on the snake controversy. Some say the snakes are a metaphor for evil in general, but others argue the snakes were actually the Druid bards that Patrick helped remove from power. Paleontologists say there have never been actual snakes here."

"Well, I don't know where the snake reference started, or what they are supposed to stand for, but the conversion of Ireland to Christianity did include removing the old power structure. The bards kept the oral traditions, which included the histories of the families and why who owned what lands. By removing them from power, the Catholic church was able to challenge land ownership. Rome's claim over Ireland could only hold if folks lost their ties to the past. The campaign took centuries, but eventually the old ways were discarded as folklore and the Roman church was accepted wholeheartedly."

"Do you think Patrick knew his missionary work would lead to such a huge change in who ran things in Ireland?"

"I think he knew he was the spark to set a new fire here. He had visions, and he faced down the Irish leaders with the conviction to make sweeping change. So yes, I think he hoped his work would lead to big things."

"Doesn't the legend include magical combat with the Druids?"

"Yes, there are some really violent stories. If that angel we found was helping him, then maybe those stories have some truth. He would have plenty of reason to believe he would be successful. I mean knowing Heaven has got your back is pretty motivating."

"Patrick displaced the old gods. You found Patrick's angel's fingerprints. And now you're bringing the old gods back. Do you see where this might anger that angel?"

He stopped walking. "If I were to try to communicate with that angel, it might see me as an enemy."

Sanantha's cell phone rang. "Hello? Oh my goodness, Desiree, you're back already? I didn't expect you for another couple of days. Oh, right, the return trip, of course. What? You brought someone back with you? A monk? Oh, he's the keeper of the Pearl. You have the Pearl? Wow. Are you back at the cottage? Great, we'll catch a cab and be there in just a few minutes. Okay, bye."

•　　　•　　　•

Desiree pulled open the front door and greeted Sanantha and Alec with a big giddy smile. "Have I got a treat for you. Sanantha, Alec, this is Abbot Renpo Kashiligan Samsuri. Brother Renpo, this is Doctor Sanantha Mauwad and Alec Doogan."

Renpo placed his palms together and bowed. The others followed suit. "I am most glad to meet you both. Desiree as told me how important you both are in her life."

"Welcome to Ireland, Brother Renpo," Alec said. "I hear you brought something extraordinary back from Mount Kailash. I guess you are here to protect the Pearl?"

"Not exactly. I accompanied Desiree and Joseph on the journey to find the Pearl. Desiree knows how much it means to me and my faith, so she entrusted it to me. I would have come along whether she gave it to me or kept it herself."

Desiree chimed in. "It wasn't on Kailash. We had to go to the spirit plane, to Mount Semeru. It was amazing."

"Mister Joseph is a very capable magician," Renpo added.

Desiree noticed Sanantha's eyebrows did a little dance at that comment.

"Where is Joseph?" Alec asked.

"He came down ill on the trip," Desiree explained. "He needed to get some bed rest and recover. So, Brother Renpo, show it off."

He pulled it from a pocket in his saffron robe and handed it to Alec. "We found it gives anyone touching it the ability to understand the complete truth within something."

"Doesn't Joseph have that talent?" Sanantha asked while staring at the globe in Alec's hand.

"Joseph can see through deceptions," Desiree explained. "The Pearl embodies the Buddha's enlightenment of seeing things objectively as they really are."

"It is the fulfillment of the Vajrasattva Buddha, the stripping away of all the veils that hide the truth, including the ones we keep inside like bias and ego," Renpo added.

"It lets you see the whole story," Desiree said.

"Really?" Alec said, hefting its weight. "How about a little game to check it out. Truth or dare?" he said looking at Sanantha.

She hesitated. "Um, sure. I guess you go first since you're holding the Pearl."

"Let's switch it up a little. You tell me something about yourself, and I'll see if you're telling the truth." He grinned mischievously. "So more like Liar's Poker."

"All right. I graduated at the top of my class from Rush University in Philadelphia."

"Oh, wow," he said looking at the Pearl in his hand. "That's kind of amazing. The answer just appeared in my head, as if I had known it all along. First of all, Rush is in Chicago, not Philadelphia. And no, you missed the top spot because a statistics professor gave you a 'B' after you rebuffed his advances."

Desiree jumped in. "Whoa, this can get ugly really fast. Clearly the Pearl works."

"No, I kind of like this," Alec said. "Here, you have a go," and he handed it to Sanantha.

Desiree knew that clinical look. She had been on the receiving end of it many times. "Sure." Sanantha rolled it from one hand to the other. "Tell me something about yourself."

He rubbed his hands together. "I got interested in magic because my father was a stage magician, and I can afford to do this because I inherited a family fortune."

"Oh my, you're right. The knowledge feels like I always knew this."

"Isn't that a rush?" he said.

"It is. Your father was a stand-up comic who wanted to be a magician. The family fortune was squandered by your uncle before you inherited." She blinked. "This could be really dangerous in the wrong hands."

He pointed at her almost aggressively. "Or as you and I discussed a few days ago, I can use it to see if my experiments are real magic."

Desiree wasn't sure she liked this belligerently excited side of Alec.

"Think of that, objective verification of supernatural events." He took the Pearl back and looked over at Desiree. "You're glowing."

Renpo said, "I saw that too. It is her god-self. It is bigger than her."

"Oh, Alec discovered that using his condenser fluid too," Desiree said. "Alec, may I show him the sensor screen?"

"Sure, but that equipment is back at my flat."

Desiree turned to Renpo. "He has this screen that makes a contact photograph of soul energy. Alec hunts ghosts."

"I have expanded far beyond that," Alec corrected somewhat rudely. "While you were gone, I performed some public magic. I found the condenser fluid not only channels my willpower, but it can gather the willpower of believers too. Sanantha, can we use your laptop?"

"Of course."

As she went into the back to get it, Desiree caught her eye and mouthed the word, "Believers?"

Sanantha mouthed back, "I know."

She returned and set it up on the kitchen dinette table. "I only have dial up here, so I can't guarantee the connection quality." She plugged it in and found Alec's website. "This is the first one last week with Alec working alone at a pond."

Everyone gathered around and watched a playback that halted every couple of seconds to load. Desiree strained to see the outline of the swirl of leaves that Alec summoned by the table. "Who is that?" she asked.

"Cu Chulainn, the Hound of Ulster. He's one of the great Celtic heroes, a risk-taking adventurer. I'm not surprised he was the one to answer my call."

"May I hold the Pearl while we watch?"

"Okay." He seemed a little dubious, but he handed it over.

She studied the spirit figure while trying to ignore the annoying halting. When the figure walked down to the pond edge, Desiree got the distinct impression the spirit was disguising himself. She couldn't tell how or why, so she didn't say anything. Maybe the poor video quality wasn't letting her see well enough for the Pearl to do its best. Maybe.

"Is that Benito filming and narrating?"

"Yes."

"I still haven't met him."

"This is where Cu Chulainn talks to Boann and gets her to agree to my sovereignty so I can leave my protective diagrams and go down to the water's edge to see her."

The Pearl did not make her disagree with his version of events. Benito followed Alec down to the water and tilted the camera to try to see what Alec was looking at in the water, but the reflections were too strong.

"If you're hoping to see Boann on this tape, you can't see her," he said. "I checked it."

"You can tell Benito is trying to angle down into the water, but the camera is just not picking it up." Sanantha said.

Desiree did not feel like there was anything in the water. Maybe you have to actually see something before the Pearl fills you in on the hidden details.

They watched as Alec's spinning dance excited the water and pushed it back. "I could feel the water drag on my arms. It was like my strength reached out of me and grabbed the water."

"That's amazing," Desiree said.

"It also makes sense," Renpo commented. "*Chi gong* moves your will and strength around in your body. Practicing magic would push that energy out into the world."

"Willpower is the key," Alec agreed. "We showed that in the next experiment."

Sanantha brought up the next clip.

"We broadcast this session live and invited viewers to direct their willpower to me. The bridge is the condenser fluid. It turns willpower into physical emotive force. Here, watch. The first time at the pond I had to coax the goddess to help me and it took a while to get the latch-on to move the water. This time the audience's willpower surged into me and I just reached out and seized the water. I only had to call on Boann for permission to distort the water."

"So is Boann present in that column?" Desiree asked. "Cause I'm not seeing her there, even with the Pearl."

"I did not see her the way I did in the pond. Is the Pearl showing you anything else?"

"Not on this clip, but on the first one, I got the clear impression your Hound of Ulster was disguising himself somehow. I'm not saying he wasn't there or that you were deceived, just that he wasn't entirely forthcoming with his identity. Sanantha, it's like the whole Erzulie vs. Isis thing. Could he be something older, but appearing here and now as the spirit of this great hero?"

"Well, these gods go back to the Stone Age," Sanantha explained. "I imagine Cu Chulainn has gone by many names and has been worshipped in many ways over the eons. They are also archetypes. He looks a lot like Hercules, and he would have filled the same role in the ancient Celtic explanations of the universe."

Desiree thought Sanantha was grasping at straws. There was definitely something about this spirit that did not fit. "I guess you're right."

12

"WHEN YOU AND JOSEPH CAME TO ME, I hoped you would lead me to the returned Buddha Maitreya." Renpo said it almost like an apology. "I struggled to not let my enthusiasm blind me to the realities we would face. Our luck in finding the Pearl makes me wonder how much karma is in motion. After watching Alec's movies, I am even more convinced Alec may be the next turn of the wheel."

Desiree pondered this while she drove them out of Dublin into the country. "The magic is impressive, but what he is doing is nothing new. Sanantha faced a magician a few years ago who wielded the same control Alec has now, but this guy was a master. She tells of how he could whip up miracles on the fly."

She reached into a paper bag on the console between them and bit into a date.

She answered Renpo's frown. "Ever since we got back from Semeru, I've had this craving for dates. Not sure what's up with that. Thankfully I found a market that carries them.

"I agree this might be something huge, like the next coming of Buddha. I just can't shake the feeling that Alec is only one part of it."

"So now you want to verify his work from the first summoning?"

"I guess you could put it that way." She looked over at Renpo in the passenger seat of the rented Cortina. "I want to use the Pearl to look around that pond, and maybe gain a little more perspective."

She looked back just in time to see a deer already in motion right in front of the car. She slammed on the brakes and the car's nose dug down. The deer bounced over the grill and crashed into the windshield. Desiree and Renpo lurched forward into their shoulder belts. The deer rolled off as the car skidded to a stop.

Desiree look angrily at the dashboard. "No airbags? P.O.S." Then to Renpo, she asked, "Are you all right?"

The deer struggled to get up, but could not. She and Renpo got out and ran to the animal kicking and twitching at the side of the road.

She started to reach for it, but the young four-point buck swung his tiny sharp hooves erratically. "I might be able to heal it if I can just put my hands on it."

Renpo walked around behind it, knelt down, and wrapped his arms around its neck, holding its head still. "Come around this side away from the kicking. I'll hold him from flipping over at you."

Desiree considered how brave that little move was, to step right up to a wounded animal. She sat beside Renpo and tried to assess the damage. Its legs seemed to move fine, but it was clearly in agony. She laid her hands on its chest and let her mind go blank seeking some sense of what was hurt. The sensation of hurt overwhelmed her, as if the whole animal was shattered. It whimpered and she felt a pang. She despaired for a moment until she felt the warmth in her heart growing and spreading. It reached her hands and she stroked the length of its body, smoothing its stiff fur, hoping to repair wherever it needed. The deer settled down.

"I think you have alleviated its pain," Renpo said.

"Yeah, but I'm pretty sure it has massive internal injuries I don't think I can cure."

"I see you are letting your *chi* passively flow out of you. I can show you how to speed that up."

"Is that the *kung fu* we saw Joseph use?"

"Yes. You are upset. You're sweating and breathing hard. The first step is to let go of that. Tell yourself you can do this because it is supposed to happen."

"So I start by convincing myself I'm in control?"

"No, control is an illusion. You are going to do this the same way a stone rolls down a hill. It is natural and inevitable. You're just there to guide the stone. You and this deer where always going to meet like this. And now you're going to heal it. Feel your breathing. Slow it down. Deeper breaths are fine. That better?"

"Yeah, I'm calmer. Now what?"

"Focus on your breathing. Take a couple more breaths until you are aware of the rhythm. Everything happens to that rhythm. Now feel your energy at its source. You told me it starts in your heart. Feel it there. Close your eyes if that helps you see it. Reach inside and caress the energy. Feel it as a substance. Mold it. Now picture your arms as hollow. Keep breathing. Move the energy up into your arms like water flowing into empty bottles. First a trickle, then a free flow. Move your arms around if it helps you feel the energy flowing down into them. Do you feel it?"

"Yes, my arms are getting hot as it moves in."

Renpo took the Pearl out of his robes and held it in one hand. "Good. Now imagine your arms full. Clench your armpits and elbows to force the energy down into your hands. Squeeze it down under pressure. How do your hands feel?"

"Like they're going to explode."

"Good. Open your eyes. Place your hands where you feel the most damage is in the deer's body. Now imagine your hands are like gates on your arms. Open them and let the energy flow out, like you are pouring water into the deer. Let it flow."

"I feel it moving. My hands are warmer that his body. I feel the heat moving in."

"Good. Keep breathing. Let the energy run out like pouring water."

She looked up at Renpo and he was watching the deer intently, one hand over his heart with the other holding the Pearl.

"My arms feel empty now. There is no more heat."

"Then you have done what you can," he said raising his free hand over his head. "Now we let the energy do its work. What happens is what is supposed to happen."

The deer took a deep breath under her hands. It twitched all down the length of its spine. Renpo let go of its head and they stepped back. The deer twitched again, then scrambled to its feet. It pawed at the ground, took a tentative step, and looked up at Desiree.

She bent down to its level. "Are you feeling better?" she asked.

It turned and bounded off into the trees.

She stood up and put her hand on her heart. "My god."

"Apparently."

"This *chi*, does everyone have it?"

"It is our essential life force. People normally cannot make it leave the body. I will train you to move it with greater ease."

"That's with the *tai chi* movements?"

"Yes. Once you train and can move it at will, there is a tempting sensation that you should be able to move it out into the world to affect things. I wasn't sure how you do that."

"I noticed you used the Pearl to really see what was happening there at the end."

"I needed to understand fully if I was going to guide you."

"What did you see?"

"Guanyin. I looked away and looked back to be sure. It was quite the revelation."

"What's Guanyin?"

"Not what, who. Guanyin is the Goddess of Mercy, the Listener of the Lamentations of the World. I do not know your goddess Isis. I do know Guanyin, and that's who I saw."

Desiree looked back at the car. The hood was caved in and one side of the windshield was spiderwebbed with cracks. "Well, whatever her name is, I'm pretty sure she can't fix that kind of damage. I guess even goddesses should be glad for rental insurance."

•   •   •

Desiree and Renpo stood at the edge of the pond in Rahin Woods in County Kildare. She held the Pearl in her hand. She saw nothing in the water. She walked around where Alec's tape showed him talking to the legendary Hound of Ulster. She saw and felt nothing. She really tried to open herself up, looking for any trace of what Alec had seen. They walked across the woods down to the River Boyne.

"Hold on. Whoa, this place has some history. It all kind of just floods in on you."

"Indeed, the Pearl takes some getting used to."

"There's so much here, it's hard to make sense of it."

"When I saw Alec's film, I read up on the history of this river," Renpo said. "People have been living here for thousands of years."

"I see that. I see joy with generations of children, I see battles, I see miracles."

"Miracles?"

"Yes, and I see where there was a goddess of the river. She was wounded. Her arm, her leg, and her eye. She was tired and just wanted to withdraw and rest. She's gone quiet. It's almost like she isn't here anymore."

"But Alec just saw her a few days ago. She spoke to him."

"Then his magic is reaching something the Pearl is not. The Pearl must only see what is here in this physical plane. I see that Boann used to be here, a long time ago when lots of people believed in her. But now it's like she's sleeping. Her stories are all myth, and she's not here to change that."

"Does that mean we cannot use the Pearl to validate Alec's magic?" Renpo asked. "He was looking forward to using it for that purpose."

"I don't know what it means." She handed the Pearl to him. "We will have to use it live and in person, while he's performing." They turned to head back. A few steps up the riverbank she turned to the water. "Sleep now, Boann. I look forward to meeting you someday."

•   •   •

Desiree walked through the high ceilinged, tan granite temple with the comfortable ease of familiarity. The flagstone floor was warm under her brown bare feet. Her black hair, all in hanging braids, swung around her neck in time with her steps. She reached out and ran her tanned fingers over the painted, carved, harvest scenes on a wall as she ambled by, her white linen wrap skirt flowing around her legs. She was home. She was content.

She turned a corner and saw at the end of the wide hall, a man with jet black skin, regally dressed in ceremonial gold and jewels. She recognized him immediately from her Art History as Osiris, the Egyptian god of the Underworld. When he got up from his throne and walked toward her, she got a little nervous. What was she supposed to do with an eight-foot tall deity? She glanced down at her own body and noticed the jeweled necklace of rainbow-colored wings criss-crossing her bosom. *Oh, that's right.* By the time she had grasped and sorted her identity confusion, Osiris was to her.

"Welcome, Wife. It has been a very long time, far too long." He came in for a hug and she had to assume this was appropriate, so she hugged him back. She had to reach almost vertically to clasp his shoulders as he bent down over her. He was cold to the touch, like a dead body. He wrapped his huge arms all the way around her and pulled her up against him in a tender if enveloping bear hug. A part of her welcomed his touch, is spite of its clamminess. She realized she was getting used to letting Isis do the driving.

"My love, I'm sorry to be the bearer of ill tidings. You must carry on the good work, for I cannot do so from where I am. For the last eight and half years I have been holding Sammael captive."

The name awakened a fury within her that she could not explain. She took a breath to calm herself. "Sammael? The Hebrew demon Sanantha faced back in 2001?"

"Yes. I apologize that it took me the longest time to realize Silas Alverado was your champion. He captured the Prince of Liars and sent him to me to keep, but the Deceiver escaped and is now back on Earth. He will come for you. You must be vigilant."

Torn between fear and anger, she let her guard down for a moment. Anger won and she blurted out, "Good, I've waited a long time for this. Let him bring it." She caught herself in shock. She stared at him wide-eyed with her hand over her lips. "Who am I to face down an ancient biblical demon?"

"You are Isis. Fight like a god. You can change fate, which no mere demon can do. When Set killed me and Paradise fell, you raised me and convinced Ra to let me rule the Land of the Dead. You are the Mistress of Magicks, the Queen of Mercy. I have learned much about this demon. He is intelligent and dangerous, but he also is driven by selfish ego. He takes chances and assumes he will win. I have no doubt your plan will prevail."

Plan?

"You have more power than you understand. Your kind nature will seem to be a limit, but it is the guiding principle you should always rely on. It's what makes you better than him, what makes you deserving of victory. The revenge you seek will bring you into great danger, and you will not be able to call on our brethren gods to help you. They would rather give up another foothold in the world than become visible to scrutiny and ridicule."

"I really don't understand what you're saying."

"You will soon." He stepped back and began to fade away. "Know that I love you. Know that I believe in you. I hope we can be together again soon. Good luck!"

He was gone. So was the Egyptian temple. In fact, she looked around and realized she was in bed, twisted up in covers. She squeezed her eyes together, shook her head, and opened them again just to make sure the dream was over.

The alarm clock showed 5:30am. She reached for the phone to call Sanantha.

•   •   •

Joseph had listened to Desiree and Sanantha try to make sense of Desiree's dream for almost an hour. The dream had a lot of good information, and the ladies had a lot of good ideas about what it meant. He had his own.

An hour after dawn, Joseph pulled his rented red Lotus Elise S into the parking lot of Maguire's Café in County Meath. He got out, crossed the road and looked over the green open expanse of the Hill of Tara Archeological Preserve. The heavy morning mist clung to his steel grey suit and obscured his semi-mirrored sunglasses. He slipped the glasses off and scanned the park for people with his bare yellow eyes. The café didn't open until 9:30am. A couple of joggers on the far side would not notice him.

Rather than teleport the quarter mile to the center, he decided a walk would help him find what he wanted. He took the path through some trees around the visitor center and the church. He paused at the statue of Saint Patrick. Indeed. He continued out into the open toward the three sets of spiral earthen mounds.

Joseph could see a mix of very old and fairly new. To one side was a set of Neolithic tombs, and on the far mound the Lia Fail, the Stone of Destiny. Although ancient, had been erected in the 17th century as a war memorial. This was probably the only thing here that dated to when he needed. It had been used in coronations over several centuries. Never mind the walk.

He teleported to the stone. The four-foot high badly weathered phallus stood in the center of an array of flagstones. It had no discernable markings. He didn't need any. He stepped up and placed his hand on it, focusing his gaze intently on the surface. Rather he focused on that surface as it appeared a hundred years before, five hundred, a thousand, fifteen hundred, back to precisely the year 433. The stone was bigger then, and smooth, and painted with runic symbols. He looked around and found it wasn't on the same hill, but further down the valley.

Keeping his hand on it as an anchor, he rolled the calendar back from Fall to Spring, to the last full moon of March. He found himself in a festival village with people coming in from across the countryside. They had decorated the shacks with flower wreaths. Even the stone was bedecked. He rolled through the days, waiting for one fateful night.

Finally, an array of men wearing elaborate robes assembled on a stage around the stone. Joseph slowed down his viewing into real time. They made speeches in old Gaelic about the return of life to their valley and what they would accomplish in the coming year. Since he could only see into the past, he had to lip read and then translate.

Some men ran into town pointing behind them, yelling that the foreign demon worshipper had violated High King Laoire's edict and lit another ceremonial fire on his hilltop.

Joseph steered his vision along the path they pointed and found a conspicuous fire set on a hill nearly ten miles away. The men called it *Dumha Slaine*. They were incensed. They took up weapons and marched off. Joseph followed with his vision as best he could.

When they arrived at the Hill of Slane, they were met by Patrick, dressed in white vestments. It was all Joseph could manage from ten miles away to make out the figures. He could only see the back of the Druids' heads, so he only picked up Patrick's side of the conversation.

"Welcome Lochru! Have you come to join me in Paschal celebration of the resurrection of our Lord Jesus Christ?"

Lochru gestured broadly while he spoke. The men he brought made their chorus with brandished weapons and fists.

"The Holy Trinity are not false gods!" Patrick renounced. "Would ye cast me out as a deceiver, a spreader of lies? I bring ye the truth."

Joseph noticed a young monk standing slightly behind Patrick. He wondered why the young man thought Patrick needed back up. The Druids were not buying Patrick's rhetoric, and their gestures became more violent.

To this Patrick cried to the heavens, "Lord, who canst do all things, and on whose power dependeth all that exists, and who hast sent us hither to preach Thy name to the heathen, let this ungodly man, who blasphemeth Thy name, be lifted up and let him forthwith die!"

To Joseph's surprise, and to Patrick's as well, the Druid flew up into the air as if lifted like a puppet, and then dropped from a height of at least forty feet to his violent death. The Druid men scattered. Patrick stood in horror at what he had caused. The monk took his arm and assured him.

Joseph could not make out what the monk said. In fact, Joseph could not make out much detail on the monk since he never came completely out from behind Patrick. If the saint was surprised and horrified at the effect of his curse, why was his acolyte so ready to excuse it?

13

"HIS NAME WAS BENEN, which was Latinized and later became Saint Benignus of Armagh," Sanantha read from her online research in Alec's flat. Alec, Desiree, Renpo, and Joseph listened and watched. "He was the son of a chieftain named Sesenen who put Patrick up when he first arrived in County Meath. The boy quickly became Patrick's favorite, traveled all over Ireland with Patrick, and came to be known as his Psalm Singer. He rose in the church hierarchy, started a few churches. There is feast day in his honor. He's quite the local hero."

Joseph looked skeptical. "Is there anything there about a Druid priest named Lochru?"

"Let's see. Yes, the episode you witnessed, in your, um, vision, is mentioned. It looks like soon after Lochru was killed, the High King Laoghaire challenged Patrick at Tara to a trial by fire. Oh, now this is interesting. A druid priest and Benen were locked in a wooden barn which was set on fire. The Druid burned, but Benen did not. This is attributed to be what convinced Laoghaire to allow Patrick to remain and spread his religion."

Sanantha turned in the chair and joined the circle of silent meaningful glances.

Desiree broke the moment. "Who's going to say it?"

Joseph did. "He's your angel, the one you found the trace for on Patrick's grave. He wasn't afraid of the horror of a man being smashed on the rocks because he performed the deed. And he didn't burn because he wasn't human."

Alec shook his head. "Wait a minute. You mean an angel took human form? Since when do angels walk among us?"

Joseph traded a silent glance with Sanantha.

"All through the Bible." Desiree said. "Religious art has often depicted angels as people, with halos and wings as symbols of their divinity tacked onto normal clothing."

"Ancient Egyptian art showed divine creatures walking among common men," Joseph added.

"The same is true in Asian art," Renpo said.

Sanantha could see Alec was still struggling.

"I'm just having a hard time believing all the miracles I was taught God performed at Patrick's request might have actually been done by an angel disguised as a human acolyte."

"Why not?" Desiree asked. "Does it make a difference whether the miracles were directly from God or if an angel was doing God's work on site?"

"Actually, there is an important distinction," Joseph interjected. "Angels don't just do what God tells them to do. There are lots of examples where angels had their own agenda. In fact, the ones that act on their own are often called demons."

"Demons?" Alec almost gasped. "You think Saint Patrick was unwittingly aided by a demon?" Alec was getting pretty upset. Sanantha watched his reactions carefully.

She wished Joseph would take a more sensitive tone, but he did not. "He was willing to kill to get the job done. By the time the conversion was complete, hundreds of Druid priests were killed or ruined. An entire religion was shelved as folklore. Sounds like this angel or demon or whatever he was, had a grudge against the old religion and wanted to make sure Christianity stamped it out. Now, I admit it's just my opinion, but that sounds like a personal agenda and not following God's wishes. I have seen where demons tried to eradicate conflicting religions elsewhere in the world."

Desiree stepped in. "Alec, we talked about this before, but now I have to ask you straight. Have you tried to summon the spirit we found at Saint Patrick's grave?"

"No. I haven't even looked at it since I started working with Benito on the Celtic spirits. As excited as I was to find an angel trace, the Celtic work has given me far more conclusive results. I've been focused on that exclusively. I'm sorry, but this talk of demons is just outlandish. I really think you all have convinced yourselves based on interesting but highly circumstantial evidence."

Renpo broke his quiet observance. "I too had a vision, that great forces would come into motion and the Buddha would return for a third time as Maitreya. You are magicians and avatars who are summoning long dead gods and finding fingerprints of demons on history. I want to assure you, all of you, that we do not need to be afraid. Buddha faced down demons, and armed with your knowledge and with the Pearl showing us the truth, we can too. Alec, have you faced down a malevolent spirit?"

"I've had a couple of very angry ghosts come after me. I used science."

"The Buddha taught us how to take the self out of our perceptions. Maitreya will bring this genius back to the world by first being the Buddha, then his reincarnation, then losing himself and becoming nothing. The mission of a Bodhisattva is to find enlightenment, and then refuse nirvana and return to Earth as a teacher. Maitreya will step up as a teacher after losing his sense of self."

"That does not sound like the path I am on," Alec said rather dismissively. "I'm not trying to teach anyone any higher way of looking at things. I've spent my life trying to find out how spirits interact with the physical world."

Desiree asked, "Are you saying we should take solace that Buddha defeated demons using his knowledge of the truth, and since we have some of that same knowledge, we should also prevail?"

"Exactly," he said with a little bow.

"That's good, because I had a really unnerving dream that I may be the target of another demon, who is after my Isis self."

Sanantha did not see Alec taking solace from any of this. He was getting more and more agitated. She had noticed him getting more irritable over the last few days. She worried he was headed for a full-blown crisis of faith. "Alec, do you have any wine in the house? I think I could really use a glass to settle my nerves after all this dangerous talk."

"Sure. I think I've got a bottle of white in the fridge. That okay?" He headed out and she followed him.

"That would be great. Would you care to join me in a glass?"

Desiree watched Sanantha with a grin. She had been on the receiving end of that tone more than once.

She spotted the electric field sensor screen on a table. "Right, I wanted to show this to you." She went to the kitchen door. "Alec, may I use a few drops of the condenser fluid to show Renpo the hand screen?"

"Sure. He took the spray bottle from the refrigerator and handed it to her. "The shocker is on the same table."

"Thank you."

Joseph eyed the bottle. "So that's the fluid?"

"Yes, it allows spirit energy to be seen in the physical world."

"Oh, I know full well what it does. Silas used it extensively."

"Oh. Well, what I wanted to show you guys is this screen Alec has. First you spray a mist of the fluid on your hand," which she did to herself. "Then you turn on the screen and this shocker. You place your hand on the screen and give yourself a zap." She did so and winced. "It only hurts a little. Now you see where the screen is all filled in. When I dial back the scale, you can see my aura extends out over a foot. Normally a person's aura extends out an inch of so. This is how we first found out my aura reflects the presence of Isis in me."

"That's what I saw in you at the bookstore," Joseph added.

'Right."

"May I try?" Renpo asked.

"Of course." She ran the test and his aura read as Alec had shown her for a normal human.

"All right. Now please do it on me again."

"Other hand?"

"Same hand is fine."

She frowned but went along.

This time his aura was over twice as deep.

"What did you do?"

"*Chi gong.* I moved my *chi* into my hand."

Desiree frowned. "Wait a minute. Neither of you looks surprised. Have I been missing the point all along? Alec said he suspected these are pictures of the soul's energy. He uses this shocker to find traces of dead people's souls. Ghosts. Are you saying *chi* energy is the soul?"

"Yes," Joseph said patiently. "I didn't know you did not see that."

"Wait," Desiree said again. "Alec uses this stuff to channel willpower. He used it to gather the will of the folks on the internet watching his demonstration. Willpower equals *chi* equals souls?"

"*Chi* exists in living things whether you use your willpower to direct it or not," explained Renpo. "Life creates *chi*. Willpower moves it."

"Sorry fellas. I've been wrestling with this stuff in a vacuum for years. To have it all suddenly fit together like this is kind of blowing my mind."

"I don't care who I offend at this point!" Alec yelled at Sanantha in the kitchen. He stormed out into the living room and demanded, "I think you all need to leave now. All this righteous supposition is sounding like so much bullshit at this point. I just need to be alone. Please put all that back," he pointed at the equipment Desiree had.

"Sure. No problem." She set them down and quietly said to Renpo, "The Pearl? Joseph, can you see what's going on?"

As he turned away from Alec, he whispered, "Something off with his body chemistry."

She took the Pearl Renpo slipped her and turned to face Alec.

"What are you three whispering about?"

Desiree blinked as she realized she already knew what was wrong. Or at least that's how the Pearl made her feel. "Alec, you're not in the mood to hear this right now, so I'm just going to say it and then we'll leave. The drugs you take for your anxiety are not working. They have nearly all flushed out of your system."

He was shocked. "Are you holding that damn Pearl? That's an invasion of privacy. You have no right to know what I take."

"But you've run clean."

"I have not lapsed on my meds. I take them every day."

Desiree looked passed him at Sanantha in the doorway. "The Pearl does not lie. Can you test his pills?"

"Yes, but not right now. Alec, if she's right, you could be in real trouble. It takes weeks for SSRIs to coax the brain into behaving. If you're cleaned out, we may need to take drastic measures."

"Like what, sedation?" he spat.

"You know what it's like. You've been through it."

"Hold on." Desiree stepped forward. She still had the Pearl in one hand as she reached up with her other and put it on Alec's cheek. "You're angry and scared, but I'm here." She felt her heart glowing with the god heat. She did not know what it wanted to do, but it definitely had a goal of its own. She knew where his hurt was coming from, as if she could see into his brain and see a bruise, a wounded place. She knew absolutely nothing about how brains worked, but she knew where his was broken. She handed Renpo the Pearl, then stepped back and pulled her arms around to shake the energy down into her hands.

Alec looked like he was about to bolt.

"I've done this three times before. It only helps. I don't think I could harm anything with this energy. Can you trust me for just a moment?"

He was breathing hard and took a moment to get to a rational answer. "If I don't, I will always wonder if I should have. Go ahead."

She reached up and placed one hand behind his head and the other on his forehead. She felt the energy leap from her hands and dive straight to where she knew it needed to go. It only took an instant and her hands felt empty as usual.

"Is that it?" he asked.

"Yes. That's all I got."

Desiree could see Sanantha was struggling. "Even if she cured you, you won't see any change until you test it over time. The brain doesn't so much heal as retrain." She turned to the others. "You should go. I'm going to stay here with Alec for the evening and make sure he's all right."

Desiree looked to Joseph and Renpo who was holding the Pearl. They turned their gaze from Alec to her. They both smiled and nodded.

• • •

"Not that I don't appreciate being treated to breakfast, but wouldn't you rather talk to Alec about the progress he has made?" Sanantha tried to read Benito's face but his perpetually cheery demeanor again made it difficult.

"I've been away all week, and I wanted to hear an unbiased view of what you all have been working on." He motioned out the second story window which overlooked the gates of Trinity College. "Besides, you are much more pleasant company on a cold, drizzly day. I was in Spain which was much drier and warmer. You say you've never been here?"

"To Kilkenny's? No. Of course I've been in town less than a month."

"Then I'm glad to be the one to introduce you. You got a scone. Didn't you get the clotted cream?"

"You know, I don't think of myself as a restaurant snob, but when you said this was the best breakfast in Dublin, I didn't expect a cafeteria over a jewelry store. Granted the selection is kind of amazing …"

"That's an impressive spread."

"… But we're eating off plastic trays."

"Did you see the write ups from the top travel sites?"

"Yes, I saw the signs up front. I take it this is traditional Irish fare?"

"Absolutely. I'm having the Weaver's Breakfast: sausage, ham, polenta, broiled tomatoes, portabello mushroom, and scrambled eggs. And it was only 9 euro. You went with the oatmeal. Always a good bet. Are you sure you don't want to try the clotted cream with your scone?"

"In fact, I didn't see any on the buffet."

"Preposterous." He waved down a busboy. "Be a good fellow and get the lady a pot of clotted cream, will you?"

"So sorry, Sir, but the chef said there isn't any today. A misdelivery or something."

"Go check in the ice box."

"The chef runs the kitchen. I don't know if …"

Benito raised a finger. "Take the initiative. People make mistakes. If you can succeed where others have failed, that's a win for you."

137

"The ice box?"

"Yes."

"Yes Sir."

Watching the boy's retreat, Sanantha was amused and fascinated. "You know, I have had clotted cream before. You didn't have to send him on a goose chase on my account."

"It was a chance to help the boy make a good choice. See?" he said with a flourish at the boy's return, with a ceramic pot.

"You were right, Sir. The chef was surprised too."

"Thank you," Benito said graciously.

Sanantha smirked. "I guess I should have some then." She smeared it on and took a bite. "Mmm, that is good."

"Now you're having the full experience," he said picking up his own knife and fork. "So what have you been up to?"

"As I started to tell you in the car, we've been really busy. Alec and Desiree had a shared vision about an artifact in Tibet."

"Shared visions? Those are cornerstones of objective proof."

"Exactly. So she went there with Joseph and they found it. It's a giant pearl. They also picked up a monk named Renpo who is, I guess the keeper of the thing. It helps you see the truth, although we haven't quite figured out how it works."

"See the truth? Like a lie detector?"

"No, it alters a person's perceptions. It lets you see the whole story."

"Is it a drug?"

"You know, I thought that too. I thought maybe a contact stimulant or hallucinogen. The effect is instantaneous, so I'm not sure there is a scientific explanation."

"You think it's magic?"

"It might be. I don't know the history or the myths behind it. Alec hopes it will show him if he is really contacting spirits or if he is seeing things too subjectively."

"He does worry about that."

"We also did some poking around the myth of Saint Patrick."

"You chose Saint Patrick because we're in Ireland?" he said with a grin.

"No, now you're just being silly. Before Alec met you, he did some ghostbusting at Saint Patrick's gravesite and found some interesting traces.

"We did some research, and Alec had a bit of a meltdown when we figured out the Saint may have had some angelic or maybe demonic help with his miracles. Desiree helped him get back on his feet. It has been an exciting week."

"Has Alec contacted this angel? Angels can be dangerous."

"No, he swears he hasn't. I warned him about the dangers too. So how about you? You said you had business in Spain?" Sanantha caught herself, surprised at acting so familiar. Benito didn't seem to mind. Of course, he was glad to talk about himself.

"It was an old matter from a previous client. I suddenly had a chance to clean up some loose ends. Alec was making good progress on his own, so I decided to take time out."

"That's amazing. What a jet setter life you lead." *Gushing? Really?* What had come over her? When she looked away, she caught a headline on a newspaper sitting on the next vacant table. It moved her to pick it up. "Excuse me a moment."

It was bad. "Oh how horrible."

"What?"

"A freighter caught fire in Barcelona harbor and when they put it out, they found the ship was filled with Cypriot refugees. All three hundred of them died, trapped below decks. Good God. Can you imagine?"

"It is a crazy world." He gently took the paper out of her hands and set it down. "That's why it is so important for us to enjoy what we can, while we can."

Normally she would have been offended by him taking it from her. Somehow she wasn't, and she found herself agreeing with him.

"Now more than ever, for you especially." He gestured broadly as he spoke. 'To see one of your gods up walking around in the flesh, to be solving spiritual mysteries that have confounded mankind for eons, to witness miracles like no one has seen in millennia. You should be as excited as I am, maybe more so."

She took a breath and nodded. "Renpo said this could be the dawn of a new age."

"Absolutely! I understand you see yourself as the rational counselor, the one who keeps an objective, cautionary eye, and that's a good thing. Just don't miss how wonderful this all is. You can indulge yourself, occasionally, the joy of what we're doing."

"I'll admit, it's pretty exciting. Terrifying, but exciting."

"We need to work on that terror part. You're a beautiful woman, in an exotic city, having the adventure of a lifetime, maybe even changing history. I'm going to go with, 'thrilling.' Is that fair?"

All right, that was a flirtation. Kind of nice, actually. "Fair enough."

•   •   •

Desiree peeked out into her living room to check on Renpo and found his bedroll was already off the couch and packed neatly in the corner. She pulled her pink plush robe snug against the morning chill. It was still dark outside at 7 AM, and she knew he was out on his daily morning walk. Sanantha's door was still sensibly closed. Coffee. This morning needed coffee.

She just sat down with her first cup and a plate of dates when Renpo came home. "Good morning, Brother Renpo. Have a nice walk?"

"Good morning. Yes, as always. Dublin is a beautiful city."

"I made you a pot of hot water for your tea."

"Thank you very much." As he started preparing it, he said, "I have been thinking of the extraordinary series of events that has brought us all together. You mentioned you acquired the soul of the goddess when a medical experiment failed. Could you please tell me how a medical event led to a spiritual change?"

"Yes, I was dead for over an hour, even though my body was still breathing. When Sanantha and my father finally got me back, it was through divine intervention. The soul that I use, what we have now seen is my *chi*, was given to me by the goddess. It's a little piece of her."

He joined her at the dinette table with his tea. He smiled and observed, "Ah, your dates."

She pushed the plate toward him. "Try one."

He picked one up and turned it in his fingers. "Unless I am mistaken, these originated in the Middle East, probably Egypt."

"Oh, shit," she let slip. "Pardon my French. I hadn't thought of that."

"I have noticed your skin has no scars or flaws, almost as if your skin is that of a newborn baby. Is that also from this episode?"

She blushed. "Yes, my skin is perfect because my body was completely changed, at the cellular level, into another person, and then changed back into me. It's like I'm fresh out of the mold of what my genes say I should look like."

"Has that episode changed how you see yourself?"

"It has made me question who I am. I mean, little girls are led to hope they will grow up to have a fairy tale life. No one told me my fairy tale would be *Frankenstein*."

"I don't know that story, but I think I understand what you mean. I sense a resiliency in you that you probably don't see." He smiled and looked her deeply in the eyes with an admiration she didn't expect.

"What? It's just me."

"I think I may have guessed wrong about the return of Maitreya. Alec denied being on the path of transcendence and return. On the other hand, you died and were reborn with this spirit of compassion."

Sanantha came down the hall in her black terry robe, blinking against the kitchen light. "You think Desiree is the returning Buddha?"

"My vision was of the return. You never know how visions will play out."

"When I healed that deer, you said the Pearl showed you I was Guanyin."

"Guanyin was with you. Many gods and spirits supported the Buddha in his quest. All of nature celebrated his arrival. May I ask you one more thing about your appearance? I don't want to embarrass you."

"That's okay."

"When you healed the deer, your eyes changed to a much darker blue."

"Her eye color?" Sanantha asked.

"I did not mention it at the time because we were busy."

"I didn't know that happens."

Sanantha proceeded cautiously. "Your eye color was how we could tell when you were Cheri and when you were you, when you were genetically unbalanced. I wonder if there is still some instability."

Desiree shook her head. "When that happened, everything changed, including my hair as it grew, my ability to tan, my memories would switch on and off. I don't see anything like that happening now. The only change I notice now is Isis is a lot more assertive then me. That's probably because she knows what she's doing and I don't."

Sanantha squinted and pursed her lips. "I'll keep an eye on that just the same."

Desiree smiled. "Of course you will. I guess you can expect to see it when Isis takes over."

•   •   •

Renpo answered the door. "Oh, Mister Alec. Come in please. What can I do for you?"

"Sanantha said she had a proper refill of my medication."

"Yes, it's right over here," he said retrieving the bottle from a table. "Did the analysis show something wrong with the old ones?"

"Yes. They were less than a quarter of the prescribed dosage. I will be contacting the chemist who made them up."

"Do you need them anymore?"

"I haven't felt anxious since Desiree did her Lay of the Hands, but Sanantha says the pills won't do me any harm. She wants to wean me off them at a controlled pace. I started to ask my regular psychiatrist, and I realized I had no way of describing what happened. I mean, how would I explain a miraculous cure to a doctor who has devoted his life to managing the incurable?"

"That would be difficult. It is a good thing we have Doctor Mauwad at your disposal."

Alec looked around. "Did they leave you here alone?"

"I do not mind being alone. I always have prayers and study. But Desiree is here. I believe she is reading on the back porch. It is a beautiful warm day."

"All right. I'll just say Hi. I wanted to apologize for the other night. I barked at you all to get out, and I see how rude that was."

"You were upset and not well at the time. I forgive you, and I'm sure Mr. Joseph and Desiree will also."

Renpo followed him out back and they found Desiree napping on a lounge chair.

"Why is she wearing white pajamas?" Alec asked softly.

"Those are her *tai chi chuan* silks. I was working with her on her *chi gong* earlier. I think she enjoys the fit. She is wearing them a lot."

"Well, could you tell her I'm sorry about the other night?"

"Of course."

As they turned to go, an alarmingly large black crow fluttered into the tiny yard and landed on the back of her chair, right next to her head. When it sniffed around her face, Alec stepped into the yard and took a breath to shoo it away.

Just then, Renpo spotted another airborne visitor. He clutched Alec's arm and whispered, "Wait! Look."

A white streak flashed down straight at the crow and unfurled its wings, claws extended. The dove did not slow, and the crow leapt out of the way, flapping furiously to escape. The dove pulled up and landed softly where the crow had stood, next to Desiree's head. It puffed out its chest and surveyed the heavens.

Alec's mouth hung open.

Renpo smiled deeply. "There is much more here than meets the eye."

14

DESIREE STOOD IN HER CRAMPED DRAB GREEN BATHROOM with her hands pressed together at her chest, dressed in her white silks, eyes closed focused on remembering what she felt when she healed the sparrow, Joseph, the deer, and Alec. In all those cases, Isis had initiated the god *chi* and Desiree had just come along for the ride. Desiree needed to learn to grow the energy herself. She started with sensing their injuries, but this did nothing. She tried remembering how the energy flowed out of her hands. Again nothing. Then she remembered the strongest emotion had always been her sorrow, her empathy, her compulsion to do something. Yes, compassion. The heat rose in her chest and she let the hurt swell with it. Yes, that was the key.

She opened her eyes, crouched down, and whirled her arms around to flood the heat out into her hands. She saw how silly she looked in the mirror and quoted Keanu Reeves. "I know *kung fu*," she mugged.

Her eyes were way too dark blue. She stepped up close to the mirror. "Son of a gun." There were none of the weird flecks of color like when she tettered into and out of being her mother. This was solid blue, darker than new blue jeans.

Her cell phone rang. She was surprised by the name on the screen. "Simon! How are you?"

"Hello Desiree! Am I calling at a good time? I wasn't sure if I got the time difference right."

"Sure, no problem. It's early evening here. What can I do for you?"

"I've actually got a couple of reasons for calling, but the first is to ask you a favor. I know Sanantha went to Ireland to see you. I don't know if she mentioned it, but she left right after we had a big fight."

"She did."

"It's been a few weeks and she hasn't called or written. May I ask your opinion if she is still too mad at me to talk? I don't want you to breach any confidences, but I would really appreciate your read."

"Actually, she hasn't mentioned you hardly at all."

"Oh. All right. Well, that brings me to the other reason I called. An FBI agent showed up here in Malaysia asking about Sanantha's involvement in a crime back in 2001."

"Do you mean the death of her patient Charles Redmond?"

"Oh, you know about that?"

"Yeah, we've talked about how she faced down a demon, literally."

"That's true. I tried to answer this FBI agent's questions to get her off Sanantha's back, but now I think she's going to come to Ireland to ask Sanantha directly."

"Did you say the agent is a woman?"

"Yes, Jill Bitterman. I'm thinking I will come along with her. The plane ride will give me a chance to find out what the FBI is doing reopening a nine-year old case. I have to admit, though, I'm just as worried about what kind of reception might be awaiting me."

"I don't want to stick my foot in it, but you should know she has started seeing someone. In fact, she's out on a date with him now. I frankly don't think it's serious. To hear her tell it, Benito is suave and charming and rich but actually rather full of himself. I think he's just a nice distraction. It's been a pretty stressful time for her. First with your fight, and then with everything Alec has been doing."

"I don't know who Alec or Benito are," Simon said.

146

"Alec is a paranormal investigator I befriended. Then Joseph showed up. You do know who Joseph is, right?"

"Joseph the Egyptian angel? Yes, Sanantha told me about him. He's in Ireland with you?"

"Yeah, that's why Sanantha rushed here, to make sure I was safe. Ironically, I was always safe with Joseph. Now it seems the demon Sanantha battled nine years ago might be after me, because of my Erzulie connection."

"You do realize we are talking about Sammael, the snake from the Garden of Eden?"

"Yes, I know, the Devil himself. I am really glad to have all these experts around me at a time like this."

"The police have always thought Sammael was a human terrorist. Something has reignited the trail. I'll try to find out what." He paused as if collecting himself. "And who is this guy Sanantha is seeing, Benito?"

"You know, I've never met him. He finances Alec's research. Sanantha and Alec talk about him all the time; it's almost like I know him, but I really don't."

•   •   •

Sanantha pulled the covers up around her and rolled to the middle of the bed. Benito wasn't there. She blinked against the morning light streaming in from the bathroom. She liked the blackout shades in his hotel bedroom.

"Sorry I left that open," he said, striding across the room in his boxers to close the bathroom door.

As he closed it, she noticed towels on the floor streaked red with blood. She slipped her hand under the blankets and found her genitals were sore.

"Is that blood from last night?"

"We did get a little carried away," he said sitting down on the edge of the bed.

"I remember that. It was kind of amazing. I just didn't remember blood. She looked under the sheets. "I'm not bleeding now. Are you all right?"

"Never better."

She noticed bruises on her arms and bite marks on her hips and shoulders. "What? Benito, you bit me."

He grinned and looked around his own shoulders. "I think I got a few nibbles too."

"I have never … Now I remember. Good grief. Did we actually …?

"Sodomy? Oh yes, and a lot more. Wasn't it wonderful?" he got up and started doing a *tai chi* routine.

She blinked and shook her head. "I'm not usually the rough sex kind of gal."

"You were enjoying it, so I stepped up my game."

She watched his well-muscled, hairy body flex and stretch. "I'll say." She wondered why she didn't feel violated. Should she? His confidence and lust for life was contagious. It was just so easy to go along with him. "Hey, did I hear screaming during the night?"

"Maybe someone else in the hotel was having fun too."

"I don't know. Maybe it was a dream. I remember hearing screams and gunshots."

"I didn't. I slept like the dead."

"I'm not surprised. Frankly, I am surprised I'm not in more pain. I mean, bruises and blood?"

He stopped. "Are you hurting?"

"No, not really."

"Good. I was hoping my fix would work for you."

"What do you mean?"

"I didn't want anything to get in the way of your pleasure, so I gave you a little boost. It's something I do for myself now and then. They're right there in the bottle on the nightstand." He returned to his *tai chi*.

Suddenly this wasn't just fun and games. "You drugged me?"

"No no no," he said with a flourish of his hands. "You remember everything, yes? I would never drug you. That would take away your pleasure. What would be the point of that?"

She looked at the bottle. "Dilaudid with Cathinone." She thought for a moment. "What a remarkably ancient mix, opium cut with khat. Pain relief without being sedated. Merde, Benito. You keep this stuff lying around?"

148

"Yes, I live with a lot of pain. I do not like to feel pain. Pain stops you from living life. I hoped it would keep you from pain, so you wouldn't have to stop, or wake up with regrets." He came around, sat next to her, and tenderly took her hand. "You don't have any regrets, do you?"

She thought she should be furious with him, but she wasn't. She took his hand in hers. "No, it was tremendous fun. Just do not medicate me without my approval," she said slapping the back of his hand.

A half an hour later, after examining her souvenirs and finding no permanent damage, she came out of the shower wrapped in a voluminous Turkish bathrobe to find him on the bed reading a newspaper. "Was that delivered?"

"Oh yes, perks," he said not looking up. He laughed to himself.

'What is it?" she asked.

"I can't believe what an absolute hash these Americans have made of this Iraq situation."

"You just now come to that conclusion? I've been watching it unfold for the last four years, and been glad to be halfway around the world." She took her hair out of the towel in front of the full-length mirror and started finger combing her curls.

"I've been busy and not really paying much attention to the details. I've got to say, the gall is impressive."

"Impressive? Not the word I would choose."

"No, really, I've got to hand it to them. They get attacked by a disaffected member of the Saudi oil regime they support, then preach 'fear' loud enough to get away with attacking the second richest oil nation on Earth. It's quite brilliant. Only it won't work."

"What won't work?"

"They want the Iraqi oil, but removing Hussein will destabilize the whole region."

"Wasn't Saddam a mass murderer despot?"

"Oh sure, but he had the zealots under control. With him gone, everyone who has suffered under Western intervention for the last fifty years is going to arm up and take the jihad fight across the globe. I predict that within five years you're going to have suicide bombings and random mass shootings in every major city in the world. It's going to be chaos. And the Americans aren't going to get anywhere near enough oil out of Iraq to make it worthwhile."

"I had no idea you were so politically savvy."

"This isn't politics, this is history. Every big lie ever told was best sold with fear. And unless someone reins them in, whenever you take the chains off an oppressed people, they revolt."

She considered his words carefully. "That's a pretty bleak assessment."

"It's not hopeless. You need a leader with the nerve to regain control. You need a Lincoln or a Gandhi or a Mandala to convince the recently freed to not burn down the world. You know, maybe it's time I got back into the game."

"You? You're politically connected? If you think you can do some good, more power to you."

He smiled. "I know lots of people. Yeah, that's a plan," he commented to himself. "Once I'm done here in Ireland, I think I'll do some travelling in the Mideast. Situation seems ripe."

"Can we order up some breakfast?"

"They're not doing room service this morning. I called down and they said there is some kind of staff issue this morning. We can go out."

"Swanky place like this?"

"I don't know. The guy was apologetic, but he doesn't have the staff."

She retrieved her turban windings from the dresser top and shook out the long strip of fabric.

Benito smiled. "I like your high crown."

She smiled back. "If I recall, it was the first thing you commented on when we met. You said you thought it was Moroccan."

"Yes, very African. Reminiscent of the high headdresses of the queens of Egypt. I remember Nefertiti wore a high conical crown of the same shape."

She paused and blinked. That connection had never occurred to her. Maybe more than just the religion of Egypt had made its way to Haiti.

Someone knocked at the door and she looked through the peephole. "It's the police." Benito joined her as she opened the door.

"Excuse me ma'am, sir. We need to ask you some questions." The young officer looked pale, as if he had been frightened. There was crime scene tape over the open door across the hall, and other officers were working inside. "We're you here all last night?"

"Yes, from about eleven on."

"Did you see or hear anything unusual last night?"

"I thought I heard someone scream and I heard some loud noises, but I couldn't tell what they were. I was asleep and thought I was dreaming. It would have been early in the morning, like one or two."

"Sir, did you hear anything?"

"No, I slept right through it. What happened?"

"I'm not at liberty to discuss details, sir."

"I understand," Benito said calmly. "We were right here. If we were in any danger, we should know."

Sanantha didn't think this tact would work, but to her surprise it did.

"I don't think you were in any danger, sir. The occupants in this unit across the hall and the occupants in the room next door were both involved in homicides. The one next door appears to be a murder-suicide with a pistol, and this one here appears to have been a knife fight with both parties succumbing to their wounds. But as I said, sir, I am not able to share any details, even with witnesses."

Sanantha was horrified and fascinated at the same time. He was telling them far more than he should, frankly more than she wanted him to, yet he still thought he was keeping to protocol.

Benito asked, "One last thing. Were these gang-related, were they all together?"

"No sir, these appear to be unrelated."

"Did anyone else hear anything?"

"No sir. These three units are all here at the end of the hall, and no one else down the hall heard anything."

"Thank you, officer. Will that be all?"

"Yes sir. Thank you for your cooperation."

•   •   •

Alec put away the last of the clean dishes and was wiping down the countertops when the doorbell rang. "Oh, hi, Benito. Is it two already? I thought we were meeting at the café."

"I'm early to catch you before you left." He held up a drink holder in one hand and a satchel in the other. "Cold drizzly day needed hot coffee and a good book. I thought you might want to stay in."

"I'm not sure what you mean, but come on in. Thanks for the coffee."

Benito slipped off his brown tweed overcoat. "You've seemed anxious the last couple of times I've seen you out in public."

Alec thought about that for a moment. "That's true, but I'm doing fine."

"Really? I know some folks just hate crowds, and I get that. Me, I thrive with people around. We've been talking about you taking your magic more public. You do realize, at some point that will mean performing in front of a live audience."

Alec wondered if Benito knew about his anxiety. Maybe Benito was just really good at reading people. "Yeah, I've thought about that. You're right, I used to get nervous, but I think I've got that under control now."

Benito still did not look like he believed him. "Okay. Great."

"You said you've had this book for a while?"

"Yes. I never took it seriously. A colleague found it and dismissed it as a fake. I held onto it as a curiosity. Now with your condenser fluid, I thought you might want to test it and see if it's got any real content." He slipped a package wrapped in yellowed paper and string out of the bag.

Alec looked at the string. "I'll get a knife."

"Oh, no need," Benito said as he pulled out a straight razor, flipped it open, and gave it to Alec handle first.

"You walk around with a straight razor on you?"

"It's from shaving this morning. I slipped it in my pocket and forgot it."

"Right." Alec cut the strings and peeled open the paper. "How long did your friend have this lying around?"

"A few years I guess."

There was a white paper strip wrapped around the leather-bound volume. "I haven't seen one of these before. Is it some kind of seal?"

"Hard to say. It's supposed to be a religious text." Before Alec could say anything, Benito kissed two fingers and made the sign of the cross over the book. He grinned at Alec's questioning look. "Best be safe, just in case, eh?"

Alec slipped his finger under the paper and broke it. He sat down on the couch and flipped through the pages. "Ancient Greek."

Benito took a breath, smiled, and then sat down. "That's the problem. Forgers know how to make ancient Greek look like antique transcriptions. Even if it was genuine, it wouldn't tell us how old the original source material was. My colleague validated that structurally the language is a translation from Aramaic."

Alec sipped his coffee and studied a random page. "Has anyone dated the book itself?"

"My friend said about 900 AD — which would be about right for a monastic transcription."

"I'm seeing references to Jesus and Lazarus. Is it an apocryphal gospel?"

Benito smiled. "That was the part I was going to let you figure out for yourself. It claims to be a gospel written by Lazarus himself."

Alec chuckled. "There have been a few of those. A first-hand account from one of the only people to go to heaven and return, that's the stuff of occult wet dreams. I can look through it. Apocryphalia like this gives insight into what the people of the time thought of heaven. It gives us a window on the research that was available at the time."

"You've got the condenser fluid to test anything you find. If you find that it's a fraud, then we'll know for sure."

"That's what you said earlier. How would the fluid validate this text?"

"It's a gospel, so there's bound to be references to the Holy Spirit. We know the Holy Spirit is what your fluid condenses, *chi* and willpower. When the book describes what the Holy Spirit can do, you try to replicate it with the fluid."

"You want to see if the book is genuine by seeing if the miracles described are reproducible?"

"What could be more scientific?"

Alec laughed out loud. "The secrets of creation Lazarus saw when he was dead in heaven?" He picked it up and examined the binding. "It is beautifully made. Somebody wanted this to last a long time." He shrugged. "We'll see."

15

Jill Bitterman walked down the aisle from Business Class into Coach with the confidence of having a target well acquired. "Doctor Herrera, how nice to see you again," she intoned with her distinct drawl.

For a relationship expert, he did a lousy job of looking nonchalant. "Oh, hello Agent Bitterman."

"I figured I'd save you the heartburn of figuring out how to come talk to me without looking like an international stalker. Is this seat taken?"

He got up to let her step past him to the empty seat. "No, it seems open. I apologize for appearing to stalk you. I am in fact going to see Sanantha. As you know, there aren't that many flights from Malaysia to Ireland. I will admit I hoped I could speak with you before we arrived."

She settled in. "We got nothin' but time."

"Since you and I last met, I spoke with a friend of Sanantha's, the friend she went to go see."

"Miss Macklin."

"Yes. Desiree said she thinks the same terrorist that attacked Sanantha back in 2001 may be in Ireland now. She said she thinks he might be plotting against Desiree."

"What's so special about her?"

"This guy is a religious zealot. We're pretty sure the attack in 2001 was some kind of jihadi fatwah. Desiree is thinking about starting a new religion, based on some experiences she had back in Malaysia. I don't have any details, but she said she thought this guy was out to stop her. I thought you would want to know that."

"What can you tell me about her new religion?"

"It's actually really old. It's a revival of ancient Egyptian rites."

"Doctor Mauwad practices Voodou. Is she part of this revival?"

"Yes, she is part of it. I know it sounds farfetched, but it turns out the gods of Haitian Voodou are manifestations of the old gods from Egypt."

"That's not the weirdest thing I've heard."

"I bet you see a lot of strange things in the field."

"Let's just say I've dealt with a lot of people who thought they had tapped into something that set them above the rest of us, when usually all they've found is a new way to be mean."

"That's the problem I have with zealots. In Malaysia I see clients from all walks and all faiths. It's a tremendous melting pot of nine ethnicities all with their own cultures and religions. Once someone starts using religion to justify bad behavior, there is no reasoning with them. Facts and logic don't even matter to them anymore."

"Well, Doctor, since you brought it up, how do you help a patient who has decided he's being called by God to break the law?"

"If I hear that a crime is about to happen, then I tell law enforcement. If I hear a crime has already happened, then I work to prevent additional crimes. The tricky part comes later, whether I turn my patient in or not. There is a judgment call. As law enforcement, I'm sure you would prefer mental health professionals reported everything we hear."

"What if you believe him?"

"Pardon?"

"What if what your patient says makes sense, if he convinces you he's right?"

"Well, I'm trained to distance myself from any delusions my patients may have."

"If I may ask, what religion were you brought up with?" she asked.

"Roman Catholic, although I don't practice anymore."

"Let's say, just for argument's sake, one of your patients told you he had been visited by the archangel Michael, and Michael told him to go out and buy eight hundred pounds of fertilizer to make a bomb. Now from what you just said, you would call the cops to stop the crime."

"That's true."

"Now what if he showed hard evidence that he really did get this message from an angel? What if this evidence rattled you to your Catholic core, made you really question everything? Would you still call the police?"

Simon thought about this for a long moment. He stroked his greying black goatee. She noted the grey was creeping into his wavy black hair too. He'd been around the block a few times. She could tell he wasn't just coming up with an answer, but was also trying to get a read on her. "I would hope I could push past my own beliefs and do the right thing. Agent, this sound like you've come across such an experience. Have you?"

"This sort of thing happens more often than you might want to believe. I depend on people like you being able to hold your water when the going gets rough."

"If I might ask, do you have a religious background you find yourself having to rise above?"

"I was raised hard line Southern Baptist. Jesus protected us from Old Testament hellfire and damnation all the way. Up until my parents were cleaned out by a couple of thieving televangelist priests. Broke my faith in churches altogether."

"Did you lose your faith in God?"

"I decided on a more practical way to serve the Lord. Faith had always been part of who I am, so I had to find something else. That's when I found justice." She pulled out her badge. "Fidelity, Bravery, Integrity, those are my trinity now."

"I imagine a lot of lawmen feel strongly about justice. Why have you elevated yours to a faith?"

"When you've seen the things I've seen, you start to hold your sense of right and wrong pretty close to your heart."

"You've been tempted?"

"That's a big one. I can tell you this story because the case is closed and the perp is off the street. I was once offered more money than I would ever be able to spend in my lifetime, and all I had to do was lose a phone number that wasn't supposed to exist. I got the number from a medium who was being extorted by a Mexican drug cartel strongman. She got it from a Tarot card reading. The number turned out to be real, the witness it led me to was real, and that drug lord is now behind bars. I kept my faith that justice would prevail, even when I had to use mumbo jumbo."

Herrera paused to think about this. "If Desiree and Sanantha are being targeted by this terrorist, I am very glad to have you and your convictions on the case."

Given that she was going to Ireland following a lead on the terrorist and not actually following Sanantha Mauwad, she decided to not dissuade Doctor Herrera's impression of her motive. This Desiree woman could be useful.

•   •   •

Desiree pulled open the door with a cheery but presumptive, "Hi Joseph! Oh, sorry. I was expecting someone else."

The tall, broad-shouldered man in a grey trenchcoat smiled and showed her a badge. "Sorry, ma'am. I am Revenue Agent Michael Archibald from the Irish Treasury Department. Are you Desiree Macklin? I'm here to ask some questions about Alec Doogan. Is Mr. Doogan here?"

Treasury Department? Why would they care about defacing a fountain? "No, he doesn't live here, and he's not visiting right now. Is Alec in some kind of trouble?"

He put his badge away and shook off his trenchcoat. It was raining, but he was under the porch eves. She wasn't sure she wanted to invite him in.

"I spoke with Mr. Doogan a few days ago. I'm following up on some things he told me about his finances. Are you familiar with a Mr. Benito Nomini?"

"Yes, he's helping Alec. I have never met him. Why don't you come in?"

"Thank you."

As he stepped up through the door, he was even bigger than he looked outside.

"When you say he is helping Mr. Doogan, do you mean financially?" he asked.

"Yes, I believe so. My understanding is he is wealthy, though I don't know what he does for a living. Should I be concerned that my friend is dealing with a shady character?"

He smiled a crooked and somehow predatory grin. "I can't discuss details of our investigation."

Someone knocked on the door.

"Excuse me." She opened the door. "Oh, Joseph, there you are."

"I was just admiring this car out here," he said pointing.

"Joseph, we have a visitor, from the Irish Treasury Department."

He stepped in and asked, "Is that your white BMW?"

"Why, yes it is."

The pleasantries stopped when the two men locked gazes. "Do you two know each ..."

Before she could finish her question, Joseph whipped off his sunglasses and Michael lowered one shoulder as if ducking down behind something. Before she could react, Joseph swept her roughly behind himself and fired blinding white bolts of energy from his eyes. The bolts bounced off something invisible over Michael's shoulder and blasted a four-foot wide hole in the wall behind him. For just an instant, Desiree thought she saw a glow where the bolt had glanced that was the shape of a wing. "Stop! What the hell are you doing?"

Ignoring her, Michael held up his fist as if holding something weighty in his hand. He shook his head and warned, "Don't make me use this."

"That's up to you," spat Joseph.

Michael grinned. "As much fun as it would be to mix it up with you, this time we're on the same side."

Desiree thought about what she was witnessing. "What? Are you an angel too?"

Joseph finally acknowledged her. Without taking his eyes off the man, he said, "Yes. He's Michael."

"I know he's … Oh shit! He's Michael? As in the Archangel Michael?" Then to him, "Don't terrible things happen whenever you appear?"

Michael grinned wider. "My reputation precedes me."

Joseph pressed. "What do you mean, we are on the same side?"

Michael stood up straight, but kept his shoulder forward. "This isn't about Yahweh versus the Neters. That ship sailed long ago. This is about truth versus deception."

Now it was Joseph who grinned. "You're after Sammael, now that he's free on Earth again."

"That's right."

"You Old Testament boys don't usually go after each other," Joseph observed. "Don't you have an edict to not fight amongst yourselves lest there be another 'falling out'?"

"That's true. I have never cared who he deceived, whether it was Ramses and your old master Silas, or a thousand other poor souls since then."

"Ah, but this is different," Joseph interrupted raising a finger. "Let me guess. That farm boy turned acolyte who slaughtered the Druid priests and left Patrick with blood on his hands, that was Sammael, wasn't it?"

"Yes."

It was all Desiree could do to contain her fear and think rationally. "This is who Alec accidentally summoned at Saint Patrick's gravesite?"

"It was no accident," Michael said. "With him, it's never an accident."

Desiree was catching up. "You're here to stop him because he pinned this heinous crime on one of your saints. Wait, you're just catching up with him now, because he surfaced with Alec? What, he covered his tracks so well that, even Heaven didn't see him do it six hundred years ago?"

Michael nodded. "He is called the Deceiver for a reason. He invented deception."

Desiree's head spun with questions. "Why would the Devil think Saint Patrick needed his help to defeat the Druids? I mean, God sent Patrick on that mission."

"We now see it was personal," Michael explained without taking his eyes from Joseph. "The old Celtic gods were inheritor reflections of his lifelong enemies, the Egyptian pantheon."

"What? How?"

Joseph whistled. "Missed that."

"Missed what?" she insisted.

"Angels, like Joseph and myself, are largely immutable. We were created to serve our gods and that never changes. Gods, on the other hand, need worshippers to exist and are influenced by the cultures of the people who worship them."

Joseph ticked them off on his fingers. "Egyptian, Greek, Gaul, Celt. Just like Egyptian, Animus, Catholic, Voodou."

Desiree shook her head trying to keep up. "So these old Celtic gods Alec is contacting are manifestations of the Egyptian gods, which are Sammael's enemies?"

Michael nodded.

"Wait a minute, there is more to a religion than just what gods you worship. What else carried over? How can we see the Egyptian world view in ancient Ireland?"

Michael nodded. "You're right. The Gaelic Druids believed in reincarnation, they did not believe in a punishment after death, they believed in a balance of life, that a life lost leads to a new life gained, and their goddesses were just as powerful as their gods."

Joseph followed up. "All of these concepts were also in Egypt, but not in Rome. They got here before the Romans conquered Europe."

"All right, if that's all true, then when Osiris warned me that Sammael was coming, he meant Sammael is coming for Isis's religion, in all its forms. He tried to stamp them out with Patrick, and now he's back to finish the job? We've got to tell Alec and Benito to stop contacting the Celtic gods. They're just making targets of themselves."

"Which is why I've been investigating Mr. Nomini. He has the resources to empower Mr. Doogan to bring the Celtic gods right out into the open. Sammael won't be able to resist such an easy target. I will be there when he sticks his head up."

Joseph raised an eyebrow. "So we should not tell Alec or Benito? If they stop, Sammael might not show himself."

"Bait?!" Desiree snapped.

"Highly protected bait," Michael insisted. "It has to be done right. There is no opponent more slippery."

Desiree was not convinced. "That means I have to lie to Alec and Benito, although I've never met him. Oh shit, Sanantha too, since she would no doubt tell Benito between the sheets. I'm supposed to let them blithely build this bridge to the gods, without telling them they are really my gods, knowing the whole time the Devil himself is planning on attacking? There has got to be a better way."

"I only managed to seize him the first time by drawing him in so deeply he could not writhe free. We just have to be ready to grab him before he can hurt anyone."

"I don't know if I can keep a secret like this. I'm supposed to be a god. This is not god-like behavior."

Michael and Joseph looked at each other dismissively.

"What? So gods lie all the time? Fine. I need your personal guarantee, if push comes to shove, you are not going to sacrifice Alec's or Sanantha's safety to get your quarry."

Michael looked her straight in the eye. It was not as comforting as she hoped. "You have it."

Joseph put his sunglasses back on. "You do realize that in clearing Patrick's name, you are going to shine a lot of light on the pagans, and the Neters are going to gain a lot of interest. You're going to lose those converts."

Michael grinned a sly smirk that Desiree found disturbing. "Not my department. You and I don't need believers. I've got people who take care of that. We'll get them back in time."

Sanantha let herself in and stopped, staring at the confrontation. Desiree saw her track the line from Joseph to the giant hole in the far wall of the living room.

"Sanantha! We have a guest of some repute. This is the Archangel Michael, come here to capture your old enemy Sammael."

The psychiatrist silently shifted her wide-eyed gaze from person to person and around to Desiree.

"I know, it's a lot to take in. Osiris's warning to me was real. It turns out the angel trace Alec found on Saint Patrick's grave was none other than the Devil. So, yes, we are all in mortal danger. Fortunately, the one entity who has ever beaten the Devil is here to help us." She turned to Michael. "Do I have that right?"

"Yes. Very nice to meet your acquaintance Doctor Mauwad."

"Likewise, I'm sure. Shouldn't we tell Alec?"

Desiree took a breath. "Alec was pretty unhappy with the idea that an incarnate angel helped Patrick. He would completely freak out if he found out it was the Devil."

Sanantha turned to Joseph. "I told you just being around angels was going to put Desiree in danger."

Michael explained, "The fact that Isis is alive in Desiree would have been enough for Sammael to find her."

Desiree jumped in, smiling, but the waiver in her voice showed her nervousness. "Now that I have two angels, I am fully protected."

16

"NOW WE GO LIVE TO THOM CASSIDY IN THE FIELD for an update on the sudden downpour that has taken Ireland by surprise." The prim thirty-something redheaded female news anchor turned away from the camera. "Thom, we usually see you here in the studio. What got you out in the storm?"

Thom was bundled up in a raincoat, wide-brimmed hat, scarf, and an umbrella, and he was still shivering. Rain poured down in sheets across the street scene behind him. "Well Erin, this storm was worth a visit. We've had our usual seasonal drizzles all week, but then air pressure dropped dramatically over the Northern Sea last night. This whipped up the same conditions we usually see in warm waters with tropical storms. Enormous amounts of water have been pulled up into clouds and high winds are driving those clouds overland. You can see behind me, the rain has not let up for several hours. Traffic has ground to a crawl as commuters are trying to navigate with windscreens that wipers just can't clear on streets that are flooded. If you can in any way stay home or indoors for the next few hours, please try to do so."

"Thom, how long is this expected to last?"

"Erin, this will persist all day today and into tonight. We don't know how much energy the storm will lose over land. Realistically, this could last for days. We are already seeing rivers swollen to flood levels."

The view switched to a crew of workmen in yellow raincoats and hardhats shoveling mud. "Here you see some municipal workers trying to divert water away from the access road to the Cannecle School which sits on the bank of the River Boyne. That vantage is usually beautiful but today the rising waters may threaten the school. They have not evacuated at this time. Workers say they have that situation under control."

One of the workers looked up into the camera and his eyes reflected a distinct violet flash.

"Thom, what was that flash of purple? Are you getting lightning out there?"

"Erin, I'm not seeing the camera feed you have, but I didn't see anything. No, we don't have lightning at this time."

Two other workers looked up and their eyes also flashed bright violet. Just then the ground gave way under them and all six men fell forward into a surge of water that washed away the access road. "Oh my God!" Thom yelled. 'The men have all fallen in. Their digging made things worse, not better. The roadway is gutted, cutting off the school. I don't see anyone in a place to save the men. They've been swept into the rushing river below. This is just horrible. The school is now surrounded by rushing water, with the river below and now the diverted overflow around the land side."

The camera jerked around trying to capture everything.

"We're seeing dirt eroded away on both sides now."

Erin back in the studio cut in. "We contacted the police about an immediate evacuation. My director just said we are going to stay live on you Thom as this situation unfolds."

"Great. We just heard from a passerby that something is happening just up river. We're going to run up there and check it out."

The camera bounced along as Thom continued to speak in transit.

"The Cannecle School is located at the very east end of Dublin proper, so just up here the buildings give way to farmland. I imagine a lot of that land is lower and already flooded. Okay, we see some people gathered at a bank head. Let's get up here to see."

The camera pushed its way through a group of people peering down into the river. The image pulled up on a man down on the bank, walking into the water.

"There's a man on the far bank right at the water's edge. He looks like he's going to jump in. He's got red hair and he's wearing some kind of long robe. He's waving his arms around. No, he's dancing and spinning. Erin, I don't know what he's doing over there. He's all alone and, oh my goodness, the water's edge just pushed back away from him. Are you seeing this?"

"Yes, Thom, we're seeing it clearly. Is he doing that?"

"I don't know, but the effect is amazing. The water is rushing by but it's moving, like it's bouncing away from him. Now he's walking out off the bank into the riverbed and the water is flowing around like there's a dam in front of him. I don't have an explanation. He's got to be thirty feet out from the edge, and he's got the water held back at bay in a wall that's at least fifteen feet high. He's still doing his circular dance. I can only guess that's how he's moving the water. The river jumped its bank on the far side, with a lot of water flowing out over the farmland. The man is nearly to the middle of the river and his invisible wall has formed a wedge, driving a lot of the water up over the banks on both sides."

"Thom, what is that roaring sound we hear?"

"The sound of the water turning out and up over the edge is like a waterfall. The water that's making it past him on either side is flowing calmly down like the river would normally. This is like something from a movie. I swear I've never seen anything like it. Oh, and you're probably also hearing the crowd here cheering."

"This is like Moses parting the Red Sea," Erin interjected.

"You're right. All the excess rainfall is being driven up and out across the surrounding flat land."

The camera swung around and looked back at the stranded school. The water level behind the man was below the bank edge, and the washed-out access road was now again above water. Fire crews were racing across the gap and ferrying children out of the school.

"The water drop behind the man has given rescue workers a chance to get the children to safety."

The camera swung around again to focus on the man dancing in the middle of the river on dry ground with a huge wedge in front of him pushing the water up and over the sides, with half the water flowing around him, gathering up, and flowing down river.

"I don't know what I can say that you aren't already seeing. This man is working some kind of miracle out in the middle of the river. Oh wait, he stopped dancing and is looking behind him now, yes, at the school. I can see the rescuers are just finishing up. Yes, it looks like they've got everyone out. The flashing lights on the fire trucks have moved away, so it looks like the school is empty."

The man turned to face his wall of water and held his arms up. The wall started to give way on the edges, with more and more water flowing around him. The river behind him filled up and rose.

"It appears the man is letting down his wall. Only he's not moving back to the bank. He's letting the water flow around him closer and closer. It's up around his feet. It looks like he's only barely holding it back now."

Back in the studio, Erin was breathless. "Is he going to let the river sweep him away?"

"That's what it looks like. Yes, he has let his wall down and, yes, there it is, the river has swept him up. That was actually pretty gentle given the speed of this water. There he goes, floating down river. Too bad, I would have loved to interview him."

"Do you think he'll be all right?" Erin asked.

"I'm sure of it. Anyone who can control hundreds of tonnes of water like that will just have the river deposit him safely wherever he wants. If anyone recognized this man, or if anyone sees him when he comes onto land, please call the station. What an amazing feat!"

•　　　•　　　•

Sammael put his foot up on the roof railing of the Aberdeen Plaza Hotel and drew a big mouthful from his Cuban cigar. Although he faced west, he did not admire the colors of the sunset. He breathed out the thick smoke through his nostrils as he watched with his mind's eye through the vision of the people on the streets around Desiree's rented cottage halfway across Dublin. The half dozen people he borrowed only momentarily lost focus from what they were doing while he used their eyes. As soon as they drove or walked past the block he was watching, they blinked back to focus from their daydreaming. He didn't care if anyone else on the street noticed the odd violet glint in their eyes while he took them over. He only held each one for a few seconds before releasing them.

In this manner, he watched Brother Renpo walk home alone at dusk. Sammael's spies unconsciously glanced over the back fence and through the front windows to see the lights go out a few minutes later. "Ah, right on time," the archangel said to himself. This wasn't the first time he watched the monk retire early. "Jet lag is a harsh mistress."

Sammael took one last drag from his cigar, set it on the railing, and transformed himself into a raven. He flew across town to the cottage's small backyard. Just as he was about to land, he transformed back into human form and silently set down on his loafers.

The back door wasn't even locked. He silently made his way from back to front and found the monk in his bedding on the living room floor. He was pleased to hear the man's breathing had slowed in a deep slumber. He bent down and peeled up an edge off Renpo's forehead with two fingers. The layer he pulled up shined from underneath with a rainbow of light. Once he got a good pull started, he lifted it up and over his head, enveloping himself in the dream.

Renpo was walking among a ruin. Sammael assumed his raven form and flew up into the tropical trees that surrounded what had once been a temple. Burmese, he guessed from the architecture. He tilted his head mischievously and squinted his round black eyes.

The monk's path took him from broken, fallen walls, to upright fragments he had to walk around. As he walked, the more the walls connected to form hallways and corners he had to walk around. When he encountered the first dead end, the bald man stopped and stared before turning back. He hesitated when he saw that the path he took in was not the same on his way out.

The raven cawed. Clouds swept in to darken the sky.

Renpo quickened his step, turning his head often to track the walls of the maze. He turned a corner and lurched to stop himself from falling into an enormous hole.

Sammael was curious when the monk did not just turn back, but stared at the hole for several seconds. He was further surprised when Renpo put his foot out onto the hole and found it was actually solid ground.

Sammael could not brook having his illusion broken.

The wall in front of Renpo exploded in a ground-shaking fireball. He fell back and covered his ears. As soon as he landed, he checked and saw he was not burned.

Sammael took to the air and swooped down while watching the monk put his hand through a seemingly solid stone wall.

The Pearl. He must be using the Pearl. *Was he sleeping with the damn thing?*

Sammael dove behind a real wall fragment and turned into a six-foot black python. He slithered up behind Renpo and took aim at his calf under his saffron robe. Renpo turned and jumped back with a yelp before the snake struck. His eyes went wide and his hands shook as he staggered back into a wall.

Sammael knew that look. That wasn't just fear, that was phobia. Desiree's spiritual guide was phobic of snakes — snakes that were a favorite manifestation of Erzulie.

Sammael coiled up in his delicious discovery. He wouldn't kill this man, even though he had found a way to beat the illusions. A curse for later, to be sure. For now, though, this phobia could be a wonderful tool.

He hissed and made a huge, flaunting leap for the monk, who cringed pathetically. He grazed the monk's temple with a fang and body slammed him out of the dream and back into wakefulness.

Renpo screamed and jerked awake. He bedclothes were wrapped around him tightly, like the coils of a snake. He pulled his hand out of the covers and looked at the Pearl he tightly clutched. Why would the Pearl, which was the embodiment of truth, show him a dream about deception and fear? He forced himself to set aside his immediate reaction of feeling betrayed, and decided to take this as a puzzle. He had to convince himself of this over the several minutes it took for his heart to slow to normal.

17

DESIREE AND RENPO SAT CROSS-LEGGED on the small living room rug facing each other taking turns reading aloud from Renpo's texts on meditation. The Pearl sat between them. Renpo wore his red teacher's robes and Desiree wore her white *tai chi* silks. "You know, I'm not sure how any of this will help me fight Sammael, but I am glad to find a way to control my fears."

Renpo had been over this several times over the last few days, but he understood her nervousness. "The mantra you selected, sitting by a peaceful pond, will allow you both something calming to concentrate on and a sense of place you can go to. By concentrating only on the pond, you will learn to push all other thoughts away, including thoughts that worry or frighten you."

"I can't go there whenever I'm frightened. I'll be busy trying to stay alive."

"True. You practice going there whenever you can, and learn what it feels like to focus on one thing at a time. You learn what being at peace feels like. That clarity of thought, that sense of peace, that's what you take into battle."

Sanantha walked in.

"Hi Sanantha."

"Oh, hi you two. Let me guess, late afternoon meditation drills?"

"Correct," Renpo answered. "The Isis *chi* appears to have enormous potential. She will need to focus with great determination to gain its full benefit."

"Sounds great," she said breezing through to the back of the cottage.

"Did it finally stop raining?" Desiree asked.

"Yes, after four days," she called from her bedroom. "The whole city has gone into damage cleanup."

"Have you heard from Alec? I've left him three messages. I'm worried."

Renpo realized the Pearl was sitting out in the open, so he picked it up.

Sanantha came out with her clothes changed from jeans and a shirt into a pencil skirt outfit. "Benito says he's gone into hiding for a while."

The monk was so distracted by the huge white snake wrapped around her shoulders, he didn't even notice she had changed clothes. Intellectually, he knew there wasn't an anaconda in the house. Intellectually, he told himself this was the Pearl telling him something. Intellectually, he understood Sanantha had stood in the role of Erzulie for Desiree in the past, and that Erzulie often appears as a large jungle snake. Unfortunately, all his intellectual musings were sweep aside by his paralyzing, irrational fear of snakes.

"To recover from the river ordeal?" Desiree asked.

"No, I think he's fine from that. He's got some new big research project he's working on. Have you seen the social media on him?"

Desiree snorted. "Yes, he's got tens of thousands of people following him on Youtube and Facebook."

Renpo dropped the Pearl and the snake turned into a white scarf around Sanantha's shoulders. He forced himself back into the conversation. "I am concerned about the fanaticism of his followers. Religious fanaticism is always destructive. Even in my own province of Purang, there is another monastery called Gongphur where the acolytes see themselves as the guardians of Buddhism, as if the faith needs defending. You are lucky to have come to my monastery Khorchag Gonpa instead, since the monks at the other one never would have helped you."

"Followers are what he needs to make the fluid work," Sanantha countered.

Desiree looked her up and down. "Going right back out?"

Renpo pushed his gaze away from the snake vision.

"Yes, Benito is waiting for me in the car."

"Oh, have him come in. You know I've never met him."

"Sorry, we're late already. Bye!"

Desiree got up and went to the window. "She seems pretty smitten."

Renpo took a couple of deep breaths to clear his head. "Does that bother you?"

"Not really 'bother,' but the timing seems off. Here we are exploring the secrets of the universe, and she, the most level-headed of us all, goes and let's herself get romantically swept away."

"May I offer a theory? She may have taken these exciting events as her cue to enjoy life more fully. Maybe she is feeling more in touch with her true nature. Although, now that I hear myself say that out loud, it does sound like a surrender to the senses."

"Thank you. I was starting to think I was being unfair to her."

Desiree's computer chimed. She walked into the kitchen and opened the laptop. "Oh, Alec finally answered. Oh wow."

Renpo joined her.

"This is what I've been up to," she read aloud. "I am ready to bring mass appeal to the Celtic gods of old. Here's a link."

"Wow is a good word," Renpo said as the new page opened to reveal a colorful, animated page advertising a public spectacle at a fairgrounds just outside of town. "'New Age Celtic Fair," he read. "Come reconnect with the old ways of Ireland's past. All faith traditions welcome. Come, celebrate Samhain with us and be amazed. Featuring the Internet sensation Alec Doogan, magician extraordinaire. Special musical guest Garbage.' I don't understand that reference."

"That's the name of a band. A really popular band. They're going to be huge draw. Which is really weird. I heard that Shirley Manson announced she was quitting the music business."

"You know this person?"

"No, but I am a big fan. Benito must be very persuasive."

"October 31st, that's only three weeks from now."

Desiree turned to Renpo. "The site is live to the public already. He's selling tickets. Just to be clear, the Archangel Michael said the only way to get Sammael to show himself would be to tempt him with the appearance of the old Celtic gods. It looks like Michael's timing is perfect. Only thing is, we cannot tell Alec or Benito or Sanantha that we're setting a trap."

"Why not?" he asked.

"I know, I didn't like it either when Michael first suggested it. If Alec hears the Devil is on his way, he will call this off, and we will lose our advantage. I need Sammael focused where I want him focused, and not plotting against me and Isis without me knowing where he is. We must let this fair go forward."

"I hear the strain in your voice. You do not seem entirely sure Michael will be able to capture Sammael."

"He's the only creature who ever has, so I've got to have faith in that. No, what I'm stressed about is lying to Sanantha. She has always been my cornerstone, my rock, I have never kept anything from her. Now I'm not telling her we want to use her boyfriend as bait. Since she is now close to him, there's no way she could keep it a secret."

"Do you feel this regret will leave you unable to follow through with the plan?"

"I hope not. That also means not telling her about the Egyptian/Celtic connection. If she knew that, she would figure out the rest of it. Do you think the Pearl can show us if this plan will succeed?"

"I agree defeating Sammael is worth the risk. I see Sammael as Mara, Death the Deceiver whom Buddha faced down, who masks the true nature of things and thereby causes mankind's suffering. The Pearl shows the true nature of things, it does not foresee the future.

"Even though your plan makes sense, I do not approve of lying to Sanantha or Alec," he said. "For people to achieve their potential, they need to be informed to make wise decisions. If Alec's fair is the best way to capture Sammael, then you should tell him, and let him do the right thing. He may know how to make the trap even more enticing. I hope the Pearl will help us when it comes time to face him. It was only by seeing through Mara's temptations and understanding the true nature of things that the Buddha defeated Death."

A knock came at the door. "Now what?" she sighed. She peeked at to the window. "Oh Jeez, it's Michael." Pulling the door open, she stepped aside and greeted him. "Hello, Michael. What brings you here this fine afternoon?"

"I thought we should start making plans." He stepped in but hesitated when he saw they were not alone.

"Oh, this is Abbot Renpo Kashiligan Samsuri from the Khorchag Gonpa monastery in Tibet. Brother Renpo, this is the Archangel Michael."

Michael pressed his hands together and bowed even before Renpo did. "Very pleased to meet you."

"It is my pleasure as well. Miss Desiree has told me of your intention to capture your brother, archangel Sammael."

"Good. Are you onboard with the plan?"

"Yes, and I am excited by the prospect of capturing Mara once and for all. As I was just telling Ms. Desiree, I do not agree with withholding the plan from Mr. Alec and Doctor Sanantha."

"Conspiracies fail because they include people who do not need to know," countered Michael.

"People can't do the right thing if you don't give them a chance to do so. How is it that I am arguing morals with an angel?"

Renpo caught Desiree's surprised look at him.

Michael grinned a disturbing half smile. "Angels have no special claim to morality. We get the job done." His Irish brogue let him hit the word "done" with gravity. He turned to Desiree. "You will note that your friend Joseph did not object to using Alec as bait when we first discussed this plan. If we are to capture the most elusive of all quarries, sacrifices will need to be made. If your faith in my integrity suffers in the process, then so be it."

"As long as Alec and Sanantha are not among your sacrifices," Desiree insisted.

"I already promised that."

"You did."

Renpo was not convinced.

Desiree brought the laptop out from the kitchen and handed it to him. "You will want to see this."

He read over the page and said, "This is all kinds of wonderful. There is no way he will be able to resist an event like this. Will you be able to get the plans for this fair? We will need ground plans, obviously. Also lists of set riggers, caterers, decorators, electricians, musicians, basically anyone who will be part of the event. It looks like he will have a huckster's row for crafts and jewelers. I suggest you volunteer to help, then make copies of anything you can."

"Sure. He's going to need a lot of help to pull it all together with only three weeks to go."

"We will need to know every hiding place, every vulnerable person he might hypnotize to do his bidding, every escape route."

Desiree struggled with a thought. "I get that he is dangerous, that he loves to cause suffering, and no tact is beneath him, but isn't he just an incarnate angel like you and Joseph?"

"I'm not sure you understand what is included in your phrase, 'just an incarnate angel'," Michael said.

"Actually, I do. Each of you is capable of deeds that exceed human understanding. I get that," Desiree conceded. "But all three of the Abrahamic religions attribute him, as Satan, Lucifer, Beelzebub, Iblis, as the source of all evil in the world. Anytime something evil happens, folks say it's his fault. How is that possible if he is not an all-pervasive force, like God?"

"It is misattribution. He is responsible for much suffering in the world, but certainly not all of it. People bring a lot of suffering on themselves, due to their refusal to accept things as they are. I'm sure Brother Renpo has shown you how destructive the ego can be. People find it easier to blame everything bad on a known enemy like the Devil than admit their part in their own suffering. God also tests people with change, and people often see change as suffering."

"We're treating this like it's just him. Won't he have a legion of demons at his side? How are we going to face all the denizens of Hell?"

"If he were going to war, then you would be right. He does command legions. But this is his own private score. He won't bring any of his subdemons on board because they would reveal his plan. His vendetta against the Neters is a very personal fight that he has kept hidden from Heaven for thousands of years. It's the same reason we should not tell Alec or Sanantha what we are doing. The more conspirators, the more likely the plan will be discovered. He will run this battle on his own."

"That's good news. Wait. You just said God tests people, and people blame their bad fortune on the Devil. Now, I get the whole, 'pain is ubiquitous, but suffering is optional'. But that doesn't cover evil. What about people taking unfair advantage, people enjoying cruelty, people excelling on other people's misery. Why does God allow evil to exist in His world? If I am going to fulfill my role as the avatar of a god, I need to understand evil." She followed up, "I don't believe you need evil to test people's free will. And I won't accept 'God works in mysterious ways' as an answer."

Renpo was proud of his pupil's grasp of what she did not know. He was also very interested in an angel's answers to such questions.

"Did you study physics or philosophy in college?"

"A little of each, actually."

"God sits in the one place in the Universe where the Heisenberg uncertainty principle does not apply. He can know both the location and velocity of any particle. He can simultaneously see the wave and particle nature of energy. He can see all the possibilities that stretch out from every action. It's not that He works in purposely mysterious ways. Rather, he can work in ways that are beyond our understanding since we live in a world of Aristotelian logic, of dichotomies, of zero-sum games, of right and wrong. We who do not have His unique viewpoint cannot see what He has done and what He has simply left undone. We cannot see all the consequences of His actions.

"If you are to embrace your nescient godhood, you should start with the Zen concept of accepting apparent contradictions and opposites. Brother Renpo can help you with that."

Michael continued. "The real answer to your question is, we can't know what else might have happened, and we should rejoice that God is there to act with His unique knowledge. The next time you see what looks to be an evil God has allowed in the world, ask yourself what greater unseen evil may have been stopped by God."

Renpo spoke up. "Thank you for being open to us asking metaphysical questions like this. Miss Desiree was recently surprised to learn *chi* energy is the same as the soul. I heard Mr. Alec call it ectoplasm, and he has shown how willpower influences it. I have seen her manipulate it when she heals. What should Miss Desiree know about ectoplasm?"

"I prefer to call it the Holy Spirit. God kept it from mankind for millennia but then He had a change of heart. The Spirit was God's gift to mankind after God withdrew his presence on Earth as Jesus. It is the bridge to allow mankind to access the spiritual plane." Michael turned to Desiree. "It is most certainly what you push into those you heal."

"After Sanantha told me Erzulie had saved my life, I did a lot of research on Voodou. Later, when I learned Erzulie is Isis, I had more questions, which Joseph eventually answered. May I ask you one last godhead question?"

Michael smiled, and this time it was nice. "Yes, of course."

"Is Legba the same as Christ?"

He chuckled. "No, Legba is a godhead who visits the Earth through his subjects, while Christ was God incarnated as a man walking the Earth. On the other hand, you've made a good connection. Horus, Apollo, Jesus, Legba — they are all, in their own way, the Son come to tell man that God forgives him after all. Without that message, mankind lives in fear of an arbitrary, unforgiving God. No one forgives himself for anything, and the sand of guilt grinds the gears of civilization to a halt. God knows this, but can't be seen coddling his children. So He sent his Son to deliver the message. Repeatedly."

"Like He used to send you and your brother angels?" she quipped.

Michael grinned and did not take the bait. "Our touch was a little too rough. Besides, it was inappropriate for this critical a message to be delivered by outsiders like us."

Outsiders. Renpo logged that for future consideration.

Desiree sighed and let her eyes wonder the room in thought. "I don't know who I am supposed to be. I have reconciled Erzulie being

Isis, but you and Joseph said people have been believing in Isis across many cultures."

"Indeed, she was called Panecea by the Greeks, and Airmid by the Celts, each time telling the stories the people believed in. You know, it may be simpler than all of that. Ultimately, you may be the vessel for the original female principal of the Universe, Ashera."

18

DESIREE NEEDED TIME ALONE to digest what Michael had said. She remembered how her mother used to run to clear her head. For Desiree it had always been walking. She had loved Georgetown's sprawling campus. Those walks had saved her sanity. Now it was Dublin's turn.

Could any of this even be possible? Alec's ghostbusting was amazing but understandable. Sanantha's stories had primed her to accept Joseph. Her healing ability still scared her. She didn't know what to make of the Pearl. *Now the Archangel Michael? On a quest to capture the Devil himself? Seriously?* Her little college graduation getaway had turned into a religious rollercoaster, with each turn more shocking than the last.

She looked at the people around her, driving by, stepping into and out of shops, going about their business unaware, undisturbed by the forces she now knew were real. Most of them were probably Catholic. Many genuinely believed in God and heaven and angels. Not her angels; beneficent, ethereal angels. Incarnate angels belonged in biblical times. Warring angels belonged in myth, along with ancient gods. How calm would these people stay if they knew better?

Yet she was calm. Amazed, confused, dubious, but calm. Shouldn't she be freaking out? Did getting kidnapped and experimented on by a madman somehow entitle her to talk to angels as an equal? What did it mean to carry within you the essence of a god? Was she supposed to live up to the hopes of all those Egyptians and Haitians and ancient Irish who had prayed to her god? Her Art History Bachelor's degree hardly prepared her to lead a faith. Yet not only Joseph, but now Michael too had confirmed her identity.

She paused and looked around to make sure she hadn't gotten lost. Cork Street, okay.

Was she insane to accept this as okay? Was Sanantha too close to the subject to make a proper diagnosis? Sanantha had battled this Devil face to face. Maybe it's not insanity if you're not making it up.

She stopped walking and stifled the urge to laugh out loud, pure, overwhelmed, nervous laughter.

Before she could make a public spectacle, an ambulance siren jolted her back. The short burst cleared the sidewalk as it turned into the Coombe Hospital driveway across the street. She couldn't tell what, but something about that ambulance seized her attention and would not let go. Waiting only for traffic to clear, she marched across, dropping all her doubts like loose change in the street.

The paramedics opened the back doors and pulled out a gurney laden with a woman heavy with child. The husband climbed down after as they rushed her inside. Curiosity melted into dread as Desiree focused on the woman's bulging tummy. Something was wrong.

She dashed in right behind the husband and strode alongside with the confident step of someone with a clear destination. She glanced sideways at the pregnant woman, trying to discern why this ordinary episode should so completely demand her obsession.

The woman was panicked, but wasn't in pain. No one asked her any questions. The paramedics handed her to the doctors who rushed her in without switching her to a hospital bed. No one said anything that explained what was happening. They must have radioed ahead.

Somehow the sounds inside the hospital were louder than she expected. She could hear every voice, even from people on the far side of the lobby.

Desiree followed them down a corridor and around a bend, doing her best to appear headed somewhere else. The further into the hospital she went, the stronger the smell of antiseptic became. The expectant mother smelled strongly of sweat and fear. She finally got a good impression from the baby. Something was missing. They turned and pushed through doors marked Surgery. She was left standing there blinking. What was missing? How did she know?

She was sweating, and not just from her nerves. She was still wearing her favorite green wool scarf. She unwrapped it from her neck and fanned herself with a hand in the cool, overclean air. She looked around and wondered what she had hoped to accomplish.

Her assessment didn't last long. She made it back to the first intersection before another urge, just like the first one, steered her feet around a corner. She did not understand this compulsion, but she felt it coming from her heart, the same place she drew from when she healed. Perhaps another facet? She dared not miss the chance to learn more.

The door stood open to an ordinary ward room with the lights turned low. An old man sat at the bedside holding an old woman's hand. She was still, with tubes and wires connected all around her. Desiree could see the man's pain in how he hung his white-haired head and the way he stroked her hand. In contrast, she appeared at peace, whether sleeping or under medication.

Peace was not what Desiree felt. She felt the woman was sad, sad and tired, tired of being in pain, tired of causing her husband pain, tired of a long life with no promise of ever getting any better. The feeling lowered itself onto Desiree like a crushing weight. Overcome, she began to cry. The old man heard her sob and turned to look, and she ducked out of the doorway.

She leaned back against the hallway wall and twisted her scarf up in her hands against her heart. The woman's loss of hope shook Desiree like nothing in her life ever had touched her. The black empty despair was almost too much to endure, yet she didn't want to turn away. She found herself sliding down the wall with her legs curled up.

That was when she noticed the scarf. In the onslaught she had wound the ends around each wrist with only a few inches left between. The pressure was painful. She flexed her hands, one then the other. Then she saw what she was doing. At the ends of a bridge, one opened while the other closed.

Realization snapped into place so hard she thought she had cracked her neck. Now she knew what the baby was missing. She also knew what to do for the old woman's suffering. She looked at her hands and wondered how to turn the idea into reality.

She stopped herself abruptly. Even if she could pull this off, should she? What right did she have? This wasn't just healing. This was also taking a life. It was also … ending suffering. Should she not try to replace suffering with joy?

She decided her left was the baby and her right was the woman. It was the last decision she needed to make.

As soon as she chose, a wave of relief swept away the sorrow. Her heart beat faster and the healing heat surged to fill her hands. No, not just her hands. She felt it all around her like she was connected to the world at some impossibly deep level. She slowly reached out and felt her grasp of the energy around her. She gently tugged at the threads. It was now easy to see her hands as these two people in need.

She realized she wasn't entirely in control of what she was doing. The power came up as if it had been eagerly awaiting her permission. She pulled a handful of the energy into her right hand, gently closing her fingers around it. She kissed it. By now her heart was beating so hard it shook her whole body. She fought back a rising delirium. Taking a deep breath, she pulled the scarf taut before opening her right hand while closing her left.

As she opened her right, and released the old woman's life, her mouth filled with the taste of the most putrid vomit, even though she had not retched up anything. She wanted to spit it out, but dared not break the bridge between her wrists. As she visualized the energy moving across to her left, she closed her fingers around it. The vile taste was flushed out by the smells of flowers and earth and wind and suddenly she felt like she had the whole world of life distilled in her breath. She closed her hand securely, capturing the energy firmly in the baby. Something boiled up within her, starting deep within her and rising like a flash flood. All at once it shook her hard and forced the air from her lungs. She sat on the floor gasping, staring at her two perfectly normal hands. She wiped her tears and her sweat, then unwound the scarf.

A low, but shrill, steady tone cut through her reverie. She stood up and confirmed it was the old woman's heart monitor alarm signaling death. The old man stood up, leaned over the body, and kissed her goodbye. Desiree still harbored misgivings about doing this.

What about the baby? Desiree ran around the corner and pushed open the surgical suite doors. The piercing healthy cry of a newborn told Desiree all she needed to hear. She let joy push away the doubts. As she turned to walk away, she heard elated voices welcoming the baby. Someone said, "It's a miracle." Maybe it was. Desiree had never thought of miracles as such tough choices.

19

T HE WALK HOME FROM THE HOSPITAL WAS SURREAL. Desiree couldn't bring herself to make eye contact with people she passed on the street for fear of her god-self reaching out and seizing their souls. Could life really be moved into and out of a body so easily? She wondered if soldiers ever got used to the feeling of taking a life, or if they had to make excuses to themselves for the rest of their lives. All these questions, and every time she got more answers, it all became just that much more intense.

She opened the door and moved directly to collapsing on the couch. It was more of a loveseat, so she was left with one leg sticking up in the air. She glanced over at the giant hole in the back wall of the living room and thought about how Joseph always referred to his god Ptah as the Opener of the Ways. *More like 'Opener of the Kitchen'.*

Sanantha came out from her room. "Welcome home. You all right?"

"No," she groaned without getting up. "I used to think more information leads to more understanding which leads to better coping. Knowing more is not helping."

"Helping with what?"

Desiree sat up. "My powers are out of control. They take off on their own and I just get dragged behind. They're frightening too, like life and death at a whim. Knowing what's going on doesn't help. All the history and mechanisms and relationships don't give me any handle. I can't tell if my conscious actions are helping Isis or not. It's like I've found this fabulous alien spacecraft crashed in my backyard. I know it can go to the stars, but with no instruction manual and all the controls in an alien language, I can't make it do anything. If it flies, I can't tell if I'm doing it or it's doing it on its own."

"Is Isis pushing you aside? Are there periods when you can't remember what you've been doing?"

"No, I'm always aware, which makes it worse. Oh, I see. You're thinking about when I would shift into being my mother and lose my Desiree identity. No, I don't feel like I'm being overwritten, just forced to be a passenger in my own body."

"That is consistent with the *loa* mounting experience. You said all your answers so far don't help. What would you like to know?"

"How to be the god I'm supposed to be. Both of our angels say I am. Osiris in my dream said I am."

"Who knows how to be a god?" Sanantha asked.

"Other gods? Alec contacted Boann. I felt for her when I went out to the woods by the river."

"Maybe. I can try to summon a *loa*. I don't know how successful I would be. I was only ever a flag mistress in my village, and it usually takes a mambo to summon a god from scratch. The only time I have ever been mounted was when Erzulie revived you."

"Joseph knows the Egyptian gods, he served one of them."

"Yes, but he was also imprisoned by them for thousands of years."

"Do we know why?"

"No, and I don't think that would be a polite question."

Desiree squirmed around on the loveseat and pulled her phone out of her back pocket. "I still think he'll have our best access. "Hello,

Joseph? It's Desiree. May I ask you a favor? Right, of course. Thank you. Can you come over to the cottage this afternoon when you've got a minute? I need your advice. Okay, sure. Thanks."

She hung up and gestured broadly toward the door. "Wait for it ..."

The knock came.

Desiree grinned overbroadly. Sanantha got the door. "Come in."

"Joseph, I need your help. You have been wonderful answering all my questions. Sanantha, you have been a rock of support in my corner. Now I need an expert, a peer. I need to talk to a god and see how I'm supposed to do this. Boann did not talk to me when I went to her. Sanantha's not sure the *loas* would listen to her. What can you do to put me in touch with a fellow Egyptian god?"

He frowned. Was that thought or caution? "I am an angel of Ptah, the Opener of the Ways."

Desiree snickered to herself.

"What?" he asked with no humor.

"Nothing. Sorry, please go on."

"As we saw with Kailash and Semeru, holy places are holy because they exist in both this plane and the next. I could open a gap at Karnak where my gods are resting."

Sanantha helped him out. "I understand your reluctance to visit the gods."

"I want to help and I will. I will have to avoid direct contact with the gods, though."

Desiree couldn't help herself. "When Silas freed you, it was against the gods' wishes? Why were they holding you?"

"Yes, my master freed me before the gods were satisfied. I had exceeded my authority, acted on my own wishes and against theirs."

"Isn't helping me more of the same?"

"No, I am assisting a goddess. Helping the Neters is why I exist."

"Actually, Isis is known for acting on her own," Sanantha added. "Plenty of stories have her going against the wishes of the other gods. So helping a rebel may not excuse you. Please be careful."

Joseph smiled what almost came across as boyishly. "I didn't know you cared, Doctor."

Sanantha smiled back. "Don't flatter yourself. I need you here to protect her. Promise me you will keep her safe."

"I promise." He turned to Desiree. "When would you like to leave? I know the place well, so we can get there in one step."

"What time is it there now?"

"There is a two-hour time difference. It's three o'clock here now, so it's five there. We'd have a little over an hour of light."

"Am I overdressed. I mean, it's the desert and I'm in a sweater."

"You should be fine. You might be warm, but it gets very windy."

"All right then. No time like the present."

Sanantha spoke up. "Please don't do it in here. Go out back, maybe. You create a cloud of black sulfurous smoke when you leave."

Desiree snickered. "Bye, Sanantha." She started to follow Joseph but stopped to retrieve her wallet.

"You won't need that," Joseph said. "We're going and coming right back."

"I dunno, traveling to another country. I'll take my passport and credit card just in case."

She and Joseph walked to the patio. She took his hands facing him and closed her eyes.

"Are you still frightened of this travel?" Joseph asked. "We have done this several times now."

"Not afraid of the trip, but the blackness is always a shock. I'll just keep my eyes closed, thank you."

With the rushing sound of air, she knew they were no longer in Ireland. She felt a gentle warm breeze on her face, opened her eyes, and involuntarily took a breath at the view. The grandiose pylon gate of the Temple of Isis at Agilika loomed behind Joseph like a fortress wall. It was huge and beautiful but there was something more, something touched her deeply. "Joseph, I feel like I'm home."

"People came from all over Egypt to worship you here. This place keeps you alive in people's minds even today when they visit and learn. Did Alec tell you about the impression prayer leaves on a place?"

"Yes, like Patrick's gravestone." She was happy to notice no tourists present. She looked around and saw they were on an island.

"This place is steeped in thousands of years of belief in you."

'Well, not me personally, but my soul, which is where I feel the connection. Is this one of those holy thin spots?"

"Oh yes, this temple very much exists in both planes."

She looked around again and felt something didn't fit. "Why does this place feel like it's in the wrong place?"

"Oh, of course. Isis remembers it in its original setting. This temple complex used to be on a nearby island called Philae. When the Egyptians built the Aswan High Dam, the Nile backed up and expanded Lake Nassar, and it flooded Philae. The United Nations Educational, Scientific and Cultural Organization declared this a World Heritage Site and spent nine years dismantling the entire complex, numbering all the blocks, and reassembling it here on Agilika."

"They moved all these temple buildings? Wow. Wait a minute. That's UNESCO. My mom worked for UNESCO." She walked across the entrance plaza, looking up at the two pylon towers that formed the front gate. "Those giant carved images all across these faces include other gods in addition to Isis. Will they be on the other side for me to talk to?"

"That's my hope. Now you're going to need to know how to part a gap to go there and to return. I can't come with you."

"Right. Do I use my god *chi*?" she asked, grasping.

"Yes and no. You will need to summon it, but not to project it the way you do when you heal. You let it flow into one hand, and then you use that hand like a knife to split the firmament."

"Split the firmament."

"The split will be narrow, so you need to line up your body flat behind your hand so you can slip through."

"Right, I saw you stand sideways on Kailash."

"Since you're new at this, don't expect the gap to be as wide as the one I made for you and Brother Renpo. Any gap will do, just squeeze through. Let me set up a shadow phase for you to practice on."

"Part of me thinks this is perfectly normal, and part of me is scared shitless."

"You know which part is which. Isis used to do this all the time when she visited this temple." Joseph took off his sunglasses and swept his gaze back and forth between them. At first, she didn't see any effect, but then she saw a distortion, as if she were looking through water at him.

"I won't even ask how you built that. I take it this is made from the same stuff as the barrier between worlds?"

"Yes. Stand like this." He stood sideways to the wall with his legs and free arm bent back to hide behind him.

"Oh my god, Joseph. Walk like an Egyptian?"

He appeared taken aback. "Of course."

"No, no. I mean you are in the same position you see everyone in tomb paintings." She pointed up at the pylons. "Like those figures. They didn't understand how to portray perspective in their art, so they drew everything flat."

He stood up straight to face her. "That's not true. They drew figures like that out of vanity."

"What? I was an Art History major."

Joseph rolled his yellow eyes. With his sunglasses off she could see him do this. She wondered how often he did this that she couldn't see.

"Once people saw this was the position gods and angels used to travel to heaven, everyone wanted to be portrayed as divinely important. So they had artists place their images in this posture whenever possible. They couldn't actually make the trip, but they wanted to be remembered as having a touch of the divine."

She stared at him flabbergasted. Standing there indignant in her sweater, cords, and boots in the Egyptian desert, she couldn't even find words.

"Surely you learned how important status was in art."

"Yes, yes. The more clothes you wore in your portraits, and the bigger you were pictured in relation to the others, the more important you were. I get the vanity thing. I'm just having a hard time believing the divinity thing was so lost to time, that we in modern times guessed so wrongly."

"Thousands of years of unspoken tradition followed by hundreds of years of silence under the sand. I think you will find a lot of things have been reconstructed incorrectly. Shall we try this?" he said resuming the position.

"Of course." She reached inward, took a deep breath and summoned the god *chi* in her heart. Then, as Renpo had taught her, she whirled her arms around and let the heat flow down into her right hand, ending with her body mimicking his.

"Now picture the barrier as a viscous gelatin, spring forward with your back leg, and bring your hand down to cleave the barrier like a hatchet."

She did this and was shocked at the sensation. "I felt my hand part something, like I was tearing through fabric."

"Good, now do it again, and this time as you feel the splitting, walk into the gap and push it open."

Again she followed his instructions, and again she was amazed at the result. She passed through and ended up next to Joseph. "I felt that. Why am I still here?"

"This is a practice wall. It has this world on both sides. The real wall has the spirit plane on the other side. Practice one more time, going back through to your side. I want you to know this sensation well. It will be your way home."

Summon, displace, pose, spring, cleave, and step through.

"Well done." He performed a bit of *tai chi* himself, ending with a sweeping away with both hands. The practice barrier vanished. "Now you're on your own."

"Do I cut anywhere in particular?"

"Anywhere here is good. This whole area is as you said, a thin spot. Oh, and don't worry about any locked gates. They won't be there on the spiritual plane."

She felt like she was about to jump off a cliff even though she was standing on flat ground. She wet her lips and took a deep breath. "A guy I knew in college said he had visited the astral plane by making espresso with Red Bull instead of water." She smiled weakly at Joseph. He smiled reassuringly back. "I don't think this is what he meant. Here goes nothin'." Summon, displace, pose, spring, cleave, and step through. The walls of her cut stuck to her as she pushed through, making her drag her following arm the last few inches. Obviously she needed more work on technique.

She found herself at the Temple, but the air was filled with mist. The sun was obscured, making it seem later. The carvings up on the walls appeared the same. Semeru had appeared different than Kailash.

She walked between the pylons, looking for any sign of life. Behind the gate was a courtyard lined with flower-topped stone columns. Behind them were rooms that probably were for priests back in the day. The other end of the courtyard was another, smaller pylon gate. She turned around and she could no longer see Joseph who waited outside. Alone in a heaven only her soul recognized.

Through the second gate was an interior court of columns. Beyond that was a chamber of high flat walls covered in hieroglyphics. She sensed this was the actual sanctum of Isis. She felt calm here, at home. She was tempted to just sit down on the floor and revel in the peacefulness.

She remembered why she came, and decided bold was better than timid. She was a god, after all. "Hello! I'm home! Anyone here?"

"Isis, is that really you?" a woman's deep voice called out from the shadows through a passage out into another courtyard.

Desiree looked closer and saw an outline emerge. It was a woman in a flowing gown, but she had the head of a hippopotamus. Even though she had imagined this moment of first contact, meeting one of the gods face to face was a lot more daunting than she imagined. "Hathor! It is lovely to see you again!"

Hathor stepped right up and enveloped her in a hug. Her huge head felt very strange. "Sister! It has been centuries. I thought I would never see you again. So many have never returned. Let me look at you." She held Desiree at arm's length and looked her up and down. Then she let go, frowned, and stepped back. "Oh no, you didn't."

Desiree wondered what the god saw. She reached up and felt a headdress of bull horns holding a sun disk. She hadn't felt it there before. She wasn't sure what to say, but words came up anyway. "Yes, Isis moved into my body, that we now share, so she can walk the Earth. She did not have the strength to manifest and travel to the material plane. I need advice on how to best serve the goddess. How does a goddess gain believers that bring strength? How can I tell which motives are mine and which are hers? I want to do the right thing."

Hathor gently swung her massive head side to side. "We do not approve of this. We are not supposed to walk the Earth unless our believers wish it. We only possess humans to give them messages, not occupy them like puppets."

"It's still me, Desiree. I'm still here. Isis gave me life and I'm letting her use my body."

"You always were a rebel. I love you for that. There are limits though, and you have crossed them. You already know we do not agree with your revenge quest."

"I'm sorry, I don't know what you mean by that."

Another figure appeared out of the misty shadows. This one was a tall muscular man. It wasn't until he came into the light that she could see he had a falcon head.

Desiree's heart jumped and she felt compelled to greet him. "Son!"

He paused and frowned deeply over his enormous beak.

Hathor said, "Yes, it's really Isis. She's sharing a human body."

Horus did not look entirely convinced. Moreover, he did not look happy to see his mother.

Isis in her heart was crushed by sadness.

Horus put his hand on Hathor's shoulder and motioned with this beak toward the front of the temple complex, toward where she had left Joseph.

Hathor and Desiree followed his gaze. "Oh no. You are not going to gain favor by bringing Ptah's exiled bastard." She held up three human fingers. "That's three bad throws in a row, possession, revenge, and the exile. Remember the pillars, dear: strength, tenacity, intelligence, and," she paused for emphasis, "discretion. You'd best be going back now."

"Please don't reject me. This place feels so much like home, and you feel so much like family. You said yourself it has been far too long. I really need to understand how I can do right by your sister goddess. To do right by you."

"I am sorry," Hathor said, "but talking to you any more will only come to a bad end. It was lovely to see you again. Perhaps we will meet again, in happier times." She and Horus turned and walked back into the mist and vanished.

The goddess inside her felt crushed. Desiree felt crushed. She hung her head and tried not to cry.

As she turned to go, something on the stone floor caught her eye. Up against a wall in dust, it looked like a bug. She pulled out her cell phone and used it as a flashlight. "No service. Big surprise." The light revealed it to be a key. She picked it up and examined it. Gold, with a hieroglyphic stamp on the thumb grip. She looked around and no one came back out to say anything. She slipped it into her pocket.

She walked dejectedly out through the courtyards and the pylons, and could see Joseph waiting. He was making eye contact, so she guessed he could see her. She raised her arms and shrugged in resignation.

He shook his head and slumped his shoulders.

She started to summon her god *chi* to open a cleft back through, when a feeling pulled at her to turn to the right. She recognized this yearning as Isis trying to tell her something. At first she only saw the river and the horizon beyond. Then she looked closer and saw ... pyramids? Yes, a grouping of three. Giza was at the other end of Egypt, how could she see them? The effect was tantalizing. The harder she looked, the closer they appeared. Her feet felt light on the ground and when she looked down, she saw the ground flying by beneath her. It felt like a dream and somehow it didn't frighten her. Apparently physics doesn't apply in the spirit plane. What was Isis showing her?

She flew up to a walled city built around the Great Pyramids. Everything was new and clean and people were working in and around the buildings, priests and bald acolytes. She landed in the middle of the complex, near the sphinx, which was intact and painted. No, she didn't land, she descended right into the ground, finally emerging in a large cubical underground chamber. A colossal painted statue of Isis dominated the room and faced a gray stone altar. The room was made of black granite and was lit by twelve torches in sconces around the statue's feet. A gold throne sat next to the altar, and in it sat a priestess. Behind the altar stood a short, pale priest.

A panel swung opened and another taller priest entered. The man behind the altar and the new man wordlessly exchanged gestures. Laid out on the altar was an assortment of utensils. The new priest reached into his robes and pulled out a case, and from the case he pulled a wand and a dagger which he added to the altar collection. The short priest assisted the taller one with his attire and preparations. This routine looked very much like what she had seen Alec do.

Almost. This gear included an elaborate metal crown and a purple sash belt. There were also more utensils here, including little copper mirrors. If Alec was working from the same rituals, why didn't he have all this stuff too?

For the first time since he entered the chamber, the tall priest looked up at the statue of Isis, dropped onto both knees and then lowered his gaze reverently to her painted stone feet, holding the rod and sword in either hand down at his sides. He began in a language Desiree did not recognize, yet did understand. "Great Isis, Goddess of Life, Protector of Humanity, hear my summons." He swung the rod up in a broad arc to hold it aloft and spoke more forcefully. "I stand at the center. I am the Master. You must hear my summons." He then stood up and drew a symbol in the air with the end of the rod and stated, "I have the power. I now walk freely on your plane. You must come forward at my command."

The priestess frowned at his bold gesture, but this was only his opening volley. He leaned back and looked the huge statue straight in the eye, pointed his sword at Isis and demanded, "I am Chosen. You must obey me. Tell me what I seek."

Desiree felt Isis wanting to possess the priestess, so she decided to play along. She swooped into the priestess and took over her body. She was alarmed at how easy it was to do. She stood up abruptly and raised her head proudly. One by one, twelve rays of light erupted from her forehead to form a wheel-like crown. She raised her hands and five more rays of light shot from each upturned palm. Desiree loved the effect. They felt like they stood for something. Were these keys of some kind?

The tall priest did not look satisfied. He commanded further, "Do not dare to withhold your powers from me! I demand that you employ all your abilities to my task. I know of the last seven rays of enlightenment. I need them to strip away all deceit to find my enemy, our enemy! Reveal the last seven Arcana to me!"

Desiree felt a profound emptiness. She did not know why, but she felt like he wanted something that had been stolen, something she should have kept safe. She felt a tear roll down her cheek. Isis was really upset.

The priest saw the tear and looked terrified.

The short priest's head transformed into the head of an ibis bird. Oh, Thoth possessed the priest.

"Faen-ka." Thoth said quietly, but clearly.

The tall priest seemed incensed by that name, and whirled on his fellow, only to see the god standing there instead. He dropped to his knees.

"Son of Earth," the God of Wisdom addressed him paternally, "the twenty-two images at your disposal, those twenty-two rays of knowledge Isis is offering you now, are the only keys I have ever possessed for your use. The additional seven you seek, the Tablets of Aeth, reveal the powers of creation itself. In all my wisdom, I do not know how to convey such secrets to the minds of men."

"Great Teacher of Mankind," he humbly addressed the god, "if these keys are not yours, then from whence did they come? And to whence did they go? Does Isis not command all the material, mental and spiritual realms?"

Really? I do? I mean, she does?

"These images were designed by the betrayer you now seek. My daughter Isis thought Faen-ka discovered them in a foreign land and brought them as a gift to the gods. Now he has taken them out of the temple."

The priest was clearly surprised and took a moment to think about it. "I have only watched my predecessor use these images. He used them just last month in our conflict with Moses. I was never given the opportunity to memorize them. I am certain neither of my fellow high adepts have ever even seen them. I may be the only person who has ever seen them, but I know they do exist. Is there no way for you to view them?"

"They are not of Our sphere."

The priest was again shaken. "Can you help me find the traitor?"

"You will not find him in this lifetime."

Desiree raced to keep up. *This Faen-ka guy brought new magic to the Egyptians, then right after Exodus, he stole it and ran away.*

"The clairvoyance your keys have given me has never failed. If I will not succeed in my mission, is it because I will die, or is it because my adversary has the Tablets of Aeth and I do not?"

"You will not die an early or unnatural death."

Desiree was still trying to grasp what had happened when Isis spoke up on her own. "If these Arcana are so powerful, then why didn't Faen-ka succeed in using them to defeat the Hebrews' magic?"

"Always the trusting one," Thoth commented lovingly at her, shaking his long beak back and forth slowly. "Why does the snake not fly through the air? It is against its nature. This man was never a son of Egypt. His intent was not to defeat Moses, but to lead Ramses into defeat."

Desiree put it together, but was horrified at the result. *Faen-ka was Ramses's trusted advisor, maybe even his High Priest. He planted new magic so Ramses would not take Moses's miracles seriously. That lead to Ramses's legendary overreaction and defeat.* She was astonished at the scale of the deception and amazed at how no one saw it coming. She felt terrible for the Egyptians. All those people suffering and dying, just to embarrass the king. This revelation outraged Isis. She was not going to let this slide.

Desiree knew she was watching something that happened a long time ago. The reactions she was feeling from Isis were what the goddess felt back then.

The priest was still trying to figure out a game plan. "If there are now powers on Earth that we cannot master, how will Egypt fare against those who have such power? We can blame the loss of the Hebrews to the treachery of one man, but if the traitor trains others and they attack us, we may not be able to defend ourselves."

Desiree thought this priest was really smart.

"Faen-ka will not attack Egypt, and he will never have any followers. Yet your thinking is correct. Although Moses was originally trained in this very temple, the secrets of power now at his command are not ours." The god raised his hands above his head and looked upward. "Seeker of Truth, know that the world is changing, and the truths I have given you, though immutable, will not always apply to the world of men. O Egypt, a time shall come when, instead of a pure religion and an intelligent cult, you shall have nothing left but ridiculous fables that posterity will find incredible. There shall be nothing left to you but words graven upon stone, dumb and almost indecipherable monuments to your ancient piety."

Desiree felt Isis decide to hold her tongue in spite of her anger, but she definitely sized up the tall priest. She decided if he wasn't going to catch his old master in this lifetime, Isis would make sure he did in another lifetime.

Another lifetime? All at once, Desiree realized she was looking at the first version of Silas Alverado and that Faen-ka was Sammael in disguise. It was all she could manage not to let her mouth drop open. She also now knew what she had to do.

With that thought, she fell back out of the priestess and tumbled through the dream space back to Agilika. She was still in the spirit plane where she had started. She looked around and wondered if she had actually moved at all. She guessed it didn't matter.

She was about to summon her god *chi* to slice her way back into the physical world when she spotted Joseph. Only he wasn't alone. A tall god with a head that looked sort of like a donkey, was talking with Joseph, right there in the real world. Joseph was very reverent, bowing his head.

Desiree pulled up the *chi* as fast as she could, whirled it down into her hand and sliced. She knew Joseph had seconds. She jumped through the split just as another split opened up behind Set, who reached to put his hand on Joseph's shoulder.

"No you don't! He's my servant now!" She ran up, ready to fight the god, but it was too late. He and Joseph slipped from view. She dove for where they vanished, but the hole was gone and so were they. She kicked the sandy flagstones and yelled, "Shit! Shit! Shit!"

She grabbed her auburn hair with both hands. No more headdress. She finally figured out her goddess hitchhiker was hell bent on going to war with Satan over a three-thousand-year-old deception, and not ten minutes later she lost her supernatural protector.

Oh yeah, all the while standing in the middle of the Egyptian desert in a sweater and boots. She thanked her good luck that she remembered to bring her passport and credit card. She pulled out her cell phone. At least it had a signal here.

20

Samantha knew it couldn't be Desiree ringing her doorbell at eleven at night. She wasn't going to be back from Egypt for another twelve hours, and she had her own key.

"Simon? What in the world?"

"I'm sorry to just drop in like this, and at this late hour. I sent you a few emails, but you haven't responded. I figured you've stopped reading them, so why announce my arrival?"

He was clearly nervous, standing there in the cold drizzle. He was wearing a black raincoat, but his hair was wet. He looked pathetic. Normally she would have tried to put his mind at ease, but this time the ball was still in his court. "I read your emails."

"Oh, that's good to know. I actually have news. Yes, I wanted to see you, but there is something you need to know. May I come in?"

"Yes, of course. How did you ever find me? Desiree rented this cottage."

He stepped into the doorway, took the coat off and shook it out over the porch before coming in.

Still his fastidious self, she thought.

"Desiree told me. I spoke with her a few days ago. Didn't she tell you I was coming?"

"No, she didn't say anything." She was pretty annoyed, but covered with, "It must have slipped her mind. She has had a pretty full couple of days."

"Did she tell you about the FBI agent who came to our apartment in Malaysia and is now here in Ireland?"

"FBI? Is that a woman with a Southern accent named Bitter something?"

"Yes, Jill Bitterman. So, Desiree did tell you."

"No. She called me the day I left K-L, asking about Charles Redmond's death."

"Well, she's still on the case. I expect she will be here in the morning. I shared a flight with her coming here."

"Why would you do that?"

"I chatted her up to try to find out what she's after, to see if they're building a case against you."

"Are they?"

"I don't think so. I think she has a new lead on Sammael, whom she thinks is a human terrorist. I told her he is a religious zealot and that the riot in DC was an act of some kind of jihad."

"Not too far from the truth, through you've got the wrong religion. You know, you could have just called me. Turns out I already knew this agent was reopening the case. You didn't have to come halfway around the world."

"Well, there's more to it. Desiree also told me she thinks Sammael is after her, because of the Isis connection. When she told me that, I felt I had to dig deeper with Agent Bitterman. I mean, if the FBI has a lead on Sammael, and Sammael is coming after Desiree, then we need to find out everything we can."

He was starting to make sense. "Did you learn anything?"

"Not surprisingly, she was pretty tight lipped about the case. She is going to interview you, but I think she has other leads to chase here in Ireland. I did find out she handles cases involving the occult. If she is up on spirits and magic, that could make it hard to hide things from her, but it could also make her a resource and an ally if Sammael does show up."

Sanantha paused and sized him up. "Are you saying you did not come here to ask me to come back?"

He raised his eyebrows and sighed. "I will not lie to you and say I didn't jump at a reason to come see you. I was going to come even before Desiree told me you were seeing Benito. That sealed it for me."

"Benito has been good to me."

He shifted his weight and put a hand in his pocket. She knew that posture. He did that when he was going to take a chance. "This is going to sound like the rantings of a jealous lover, but please hear me out. On the long plane ride, I had a lot of time to think. If the FBI has other leads on Sammael here in Ireland, and Sammael is after Desiree, and a stranger shows up out of nowhere, starts paying for everything, gives Alec the keys to start performing actual magic, and sweeps you off your feet, doesn't that worry you that you all are being played right before the Devil shows up? I'm not saying Benito is knowingly doing the Devil's work, but people fall into the Devil's plans all the time without knowing it."

"Are you suggesting all the great things Benito has been doing are setting us up for a fall? Are you hearing yourself? This isn't just jealousy, this is narrow-minded pessimism at its worst. Benito has done nothing but good things for all of us."

"I'm just saying the timing is worth being cautious."

"Did you really think maligning Benito, a man you have never met, with doing the Devil's work was going to drive me back into your arms? I bet you still haven't signed your divorce papers either. Get out, Simon. Just turn around and walk away. I don't want us to end with an ugly fight, but you have got me right to that edge."

He put on his coat and turned to go. At the door he looked back. "I love you Sanantha. Please be careful."

● ● ●

Desiree paid the cab and staggered to the door. She was fumbling with her keys when Sanantha opened the door.

"Welcome home, wayward one!" she greeted her with a hug. Sanantha rarely gave hugs.

'Thank you. What an ordeal. One second to get there and fifteen hours to get back." She stepped in. "At least I'm finally dressed properly for my location."

"You can thank Benito for the travel money." Sanantha stepped back and smiled at her. "You look different."

"I'm desperate for a shower."

"No, it's a good thing. I can't place what it is."

Desiree raised an eyebrow and smirked crookedly. "Maybe there is something. I've had no less than eight people hit on me on the way back, from cab drivers to check-in clerks. I even had a woman flight attendant hit on me. I must have picked up a smell on the other side. Actually, that appeal came in handy when Egyptian customs tried to stop me from leaving the country since my passport had not been stamped from entering the country."

"And so, Set took Joseph back into custody."

"Yeah, and from the look of it, Joseph couldn't do much about it. I have to figure out how to negotiate his release. I don't know what I can bargain with."

"Negotiate? It sounds like the other gods aren't willing to talk to you at all."

"Well, that's where it got interesting. I didn't tell you the best part. Hathor said the gods did not approve of the revenge quest I was on. I had no idea what she meant, so I started to leave. Then Isis flew me into the past and up to the necropolis at Giza. She showed me a conversation Silas's previous incarnation had with Thoth about how Sammael had tricked Ramses into overplaying his hand with Moses and epically failing."

"Silas told me about that in D.C. nine years ago. That was at the heart of Silas trying to capture Sammael."

"Isis was furious to learn about the deception. It was at that moment that she chose Silas to be her champion."

"He always referred to himself as 'Chosen'. That means Isis wants revenge on Sammael for Exodus."

"Yes. Silas succeeded in capturing Sammael, but I guess she could tell he would get away. Then, when she saw me with no soul, she chose me as her avatar. I guess she figured, if you want something done right, do it yourself. She's still out for justice."

Sanantha sat down on the couch and checked her manicure.

Desiree wondered at her distraction but pressed on. "When Osiris said Sammael was after Isis, apparently it is mutual. I would give anything to find out how she plans on confronting him." Desiree got the impression Sanantha had checked out of the conversation. This was really not like her. "Remember how I sat on that couch, day before yesterday, and said knowing more didn't help me cope better. Now that I know the whole story, I am terrified. On top of that, I've lost my Egyptian angel!"

Sanantha finally looked up at her. "I bet you are. Who put you in this danger? I can't say I'm unhappy about Joseph being taken back."

Desiree stood there shocked. "Seriously?"

"Can I ask you something? Why didn't you tell me Simon was coming to Ireland?"

"Oh, damn. Sorry I forgot. I take it he came here. Oh…and things didn't go well."

"That's the understatement of the day."

"He told me there was an FBI agent asking questions about the attack in D.C. I'm really sorry I didn't tell you all of this at the time."

"The FBI agent has arrived in Dublin, and will probably be by this morning to question me. Simon says the agent handles occult cases."

"Is that good or bad?"

"I'll find out."

"But Simon's visit was bad? Did he ask you to come back with him?"

"I expected that. He went much farther. He said Benito might be bringing the Devil down on us by giving Alec the keys to perform magic."

Desiree was amazed at how close Simon's instincts had come to their secret plan to use Alec's magic as bait for Sammael. "Wow, he went straight for Benito?"

"Of course he did. Jealous goat. He said we had all been blinded by Benito's money and charisma, that Benito's timing was suspicious with the FBI's investigation. He made himself ridiculous grasping at straws."

Desiree wasn't sure what to say. "I guess caution is always a good idea."

"What do you mean by that?"

Sanantha being openly defensive was not a pretty sight. "Oh, don't get me wrong. I'm just saying Alec unearthed a demon's mark, then Benito shows up making magic easy, and now we find out Isis and Sammael are at war with us in the middle as pawns. I think we're way in over our heads, and every new unknown adds more risk. Benito is making things happen really fast. Maybe we should slow down and be careful."

"Alec swears he never did anything with that signature, and he surely isn't going to touch it now that we told him it could be a demon. I think you and Simon are both boxing at shadows. I faced Sammael in person nine years ago. I know what he is capable of. Don't you think I would see his influence if he were playing Benito for a pawn?"

•   •   •

Jill Bitterman walked down the quiet lane looking for a house number. With many houses tucked in behind others, the numbers facing the street skipped a lot. She noticed the tall, broad man in a grey trenchcoat coming toward her but kept her focus on the number search. That is, until he slowed down. He was looking straight at her. "Can I help you?" she asked boldly.

"I believe you can. FBI Special Agent Jill Bitterman, if I'm not mistaken. Very nice to meet you. Interpol Special Agent Michael Archibald," he said showing her his badge ID.

"How do you know me?" She said, shaking his hand perfunctorily.

"You are mentioned several times in the files of the case I'm here working on. I believe Interpol played a part in getting you cleared to investigate here in Ireland. It seems you and I are after the same terrorist."

"The Shadow?"

"After the 2001 attack in Washington D.C., he went underground. Disappeared with no trace, but he has now resurfaced here in Ireland."

"That's extraordinary. I'm here to question a witness to the 2001 attack."

"Would that be Doctor Sanantha Mauwad? I've already spoken with her. As it turns out, she is here for entirely different reasons and has no information about the Shadow."

"That's a heck of a coincidence, him and her being here independently at the same time."

"It is," he agreed.

"I found her in Malaysia, but she flew here suddenly, rather suspiciously. I'm told she has a patient here that she met in Malaysia a few years ago. I want to make sure that story checks out. I'm also sure she knows more about what happened in D.C. than she told the police."

"Forgive me, but I need to ask you something rather personal. When I saw your work in the file, I thought how unusual it is for an agent to pursue leads on an eight-year old case like this. I commend you on your persistence. It may lead to finally capturing a very bad man, but is there more here than meets the eye?"

"I don't catch your drift."

"Didn't you start your career in a special FBI unit that investigated crimes that, shall we say, didn't fit in the box?"

"Yes, we solved a number of supposedly unsolvable crimes."

"Crimes that often included cults and mentally ill criminals, yes? Do you suspect the Shadow of dealing in cults and the supernatural?"

"I have learned from several independent sources that he is a religious zealot, with convictions that excuse his extremist actions. The part that doesn't fit is, he has no followers. Cult leaders have followers."

Archibald nodded. "That's true, he infiltrates, instigates, and then disappears."

"You seem to know a lot about me. Let me ask you a question. When you were given this case, did it seem like a wild goose chase to you?"

"I think I understand the colorful metaphor, but not your meaning."

"Is your primary lead the money movements?"

"Yes," he confirmed. "Same pattern of wire fraud we saw just before the 2001 attack. This time it leads to Benito Nomini, but he checks out clean."

"There's a lot of money being moved around, but you can't tell what's really being bought," she walked it through. "Your bosses told you somebody must be doing something illegal, and go check it out."

"That's accurate."

"That's like someone saying there is a wild goose in the woods, and everybody gets excited about a goose dinner and runs off to hunt it down. Only there never was a goose. How do you know the Shadow is one man, or if it is always the same man?"

"Do you think it's a crime ring or a conspiracy? You're right, I assumed it was one man, but it doesn't have to be."

"I am suggesting, with someone this slippery, we need to be open to any possibility. I can't imagine the red tape we would set in motion by making a formal pact, so can you and I agree informally to share any developments?" She handed him her card.

"Absolutely. Here is my card too. By the way, the cottage Doctor Mauwad is staying in is this one back here," he said pointing.

"Thank you kindly. Were you coming to see her too?"

"I was, but I met with her before. You go on ahead this time."

"Thank you again."

Polite is good, she thought. Even so, she was pretty sure he wasn't telling her everything. She walked to the door, took out her badge, and knocked.

Sanantha Mauwad looked exactly as Jill had pictured her, complete with the tall patterned fabric turban.

"Agent Bitterman, I assume?"

"Correct, Doctor Mauwad. I take it Doctor Herrera told you I was coming. May I come in?"

"Yes, please do."

She noted the enormous hole in the back wall of the living room, and chose to not mention it. "I don't usually pry into witnesses' personal lives, but I think you will understand I needed to clarify why you took off halfway around the world right after I called you."

"I appreciate that probably looked suspicious."

Jill noted the psychiatrist did not offer her a seat. "I did learn you had other pressing matters here. If I may digress, is Ms. Macklin here?"

"Yes, she's in the other room sleeping."

"Oh, good. As I said on the phone earlier, I have been researching the incident where your patient Mr. Redmond lost his life. Have you had the opportunity to refresh your recollection of those events?"

"Yes."

"How long have you known Benito Nomini?"

Two whole eye blinks and a glance to the right. Okay then.

"I met him on the plane here. That's almost four weeks."

"What has he told you about how he makes his living?"

"He told me he is an image and branding consultant."

Jill could see she really wanted to fold her arms defensively, but caught herself and just clasped her hands in front of her stomach.

"I expect you will tell him whatever we talk about today, so I will not sugar coat this."

"Why would you expect that?"

"The police report from the murders at the Aberdeen Plaza Hotel three nights ago stated that you and Mr. Nomini were interviewed in your bathrobes in his hotel room. We're all grown-ups, Doctor. Have you ever heard the names of any of his clients or business associates?"

"No. He has never conducted business in front of me. We don't talk about his business. Did Simon tell you anything about Benito? I just want your record to show that anything Simon may have said should be taken in the context of a jealous ex-lover."

"Duly noted. I understand Mr. Nomini is financing Alec Doogan's paranormal research, and Mr. Doogan has produced two videotapes which he posted to the Internet. Are you aware of the reaction the public has had to these tapes?"

"Yes, he has a large following."

"Do you know if it was Mr. Doogan who was filmed by a television news crew last week assisting rescue workers with floodwaters?"

"I believe it was."

"How familiar are you with Mr. Doogan's research?"

"I have some knowledge of what he is doing."

"Are you aware of any plans Mr. Doogan or Mr. Nomini may have to use Mr. Doogan's research to cause destruction or harm?"

"No. Alec and Benito are good men. I have only ever heard of them doing good and helpful things, like saving that school from the river."

"Do you know if Mr. Nomini is teaching Mr. Doogan, or just financing his research?"

"I believe his support is mostly financial."

"Going back to the events in 2001, were you aware of any criminal activity by the terrorist prior to the day of the shootings at the Washington Monument?"

"I knew Charles was afraid of the terrorist prior to that day, but I didn't know what crimes the terrorist had committed."

The psychiatrist was clearly more at ease discussing events nine years in the past than events today. "Did you know why the terrorist was after Mr. Redmond?"

"I'm not sure the terrorist was specifically after Charles. Charles suffered from delusions. He was trampled in the riot, not gunned down."

"Do you maintain that Mr. Redmond had no connection to the terrorist?"

"I don't know. Charles said a lot of things in confidence to me that left me with unanswered questions."

"That was not your testimony at the time. Why did you not elaborate then?"

"I wasn't sure how much trouble Charles was in with the law, given his Haitian past with the Duvalliers. I didn't want to add suspicion to him by saying too much. I knew he was just a victim. He had done some terrible things earlier in his life, but he had put all that behind him."

"You said remarkably little to the police about how the terrorist executed the attack, even though you were at a place on the venue that should have afforded you an excellent view of everything that happened. Why was that?"

"It all happened so quickly, I didn't realize we were under attack until it was too late. I told the police everything as accurately as I could recall."

"Were you aware of any paranormal research being funded by the terrorist prior to the day of the attack?"

"No, I had no first-hand knowledge of the terrorist until that day."

"Do you know who paid for all the ancient Egyptian artifacts that were found around the base of the monument?"

"No, I don't."

"Would you characterize your understanding of spells and occult rituals as being an expert in such matters?"

"No, I'm not an expert."

"Doctor, I am not here to argue with you, so please forgive me if this sounds confrontational. You have a history of clients who are somehow involved in cults or ritual practices. Have they not depended on you to understand their situations — including their less traditional beliefs?"

"I guess so."

"Ma'am, when someone in trouble trusts you to help them, I would tend to call you an expert."

"That's fair."

"In your expert opinion, do you think the rituals conducted during the 2001 terrorist attack are in any way related to the research Mr. Doogan is conducting now?"

Deep frown, halted breath. That one rocked her back. "No. They are completely unrelated."

A twenty-something woman with tussled auburn hair came out of the hallway blinking against the midday light. She was eating dates out of a paper bag. "Oh, excuse me. I thought I heard a new voice. Are you with the police?"

"Yes, ma'am, I am FBI Special Agent Jill Bitterman. Are you Desiree Macklin?"

"Yes."

Jill wasn't sure why, but she could not take her eyes off this fascinating young woman. "I was hoping to have a word with you too. Doctor Mauwad, I have no further questions at this time."

"All right."

"Ms. Macklin, what do you know about the terrorist that attacked Washington, D.C. in April of 2001?"

"Only what Sanantha has told me. He's a religious zealot and a ruthless killer, seems to pop up and disappear, nobody knows much about him, he's never been caught."

"Do you have reason to believe he is targeting you?"

She yawned and scooped her hair away from her face in a remarkably sensuous motion. "We suspect he is. We have heard rumors and we have deduced his possible intentions, but we have no hard evidence."

"Who did you hear rumors from?"

"There was an Irish Treasury inspector named Archibald who asked me if I had been threatened."

"Oh. All right. You said you had deduced his intentions. How did you do that?"

"Well, I guess the best way to describe it is with rituals, and scholarly research."

"Ms. Macklin, would it be accurate to say you are developing a religious practice that may have attracted the attention of this terrorist?"

She smiled charmingly. "Yes, that would be putting it better than I could."

Was it her clear blue eyes? Jill had to force herself to focus. "Is this practice a revival of an old religion?"

"Yes, the rites are ancient Egyptian."

"Are you aware that the terrorist attack in D.C. in 2001 centered on ancient Egyptian rites?"

"That is why we think he might be after me."

"Have you sought police protection?"

"Not yet. We have no evidence."

Dimples, it was the dimples. "Yes, of course. Let me leave you my card. Please call me if anything concrete surfaces. Any strange emails or phone calls, anyone following you in traffic, don't hesitate even if you think it's excusable. Let me decide."

"Thank you. That's very reassuring." She stepped up and extended her hand.

Jill found herself happy for no reason at the prospect of touching her. She shook her hand using her strictly professional handshake, but it still felt really nice. "I may call you if other questions come up. Goodbye Ms. Macklin. Goodbye Doctor Mauwad."

"Goodbye."

"Goodbye."

Jill stood outside the closed door for a moment. Her heart was racing and her brow was sweating. What in tarnation had just happened?

•   •   •

As she reached to knock on his door, Desiree braced herself for Alec to have the weirdly romantic reaction that everyone was having toward her.

"Hi Desiree, come on in." He turned away from the door and headed straight to his computer.

She stood in the doorway a second, then closed the door behind herself.

"I've been doing some preliminary image searches for ancient Egyptian keys. Can I see it?"

She handed it to him, and again he didn't even look up at her. Was she disappointed?

"Ah yes, that's the one I was thinking." He brought up a tomb wall painting of Osiris. There on his belt hung the exact key she found in the spirit realm Karnak. Alec held the key up to the computer screen. "Pretty exciting stuff."

"What does it do?" she asked.

"I don't know. I cannot find any reference to it. It's an easy assumption that, being the Lord of the Dead, it opens the gates of the Underworld."

"In my dream, he said he could not help me in person because of where he was. I assumed he was in the Underworld. Makes me wonder who took his key from him."

"Maybe he gave it to someone to leave in your temple so you could find it."

"He wanted to help me, that was clear."

Alec spun his chair around and looked at her full on for the first time. "Did you do something with your hair?"

She smiled and sighed. "When I went to the spirit realm, I think I picked up some kind of god pheromone or something. People keep saying I am suddenly more attractive. It was kind of annoying at first, but now I'm starting to like it."

"Well, I am feeling emboldened to say I have always found you attractive, but you made it clear early on we are fellow adventurers and nothing more."

"Thank you for your honesty. Let me be honest too. I am lucky enough to be able to attract boyfriends any time, even without the god attraction thing. I don't make friends that easily. You and I hit it off right away as friends and I thought that was frankly more valuable."

"I agree. I don't attract girlfriends easily, but I'm glad we got to be such fast friends."

"I have other news, and it's not good. I lost Joseph. He ran into some old enemies and he won't be able to help us anymore."

"While we're being honest with each other, let me just ask you."

Desiree held her breath. Which lie had he figured out?

"Joseph isn't human, is he?"

She pursed her lips. "No. He's one of those incarnate angels we were talking about."

"Right. That whole 'talented magician' thing stopped holding water once he took you through an interdimensional portal to Mount Semeru. Then he taught you how to do it at Karnak. I figured the truth would come out eventually."

"I was afraid revealing his identity would distract you from the important work you're doing. The whole Egyptian thing is my journey, and that includes Joseph and Sanantha. You and Benito have your own path with the Celtic magic, and I didn't want to confuse one with the other. I'm sorry. I hate keeping secrets."

"Joseph is an Egyptian angel?" Alec asked.

She was relived he come around to accept incarnate angels. "Yeah, remember you hit him with that Egyptian flail and it almost threw him out of his body. He's an angel of Ptah, the Opener of the Ways. His magic wouldn't help you with the Celtic gods, so I kept him out of your work."

"What happened to him?"

"He was taken back into captivity by the gods. He was only free because his old master broke him out of prison."

"An angel is a huge resource to lose, especially with Osiris's warning about Sammael outstanding."

She paused to get this next part right. "There's more to it. Things have been moving really fast. Benito has given you some frighteningly powerful tools, and I'm finding my hitchhiking god has some scary abilities and plans of her own. Whatever happens, I want to assure you, promise you, that I will be there to protect your back."

"Wow. You're scared, and scared for me."

"Gods and magic and demons and you're right in the middle of it."

"Hell yeah. Even with your goddess powers, you have no idea what a rush it was to move an entire river out of the way. I've been hoping for this my whole life. I'm not blind to the dangers, but so far so good." He smiled at her. "Thank you for the promise."

•   •   •

Jill Bitterman stood up and closed the laptop on her hotel room desk, rolled her head around to stretch her neck, giving her shoulder length, straight blonde hair a shake for good measure. She straightened her oversized Star Wars nightshirt and crawled into bed. She propped up the only other occupant on the pillow next to her, a small soft sculpture doll of a large-eyed gray alien. She retrieved her copy of the New Revised Standard Version Bible from the nightstand and pulled out a booklet she had tucked into its pages.

"October 2nd. Day 275 of Read Your Bible in a Year. Matthew 2nd," she read from the pamphlet. She nodded to her companion. "Right, the Wise Men."

"In the time of King Herod, after Jesus was born in Bethlehem of Judea, wise men from the East came to Jerusalem, asking, 'Where is the child who has been born king of the Jews? For we observed his star at its rising, and have come to pay him homage.' When King Herod heard this, he was frightened and all Jerusalem with him; and calling together all the chief priests and scribes of the people, he inquired of them where the Messiah was to be born. They told him, 'In Bethlehem of Judea; for so it has been written by the prophet: 'And you, Bethlehem, in the land of Judah, are by no means least among the rulers of Judah; for from you shall come a ruler who is to shepherd my people Israel.' Then Herod secretly called for the wise men and learned from them the exact time when the star had appeared. Then he sent them to Bethlehem, saying, 'Go and search diligently for the child; and when you have found him, bring me word so that I may also go and pay him homage.' When they had heard the king, they set out; and there, ahead of them, went the star that they had seen at its rising, until it stopped over the place where the child was. When they saw that the star had stopped, they were overwhelmed with joy. On entering the house, they saw the child with Mary his mother; and they knelt down and paid him homage. Then, opening their treasure chests, they offered him gifts of gold, frankincense, and myrrh. And having been warned in a dream not to return to Herod, they left for their own country by another path."

She thought about that and turned to the doll. "You know, if my boss sent me on an assignment, and I witnessed something Earth shattering like that, would I have the nerve to not tell him what happened, and maybe even cut out for points beyond? It says they had a warning dream, but I'll bet they realized Herod was going to come kill this kid.

"I've seen some crazy things, but never anything big enough to throw in the towel. I guess it helps that I've never had a murderous despot for a boss. Still, it makes me wonder how I would have reacted."

21

Jill Bitterman stepped to the curb and raised her hand at the yellow Hail-O taxi that didn't even slow down. She looked back down the block and saw a green Dublin-15 cab coming. She stuck her fingers in her mouth and whistled so loud the first cab slammed on the brakes.

As she stepped off the curb to the slowing second vehicle, she heard the distinctive winding up noise of a rapidly backing car. She looked up and jumped back just in time as the Hail-O slammed back into her taxi. "Oh fer Chrissakes!"

The drivers jumped out and started arguing, both ignoring her completely.

A city bus rolling up the street caught her attention. Its destination marquis read Ballsbridge. "That's convenient." She looked around and spotted a bus stop just a few yards behind her. "Better yet."

As she mounted the bus stair, she glanced back at the still combative cab drivers and caught a violet glint in the eyes of the man who had backed up. She tried to get a better look, but he turned away.

"You coming on, missy?" the bus driver asked.

"Yes, of course. How much is the fare?"

"How far you going?"

"The U.S. Embassy, Elgin Road," she said, fishing change out of her suit skirt pocket.

"Sixty pence."

"There you go." The bus was more crowded than she expected. She sidestepped her way through standing passengers to a clear spot five rows back and grabbed an overhead hand loop.

She expected to see something architecturally interesting on a long bus ride through downtown Dublin, and the gothic palace they soon rolled by caught her attention. When they got to the end of the block, she saw a sign that read Rotunda Hospital.

Some hospital.

She heard a commotion in the back of the bus. At five-foot five in heels, she had to peek between her fellow passengers to see. A dark-haired man waved his arms around causing others to step back. He did not appear to be striking anyone, but rather dancing. She has seen plenty of high people dancing on busses and trains. This seemed more deliberate. She pushed around someone and got a good look. He was performing a *tai chi* routine.

The man had his neck scarf wrapped up over the lower half of his face. Benito Nomini? He made eye contact with her and without understanding how, she suddenly knew this was the Shadow. In that same moment, she also realized this was no passive exercise.

She reached inside her jacket and unclipped her pistol while yelling, "Everyone down! Law enforcement!" By the time she got the gun free, the man finished his moves with both fists thrust forward. As she leveled her aim, people all around him started dropping, not from her command, but falling unconscious. She saw a couple of people clasp their own throats as they fell. Something in the air. She took a hasty deep breath.

His eyes grinned at her and she felt a shiver run up her spine as she squeezed off a shot. He jerked to the side faster than she had ever seen anyone move, but she still hit him in the shoulder. Then he was gone. He hadn't gone down among the fallen passengers, he was simply no longer on the bus. In the one second that had passed, the wave of falling bodies had reached her. She felt her skin tighten, like she was under some kind of suction. She looked forward and saw the rest of the people fall, including the driver. The bus veered in traffic. She was too far back to get to the wheel. The bus hurtled at the low rail wall of the O'Connell Bridge.

She hated having to decide there was nothing she could do for all these people, but she saw only one way out. She fired three rounds in the nearest window on the street-facing side and, stepping on the fallen bodies, dove through the shattered window. The bus crashed through the wall with a sound as loud and low as thunder, then tipped down toward the river below. She hit the pavement hard and rolled as best she could. She flinched at the deafening sound of metal scraping against stone and the bus twisting under its own weight. She watched helplessly as the bus flipped off the bridge and splashed onto its back in the water. She limped to the gap and saw it sink with all onboard.

•   •   •

The doorbell woke Sanantha with a start. She must have nodded off on the couch. She glanced around and saw Benito had left. She got up and answered the door.

Agent Bitterman's head was bandaged, her arm was in a sling, and she looked furious. "Doctor, may I ask if Benito Nomini is here?"

"No, he just left."

"How long ago?"

Sanantha checked her watch. She had slept for an hour? "Fifteen minutes ago. Why?"

"How long was he here prior to his leaving?"

"A couple of hours. We had lunch and hung out for a while. What happened?"

"Are you saying that a half an hour ago, he was here with you?"

"Yes. Where else do you think he was?"

The agent stared at her in locked gaze for a long second. Sanantha knew how to keep a straight face. "May I have his cell phone number?"

"I don't think I should do that without a warrant."

"Then I will get one. It will go better for him if I question him before the local police find him. Have him call me. You have my number. I advise you to not leave town without telling me in advance."

22

MICHAEL SAT ON THE ROOF PEAK of Christ Church Cathedral listening to the chorus within singing Evensong. He sat near the bell tower so people on the ground didn't spot him. He wrapped his grey trench coat around himself to look like a shadow if someone did see him. The voices welled up better through the bell tower windows there as well.

He closed his eyes and let the music remind him of home. The sopranos didn't get quite as high and the baritones didn't get quite as low as he was used to, but the harmonies stirred him just the same.

In the midst of this reverie, one sound didn't fit — the whirring whistle of a whip slicing through the air at him. He opened his eyes and quickly rolled away from Sammael's weapon, coming up on his feet, flaming sword drawn as the whip cracked next to him. "Benito Nomini after all," Michael declared. Michael charged him as he yanked the whip back. Michael brought the sword down and Sammael drew up his other hand, a trident materializing as he thrust it to intercept the sword.

Michael grinned enthusiastically. "You want to dance?"

The whip came down across Michael's back, but he expanded his huge white wings in time to block. His wings shredded his white shirt and flipped up his trench coat. The whip end cleanly sliced off his coat tails.

"Let's dance," Michael said as he brought up his left fist and caught him under the chin, sending him flying back along the rooftop. Michael dove after him, gliding on his wings, sword hissing furiously. Sammael rolled off the rooftop and landed on one of the buttress peaks below. Michael swooped down after him as he leapt from buttress to buttress back down the length of the nave, his brown tweed overcoat flapping like a cape behind him.

He flew after Sammael, closing the distance. Sammael suddenly jumped all the way to the crenulated top of the bell tower, above Michael. Michael realized if he flew above him, the entire block below would see them. Was Sammael's plan to expose him? This was hardly a problem.

He flew up and turned down, but to do so he had to extend his wings to their full length. Sammael snared a wing tip with his whip and yanked him off balance. Michael twisted in midair as he fell, bringing the sword around to deflect the trident point thrust up at him. He bounced the sword back into Sammael and slashed him across the chest as he fell. He also managed to reach out with his left hand and grabbed Sammael by the ankle. He dragged him off the tower and the two fell straight into the roof. They crashed through the green copper shingles and landed on the tile mosaic floor. The audience in the pews fled screaming.

Sammael sprung onto his Italian loafers, ignited his whip, and turned it on the crowd. Michael scooped up a couple of chairs with one hand and threw them across the whip's path, entangling it, extinguishing the flames, and bringing it down harmlessly.

"You should know better than to tangle with me head on," Michael warned. "I've always been better at this than you."

Sammael scooped up three chairs with his trident and flung them at Michael. When Michael pumped his wings to leap up out their path,

Sammael brought his whip up and snared him around the legs. Michael twisted in midair to untangle himself, then pulled out of the maneuver to swoop down on his enemy.

Sammael swung his trident around and Michael easily parried it away. He grabbed its length with his free hand, spun around inside its reach and elbowed Sammael in the face hard. Michael held onto the long weapon as Sammael tumbled back through rows of chairs. Michael threw the trident to the other end of the cathedral and advanced on his adversary.

Sammael jumped up and launched the whip but Michael caught it around his arm and seized it. He grabbed Sammael by the throat and flew up through the hole in the roof if only to get him away from the innocents still cowering in the sanctuary. Out of the corner of his eye as they left, Michael saw the trident stuck in the floor in front of the altar. He thought that would make an interesting relic.

Michael wondered at his enemy's plan, given he was roundly winning this battle. Why hadn't he used any magic? He thought Sammael might have in mind to desecrate the cathedral, so he aimed them down to the roof of the walkway bridge that connected the main building with the others on the campus. He reached around behind himself and grabbed the golden armcuffs he carried that would restrain Sammael's powers so he could take his quarry back to heaven. He looked down at his struggling adversary who met him with a knowing grin. Sammael also reach into his pocket for something.

"What, do you still carry that straight razor of yours?" Michael taunted.

Before Michael could react, Sammael slapped a black iron cuff around the wrist of the hand that held his throat.

The moment the cuff latched, Michael found them no longer in flight, but standing in a stone cavern. The iron cuff was at the end of a chain mounted to a large rock.

"Brother!" Michael cried cheerfully in Angelic, covering his own disorientation.

"Don't 'brother' me," Sammael dismissed in the same tongue. "I got the drop on you while you were napping on the job." He bent over in pain from his still smoking burn wound. He held up the edges of his slashed pink shirt. "That was my favorite. What is it with you heroes, taking days off?"

"It's called appreciating His world."

"Winners do not take days off."

"Villains do not take days off."

Sammael shrugged. "If the shoe fits."

Michael slashed at the chain with his flaming sword and nothing happened. He tested the rock and it too held. He looked around. "Where have you brought me?"

This little corner of His world was found for me by Silas Alverado. That chain is angel proof. Osiris used to bind me to that rock when he found my banter annoying."

"Where's Osiris now?"

"Back with his adoring subjects in the Land of the Dead. That was the temptation that finally got me out of here after nine years."

"Temptation. Some things never change. Your hieroglyphics bracelet is glowing. Let me guess, another present from Alverado? Designed to bring you here and hold you? It's still trying."

"Let it. I broke the curse even if I can't break the bracelet."

"Nine years. So you're only just returning to Earth. Oh, right, the total solar eclipse back in July, just before the fires across Europe."

"My Welcome Home present to myself."

"Nice bullet hole in your shoulder."

"Another present, this one from your FBI agent. It will heal."

"My cut won't," Michael said with a grin. "Did you kill Jill?"

"Oh, you like her? She's tougher than she looks. I will be sure she dies a grisly death."

"Before you go, answer me this. I understand you trying to cover your tracks from helping Saint Patrick. I also understand you setting all those fires in countries that have persecuted Jews from since before the Inquisition. Desiree knows you're coming for her, but at the same time you're helping Alec summon Celtic gods, whom you hate. That makes no sense."

Sammael leaned back on one foot and folded his arms, but he couldn't with his chest wound. He covered his painful flinch by casually shifting to supporting one arm while touching his jaw. "I should leave you like that to ponder my scheme for all eternity."

"I'll just have to think like you. All right. You're using Alec to draw the Neters out into the open so you can do something heinous to discredit them."

"You don't know the half of it," Sammael said with obvious pride. "But that's not bad. All that time masquerading as a detective seems to have rubbed off on you."

"By helping Alec, you escape suspicion of being the enemy who is after Desiree. By the way, nice work hiding in plain sight. Very you. But you're not after Desiree, you're after her whole pantheon." Michael finally saw the evil seed of the plan. "Turn the believers away once and for all and the gods lose all their power. They dissipate."

"There, that didn't take but a moment once you saw through my Benito disguise. On the other hand, these mortals will never figure it out."

"You nearly wiped them out when you helped Saint Patrick, and now you're back to finish the job. After all this time, is this still punishment for the Israelite bondage? I thought that water had long since passed under the bridge."

"Any mercy I might have shown them was wiped out by their champion chaining me down here for nine years. No one has ever managed that. I hate them. It's that simple. I hate them because they exist. I hate them because I can."

"The Neters are His creations too."

"They don't think they are. That makes them an abomination that must be expunged."

Michael regarded him and sighed. "Always justice issues with you."

"Fuck off. Look how high and mighty you are now."

"I didn't know you could say that in Angelic." Michael looked around and chuckled. "This is kind of poetic."

"Yeah, I thought so. You who threw me out of Heaven into the Pit. Now I get to return the favor! Enjoy your day off, brother."

23

SANANTHA ADJUSTED HER TALL YELLOW TURBAN against the hot breeze blowing across the desert. She lined up video cameras on tripods while talking on an enormous satellite field phone to Desiree back in Alec's apartment in Ireland.

"Wadi what?" Desiree asked. "The wind drowned out the last part."

"Wadi Halfa in the Sudan. We're just south of the border with Egypt, near the coast of Lake Nassar. I guess they call it Lake Nubia on the Sudanese side."

"Oh, it's on a lake, but you said it never rains there?"

She lined up another camera, framing Alec with the lake behind him. "Yeah, the winds blow in off the desert and no clouds ever form. The countryside is low hills and lots of flat, rocky sand, with nothing to stop the winds. One of the locals said it rained like half an inch five years ago. That's why Benito picked this spot. Alec's here to make it rain. Are you getting these feeds?"

"Yes. By the way, the numbers you've got on the cameras don't line up with the numbers on this end. You just keep lining up the shots and I'll find which camera you've got pointed where. I've got the live feed set up ready to go, with all the recording decks, just like Benito's typed instructions said."

"Good. I don't know how long this will take or how long we have to film. The townspeople were not too happy about us landing the charter jet on their main road. Benito says he cleared everything with the Sudanese government, but I'm expecting to see a column of military vehicles come up the road any minute."

"That would make for interesting viewing," Desiree quipped.

"It would, but that's not what we're here for. Hang on a minute. Benito is calling me over. I'm setting the phone down, but don't hang up."

"I won't. It took four tries to connect." Desiree scooted the chair back to look again at the stack of external hard drives Benito had set up for Alec's computer. Everything looked connected. She spun around in the chair to watch Renpo walking the apartment looking at Alec's artifact collection while holding the Pearl in one hand. "Find anything interesting?"

"Oh yes. A couple of these weapons were used in heinous crimes. That necklace on the shelf over there nearly caused a war."

"Well, don't move anything. Alec is very particular about his stuff."

"Desiree?" Sanantha came back on the phone.

"I'm here."

"Benito says he wants to go with the tape delay option. He thinks it might take a few hours for the clouds to form once the spell is cast. He wants you to just tape the first part, then broadcast it just before we go live with the rain coming down."

"Sure, that makes sense. I've got the drives ready whenever you are."

"Okay, I'll let you know in a few minutes."

Desiree noticed Renpo had found Alec's aura detecting screen.

"Did you know this device has a memory?" he asked.

She held her hand over the phone. "What do you mean?"

"It stores all the images it has taken." He brought it over. "Look, there is a list that appears."

"That's called a drop-down menu. Let me see." She cradled the phone handset under her neck and took the device. She scrolled through and found the one they took off Saint Patrick's grave. She was both pleased and alarmed to find it saved here. She hesitated to pull it up.

"Is that the angel signature?" Renpo asked.

"Yes. I only ever saw the original messy collection of impressions, and never saw the final image that Alec sorted out. Can there be any harm in looking at it?"

"The Pearl will tell me if we are in danger. Be ready to close the image right away if that happens."

"Fair enough." She clicked on the menu listing and the screen filled with a jagged set of blade-like curves that formed a hook shape. The image stirred something deep inside her. She closed it before Renpo said anything.

"The Pearl is not telling me we caused any result."

"Good. I'm pretty sure Isis did not like seeing that."

"Desiree," came Sanantha's voice. "We're ready to start."

She hit Record. "We're recording all six cameras."

Sanantha stood up straight in front of one of them and spoke into the lens. "We are here today in one of the driest places on Earth, the town of Wadi Halfa in the Sudan. This is also one of the sunniest places on Earth. Cloud cover is extremely rare, and it has not rained here in five years. Today Alec Doogan will perform a genuine miracle by making it rain. Alec will be calling on the ancient Gaelic god Ambisagrus, who also is known by the name Bussumarus. This god controls wind, rain, hail and fog, and especially weather magic.

"You can see Alec down near the shore of Lake Nubia. With Ambisagrus's help, he will be coaxing water from the lake up to form clouds which will then drop their rain on this parched ground. You've seen Alec perform magic using water before. This will be his biggest spell to date.

"Alec has started his incantation. You can see him doing his summoning dance. This is a new spell, and his motions are different than what we have seen before."

Indeed, he did not do the twirling jumping steps Boann had taught him. Here he was sweeping his arms in giant shapes, reaching from the ground to overhead and back again. He appeared to be making hand gestures at the same time, almost like sign language.

Desiree noticed one of the cameras had swung around in the wind and wasn't viewing anything in particular. She couldn't tell Sanantha because she was on camera, even if this wasn't live. Then she spotted a movement at the edge of the screen. It looked like a man's arm swinging into and out of the frame. Then his leg. "Is that Benito?" she asked Renpo who was looking over her shoulder.

"Yes, I think so. That's the direction Doctor Mauwad walked when she consulted with him."

"What's he doing over there?"

"It looks like a *tai chi* exercise. I can't tell you which motions since we only see him at the end of his movements."

She compared what little she could see of Benito's movements with Alec's big arm motions. They were not the same.

Sanantha continued her narration. "Okay, so now we see Alec winding up his spell. Just a few more gestures, and there, he's done. Now we wait and watch for the clouds to form. She smiled into the camera, then said, "Cut."

She picked up the phone. "Did you get all that?"

Absolutely," Desiree said. "Can I ask you something? Over to the side, what for the cameras is the right, is that Benito over there doing *tai chi*? The wind kicked one of the cameras around and we saw him dancing."

"I'd be really surprised if he was moving around like that. He was in a car crash and he has this huge cut across his chest." Sanantha disappeared from the camera view and the phone went silent for a moment. She came back to the camera. "Yes, he does that to relax. I guess he was nervous about the new spell. Once Alec starts his routine, there isn't much the rest of us can do but sit back and fret that it's going to work."

"Where did he get this new spell? It looks very different than his previous work."

"Benito gave him a book to translate and it turned out to be a Gospel written by Lazarus."

"The guy Jesus brought back to life?"

"Exactly. He wrote down what he saw of heaven while he was dead. Alec found a description of how to make rain."

Renpo grunted behind her. She looked over her shoulder to see him frowning and shaking his head. "What?"

"Nothing. Please excuse me."

She turned back. "Sanantha, I'm seeing something on the cameras. Is it getting dark there?"

On the screen, Sanantha looked up and stared. "Whoa."

"What is it? Tilt the camera up so I can see."

The view rotated and showed a swirl of thickening clouds. Desiree hit record. "Are you still there? Is this as weird in person?"

"Yeah, I'm here. This is really freaky. It looks like something out of a movie."

"That's what the camera is getting too."

"No, I mean it looks like some Hollywood special effect. It doesn't look real. The wind changed direction. What was a breeze off the desert is now a steady cold wind off the lake."

"It looks kind of dangerous." Desiree regretted saying that as soon as she heard the words. Her friend was out in the open with no shelter in the middle of some biblical weather summoning. "Maybe you should find someplace safe to watch this," she said into the phone.

"It's only supposed to rain. I can't get over how fast this came up. I mean, Alec just finished the spell what, five minutes ago?"

"That's why I'm worried. The spell might have set something loose that is growing out of control. Did Alec or Benito say anything about a ritual to stop this?"

"Um, no. I smell moisture in the air, you know, like just before rain falls.

Desiree was sick at how powerless she was a thousand of miles away. She looked back at Renpo who only shook his head. All she could do was tell her friend to run. Her friend did not see the danger. "What about lightning?"

"There is none, not out on the lake, and not here on land. Are you recording this?"

"Oh yes, ever since you tilted the camera up at the clouds."

"Ah, there it is. Raindrops." She tilted the camera down to show herself against the darkened landscape. The drops visibly showed on her yellow turban and white blouse. "Rain, in a place that never gets rain, brought here by Alec Doogan and his magic."

Just as she was getting back into her dramatic narrative, someone distracted her from off camera. "What? We're recording," she dismissed the unseen interrupting person. She frowned at them, listening for a moment. She turned and looked up at the clouds. The rain was coming down steadily now. "Really?" she asked dubiously.

Desiree listened at the phone carefully and caught snatches of the male voice Sanantha was talking with. "Just go ahead and shut it all down," he said.

Sanantha turned back to the camera. "Des, go ahead and stop recording. Benito says the clouds formed up so fast no one will ever believe this really happened. It was amazing and we saw it, but people seeing this online will have to believe it or we just destroy our own credibility. It will be much more convincing in person."

"In person?"

"Yes. This was the test run for the spell Alec is going to use as the finale of the Celtic Fair next weekend."

"Oh. That'll be exciting. I'll let you go. You've got to get all those cameras packed up in the rain."

"Bye bye! See you Monday!"

"Bye Sanantha! Safe flight home."

She hung up, fished a card out of her jeans pocket, and dialed Michael's cell number.

Renpo was still standing behind her chair. "Do you want to tell Michael that we saw Benito perform *tai chi* in the middle of Alec's spell?"

She spun the chair around and looked up at him. "Exactly."

The phone clicked a couple of times like the connection did not go through.

"Weird," she commented, then dialed again more carefully while looking at the card.

A recorded message announced, "We cannot complete your call as dialed. The number you dialed is either out of order or has been disconnected. Please check the number and dial again."

"That's not good. It won't even go to voice mail."

"Voice mail?" he asked.

"Our phones will record a caller's message if you can't answer. He said this was the best way to reach him, and he would always pick up."

"What do you think Mr. Nomini was doing?"

"I don't know." Her voice came out more tense than she intended. "How much trouble can a human cause with *tai chi chuan*? Joseph taught me to use it to channel my god magic, but I've got powers already. Back in Malaysia, the guy who kidnapped me used his own form of *kung fu* to do seemingly magical things to people. I saw him use his voice to paralyze someone."

"I am sorry, but my understanding of *chi* energy stops at focusing strength and healing."

"The angels seem to have the best grasp of it. Joseph has unlocked amazing things for me, and I'm sure Michael uses it the same way." She had an awful thought. "What if we can't reach Michael at all? I had two angels at my side, and now I've got none."

"He knows the Celtic Fair is next weekend. That is the focus of his plan to capture Sammael. Surely he will contact us soon about that."

She felt a shadow of despair. "Brother Renpo, what if I have to face the Devil alone?"

"The Buddha faced the Devil alone, armed only with is knowledge of the truth, and he was victorious. We have the Pearl, and you have a god's powers. It would be an easier battle with angels helping, but you can still win this fight."

He could see in her eyes that her faith had been shaken.

"We're screwed," she said quietly. "Excuse me, I have to pee."

He was sorry his encouragement speech had failed to connect with her. He looked down at the computer screen that was cycling pictures of beautiful libraries from around the world. He glanced up and was taken by the framed picture of a hooded woman holding lilies. He assumed it was a religious icon. He did not know who she was, but he had spent his life looking at similar depictions of holy people. This must be someone Alec took solace from, for it to be right above his desk.

He reached into his robes and held the Pearl while looking at her. He expected to suddenly understand who she was, but he did not expect to see what she then did. She smiled and looked back at him.

He dropped the Pearl back into its pocket, and she snapped back to her original pose. He picked it up again and she came back to motion. He knew her name was Catherine, and that she had sacrificed herself to defend her pope from demons. He was impressed. She nodded at him.

She let go of her flowers with one hand and reached down, not just down in her picture, but down out of the frame, and pointed at an elaborate bronze key that was sitting on the shelf next to her picture. He looked at the key and the Pearl showed him it belonged to the Egyptian god Osiris, and that Desiree had brought it back from the spirit plane.

She leaned forward and stretched her arm towards it. Renpo reached up and slid it closer so she could reach it. When she touched it, the vision broke, and she appeared in the frame as she had originally. He touched and retouched the Pearl, but she remained a stationery picture.

He felt lightheaded, confused, but at the same time filled with joy. He knew he had seen something enormously important, but he had no idea what it meant. On the other hand, he was confident it was a good sign, that forces were working in their favor.

24

"ARE YOU SURE THAT'S AS MUCH AS WE CAN FIND OUT?" Desiree asked the phone operator.

"Yes, when we send out a test signal and get these error messages, it almost always means the phone has been broken badly. The chip inside the phone isn't even responding. As I said before, if your friend has been missing for more than a couple of days, I can connect you with the police to file a Missing Persons report."

"It's Tuesday, it's been three days. I may do that, but not right now. Thank you for all your help."

"You're welcome. Thank you for calling Vodafone. Goodbye."

"Bye." She hung up and stared at her living room floor. *The Devil. Alone.*

Renpo joined her from the back of the house. "That did not sound encouraging."

"No. I'm thinking I should just pull the plug, tell Alec that he is playing into Sammael's hands, and have him cancel the fair. I don't think I can do this alone. Why invite Sammael to surface when we can't stop him?"

"That is a reasonable option. I do not agree that you cannot do this. When I think of all the coincidences that have fallen into place, all the dreams and visions, the appearance of two angels, even if they then disappeared, I can't help but think this is all headed somewhere. Isis saved your life so she could get this opportunity to capture Sammael. Do you feel her backing off or wanting to wait for a better chance?"

"No, she gives me power whenever I ask for it."

"What if Sammael knows of Michael's trap? What if Joseph and Michael disappearing is Sammael fighting back, evening the odds? Sammael could have told Set were to find Joseph. Now that he has removed the two angels, he may feel confident in going forward."

Desiree thought through the pieces. "Osiris told me Sammael's weakness is his overconfidence."

"Good. Let him think he has the upper hand. Didn't Osiris tell you something about changing fate?"

"He said the thing I can do that no angel can do is change fate."

"That's your secret weapon," the Tibetan threw out a hand in emphasis.

"Brother Renpo, I don't know how to change fate."

"Isis has already started the process for you. Her moving into your body changed the entire timeline. You meeting up with Joseph lead to you finding me and the Pearl. Isis has placed you at the center of many forces and pathways. By choosing wisely, you can push events away from him winning and toward you winning."

She held up her hands and shook her head. "I may be in the center, but I'm still just a twenty-four-year-old Art History grad. You speak of having the wisdom to choose fate. I have no special wisdom."

"Prince Siddhartha was just a young man when he discovered Nirvana. The peace and perspective that experience gave him were the tools with which he defeated Mara."

"Nirvana?" she asked, not even trying to hide her doubt.

"The only thing you need is focus. Your focus is being blocked by your fear. The meditation we have practiced together lets you set aside fear. You have the powers of a god. You just need to get out of your own way."

"No self. You're talking *satori*."

"Exactly."

"*Satori* takes years of meditative practice. I've got four days."

"How long did it take you to cure Alec's brain chemistry imbalance?"

She did not see that coming. "The Pearl showed me something was broken. Isis gave me the power to fix it."

"What if I showed you, with the Pearl, what a brain looks like in *satori*, and you let Isis put your brain in the same state?"

She looked at him in astonished curiosity.

"I've been thinking that we might need to do this, so I've been planning on how we could."

"You can go into *satori*?"

"It takes me a little while to dive that deep, but yes I can."

"What is it like?"

"The sense of self vanishes, and you feel entirely connected to everything, the whole universe. You can think with crystal clarity and with such speed that nothing surprises you. Solutions that might normally take you weeks to figure out take seconds once you are unencumbered with distractions and the limitations of ego. It is like nothing else a person can experience. It is the highest, purest form of thinking."

"Why would you ever want to come down?"

"If one devotes their entire life to entering and maintaining *satori*, it becomes the new normal and the person passes into full enlightenment. Very few people have ever achieved this state. Some of them decide to leave the material world and pass entirely into this form of mental heaven. Their bodies die, but their minds go on forever. The very few see how much can be done in this state, and choose to abandon personal heaven to return to Earth as teachers."

"The bodhisattva."

"Yes. They are how we know Nirvana exists. In this heightened state, you will be able to see which thread to pull to unravel Sammael's plans. Without fear and self, you will think fast enough to foil his attacks. You will shrink his chance of success to none."

"Changing fate. I know the Siddhartha story, that Mara's temptations of power and wealth meant nothing to him once he had shed his sense of self. Sammael won't be here to tempt me. He wants to ruin my pantheon."

"Mara did not want to kill Siddhartha," Renpo agreed. "The young prince had found that all suffering is caused by the delusions of ego. Mara wanted to prove him wrong. Killing him would have been admitting defeat. We have to assume he has a bigger plan than just killing you."

"We don't know what he will do. Probably some sabotage to embarrass and discredit the gods, but realistically, everything is just a guess until it goes down. I will literally have to be ready for anything."

"Shall we begin? I will need to borrow your bedroom for a few hours to work myself down through layers of consciousness."

"Absolutely. Do whatever you need to."

Renpo handed her the Pearl. "You're going to need this." He picked up his bedroll, walked into her room and closed the door. She stood there and wondered if any of this was going to make a difference.

Sanantha opened the front door and startled Desiree. "You look like you saw a ghost."

"I'm pretty freaked out about this weekend."

"The fair preparations are coming along beautifully," Sanantha countered.

"Oh, that's good. No, Michael has disappeared. That means I have to face Sammael with no angels. Renpo is getting ready to teach me deep mediation so I can face him with no fear."

"Whoa, this weekend? Why do you think Sammael will surface at the fair?"

"Before he vanished, Michael said that would be the most likely time."

"Hold on." She sat down in the armchair and waved for Desiree to sit on the facing couch. "Have a seat. You do realize the only reason you think Sammael is coming for you is a dream. You have no actual evidence."

Desiree blinked. "We deduced the angelic trace on Saint Patrick's grave was Sammael."

"Alec says he never summoned with that symbol. If Michael really thinks his enemy will surface at the fair, why would he take off? I faced Sammael in Washington. If he were coming, wouldn't I be having dreams and portents? I think you may have gotten yourself worked up over nothing."

Desiree was astonished her friend, her confidante, her therapist, was dismissing her feelings out of hand.

"I thought you were here making vendor calls," Sanantha commented.

"Is Benito helping with the fair preparations?"

"Yesterday he was in London signing musicians. Tomorrow he is going to Brussels to oversee the installation of a statue at a museum." Sanantha paused and frowned. "Even if Sammael is coming, why would he come during a Celtic fair, with Alec summoning Gaelic gods?"

Desiree desperately wanted to tell her the Egyptian-Celtic connection, but she could feel Isis holding her back. She had waited thousands of years for this chance. "I figured with all that magic being thrown around, what better time for the Devil to show up and make a hash of things?"

Sanantha nodded. "I can see that. Still, not much to get worked up about." She got up, went into her room, and grabbed an already packed duffel bag. As she walked out, she turned and said, "If you find anything more concrete, let me know. I'm sure we will all be happy to help you feel safe at the event. It's going to be great."

Once the door closed, Desiree sighed. "Yeah, just great." She went in and peeked at the door on Renpo. He was in Lotus position on his mat on the floor, eyes closed, not moving. She went into the kitchen and made herself a cup of chamomile tea. While the electric kettle heated the water, she looked out the front windows through Joseph's hole in the wall. Even that didn't seem funny anymore. The empty bag on the counter that used to have her dates taunted her.

To pass the time, she read the local newspaper. Sanantha had taken her laptop with her. There was the half page ad for the Celtic Fair. The rock group Garbage was headlining the music stage. Dozens of booths would carry handmade Celtic crafts and jewelry. Local breweries would have their specialty beers. In the center of it all, both figuratively and literally on the ad, Alec Doogan would contact Celtic gods to bring back old country beliefs and traditions. It sounded like a wonderful time, if she wasn't expecting a biblical showdown in a crowd of hundreds of innocent fairgoers.

"Desiree, please come. I am ready," Renpo called.

She entered and he motioned for her to join him on the mat.

"Are you in *satori*?"

He smiled. "Oh yes. What does the Pearl tell you about my brain?"

She knelt down and sat back on her feet while holding the Pearl in both hands. "Oh my, your brain looks very different. Parts of it are just lit up while other areas are almost completely silent. Are those quiet areas that sense of self you described?"

"Yes. I am entirely at one with the room, with you, with the whole world. Call on Isis, gather her god *chi*, and move it upward into the second chakra which is your mouth and throat."

She did as he said, first feeling her presence in her heart where it always started. She envisioned her throat opening and letting the *chi* flow up to fill. "Will this give her a voice?"

"It would if we left it there. We're going to use what the Pearl showed you as a map, and let Isis change your brain activity to match mine. Now think of your mantra, close your eyes and imagine yourself sitting by that calm pool, surrounded by green grass. You are alone with the water, Isis is warming your throat, the Pearl is showing you where to let her flow. The only sound you hear is my voice and your breathing. Concentrate on being there. Feel your breath slow as the calmness of the pond soothes you while the *chi* warms you. Are you safely in that place?"

She nodded.

"When we brought you to this pond before, we let you learn what it felt like to stay here for hours, to let the calm soak into you while you learned to stay focused. This time you need to stay focused on being there. Your thoughts will try to wonder as she changes your brain activity, but you must stay there, focused on your mantra. I'm going to let you stay there for a while and get anchored. Listen to your breathing. Feel the warmth. Be one with the pond."

She focused on every detail of being there. The shine of light on the still surface, the dark green of its depth, the brown of the muddy edge with moss and grass growing up to cover the ground, the green grass growing out over the plain round her. Even though it was the only sound she heard, she lost track of how many breaths she had taken. Was it a dozen, a hundred — it didn't matter. All that mattered was being there.

"Do you feel completely anchored in that space?"

She nodded again.

"Then invite her to flow up into your first charka to do your bidding. Let her follow the map the Pearl has given you."

She had let the god *chi* flow into her hands enough times that the sensation had become expected and normal. Letting it flow up into her mind felt like opening up a part of herself that was never supposed to be opened. It was like losing her virginity all over again, letting something wonderful but new and scary into her innermost self. She tried as hard as she could to only think about being at the pond, but she could not help but ask the goddess to please be careful.

The water level in the pond slowly began to rise. At first, she wasn't sure if the shore had always been that close. When the water crept up to her legs as she sat, it was clear that something was changing. She looked around to find the water had spread around her, and she was sitting on a peninsula that was rapidly becoming an island. She wasn't worried, it was only a couple of inches of water. She needed to follow Brother Renpo's advice and stay grounded here.

The higher the water rose, the harder it was to calmly stay focused on being present. Too late, she realized much of the peace she found in this place was from her control to shape the look, sounds, and smells. Now, she invited Isis into her safe place and the goddess brought change. When the water got above her knees, she stopped trying to force it back into its pool. Wherever Isis wanted to take her, she agreed to go. Calm was key.

She looked around and saw the water extended far to the left and right. It began to flow. She stood up to keep her head above water. The current quickened and she let it carry her. *Shall it be a river, then?* Treading water proved easy. She looked to shore and saw people in loin cloths harvesting grain, with a sandy desert behind them. The sun shone brightly overhead in a clear blue sky. The goddess had taken Desiree to her own safe place, the Nile. She felt honored and thankful.

The water did not stay calm. The river started rocking her and churning as if it were coursing over boulders on the bottom. It got rougher and she had to swim harder to keep her head up. The eddies and sloshing swamped her a few times. She tried to swim to shore but the river had her in a slipstream. Remain calm. This is an exercise in calm. She had to remind herself to focus only on where she was.

Just as she thought to surrender to her trust in the goddess, a wave tumbled her under. She opened her eyes to find the surface and saw herself dropping her bicycle on the front walk of her parent's house. She heard her mother inside the house and her heart jumped. She flung the screen door open and ran in to find her mother baking cookies. Her mother rarely baked cookies, even when she was home from overseas. Her mother knelt down and opened her arms and Desiree ran into them for a hug.

She popped up, but the water spun her around in its grip and she gasped for a breath. She wanted the happy moment with her mom back. No, she needed to focus on being here. She tried paddling toward shore again.

Another wave caught her from behind and drove her deep under. She twisted around to get her bearings and found herself twisting around in the passenger seat of her father's car, snatching a CD from his hand as he started to put it in the dashboard player. "Deep Purple? Seriously?" she chided him. His knowing smile warmed her heart.

The warmth in her heart reminded her. *Where was Isis in all this turmoil? Was this some kind of test?* She knew questioning the experience was breaking the concentration she needed to keep up. She swam with all her might back up to the air.

She got one breath before her back slammed into a rock in her path. She whirled around under the surface, losing all sense of direction. Stay calm. Ignore the pain. Push out the fear. Just ride with the water. She curled up into a ball and only let herself think about the water all round her. She opened her eyes and found herself standing in the front doorway of her cottage, arms open, welcoming Sanantha to Ireland. The warm hug they shared felt like love. All these visions showed her love. Her mother, her father, her best friend. She may not be safe tumbling randomly through rapids, but she was loved, deeper and wider than this river.

Sanantha's hug felt different. She opened her eyes and she was dry again, curled up on the ground by her calm pool. She looked around. The green grassland around was as pastoral as ever. "Be one with the pond," Brother Renpo had said. She leaned forward onto all fours and crawled to the edge of the water. The green of its depth was fascinating in a whole new way. She leaned forward and saw the reflection - not her reflection, but Isis's. It was her, swinging black braids framing that beautiful olive brown face. Desiree smiled, and of course the reflection did too. "We're really one now, aren't we?" she asked the goddess.

In that moment she realized she was able to focus on whatever she wanted. If she watched Isis's face, she could forget, at will, everything else around her. The sensation was invigorating and shocking at the same time. She knew what to do.

She tipped forward and put her head in the water, then leaned in and let herself tumble into the water.

She opened her eyes and smiled hugely at Brother Renpo. He smiled back knowingly just before he slammed two metal pot lids together between them in a resounding crash.

Desiree saw it coming, expected the sound, and chose not to flinch.

Renpo watched this, then threw the lids to the side and leapt to his feet. "You're there! Praise Buddha, you made it!"

It took her a while to make sense of all the sensations that flooded in on her. She could see every texture of every surface, hear every harmony of every sound, smell every nuance of every odor. More than any of this, she realized she had no sense of where she stopped and any of these things started. She was everywhere in the room and nowhere in particular. Everything seemed to move slowly enough she could see what came next. She tried not to be overwhelmed, but it was too much. Tears welled up in her eyes and spilled over.

"I'm awake," she said breathlessly.

Renpo sat back down. "Yes, for the first time ever, right?"

She nodded, smiled, and cried more hot tears of joy.

"I see you communed with the goddess too."

"She is beautiful and so full of love."

"Your eyes are so dark blue they're nearly black."

"How long does this last?"

"With all the distractions of seeing what *satori* looks like, you will slip out of this heightened state in just a moment. I dropped out as soon as I saw you go inside. While it lasts, remember everything. Know where this state is inside you."

"It's in the pond." She frowned at him and tilted her head. "Brother Renpo, are you feeling well?"

"Yes. What do you see?"

She leaned forward and braced herself on one hand while reaching up to his head. "There is something wrong here. I see a needle stuck in your brain."

"A needle? Do you mean an actual metal needle?"

"I don't think so. I think I can touch it." She saw her fingertips pass right through his skin and felt contact with the sharp metal. She looked deeply at where it was and what it pierced and saw it was not dangerous unless if went a tiny bit deeper.

"Your fingers are actually crackling with *chi* against my skin. What is it?"

"I think it's a trap." She pinched the end and pulled it straight out. It dissolved as soon as it was clear of his scalp. "It's gone now."

"A trap that could hurt me?"

She stared at her empty fingers. "Oh yes. Someone planted it to kill you at some later time."

"A curse? Can Sammael do that?"

She looked up at him. "Who else? Do you recall when he might have planted it?"

Renpo thought for what seemed like far too long. Desiree realized it only seemed that way because she was thinking so quickly. "I had a nightmare about deception. He must have found me." The monk looked back into her eyes and brightened. "It is this level of perception, understanding, and assimilation that will allow you to react faster than even a magical being like Sammael."

25

THE VERY REVEREND DERMOT MARTIN PATRICK DUNNE, Dean of Christ Church Cathedral Dublin, walked up to the altar to retrieve a note he had left there at this morning's services. At first, he thought nothing of the well-dressed man who was walking up the center aisle. There were always parishioners wandering the cathedral. Then he realized the man was not approaching the sanctuary, but rather the black iron trident planted in the floor tiles twenty feet in front of the altar, planted in a fight between angels three days before.

"Excuse me, sir," he called to the man. "Please do not come near that weapon. That Caution tape is there for a reason."

The man's smile would have been charming, if Dean Dunne had not recognized him from the security camera tapes. "Oh, I know it's dangerous."

Dean Dunne stepped quickly to a silver cabinet in the side wall and grabbed a cross and a small pitcher of holy water.

The man stopped next to the four stantions wrapped in yellow police tape and folded his arms, patiently waiting for the priest. "I just came to fetch my spear. Mind you, I am not one to pass up some fun while I'm here."

Dunne pushed his glasses up on his nose and felt perspiration bead up on his high, wide forehead. He did not want to show how nervous he was but realized he probably had already. "If you are who I think you are, you know you are not welcome here. I will defend this sanctuary."

"I am here to take this hazard away. Frankly, I'm surprised it's still here. I expected you would have it under a microscope in some lab by now."

"The Vatican is sending a team of experts this afternoon."

"Surely you would agree we shouldn't leave this sort of thing lying around for mortals to hurt themselves."

"The other angel who defended this church took that away from you."

"Yes, well, Michael isn't here now, is he? In fact, he's in the Pit. We sort of traded places." Sammael walked up to Dunne.

Dunne thrust the cross out at him and cocked his arm back to throw the water. Sammael stepped up, directly but not aggressively, and Dunne hesitated, not sure what came next. "Get behind me, Satan!"

Sammael gently pushed the cross away. "What does that mean, anyway?" He reached up and took the cut crystal pitcher from him. He smiled right into Dunne's face, and drank the water. "You forgot, Dermot, I am an angel. Fallen or not, I exist to serve God. You are in my way."

Dunne held his breath, clenched his jaw, and steeled his stance against the fear that strained to make him run. He glanced up at the half dozen clergy who had stopped in their tracks to watch. He met Sammael's gaze. "You are no angel," he accused quietly face to face.

He let the pitcher fall to the floor and smash to pieces as he stepped back and held his arms up theatrically. "Oh, you prefer the horns and wings and claws? Too bad, so sad. He pumped his fist straight up and everyone else in the church chamber fell flat, three dozen clergy and visitors, their faces pressed to the floor. "Time for little respect. You've let your new post as Dean go to your head,

Dermot." He tightened his other fist and Dunne felt a tremendous weight crush down on him and buckle his knees. "You know the words."

Dunne felt his throat twist inside as if the angel's clutching fingers were wrapped around his trachea.

"The old words are the best."

Dunne felt something push up, trying to get out of his lungs. He felt helpless, like a puppet. He pulled the cross up in front of himself defiantly with both hands, but couldn't make the words he wanted.

"You don't know the old words, do you? Oh, but you used to be a Catholic, so you do know Latin. Shall we, in front of God and country?"

Dunne tried to keep his mouth shut, but could not resist the power surging up. "*In nomine Dei nostri Satanas, Luciferi excelsi.*"

The angel put his hands on his hips and chuckled. "Now that wasn't so hard, was it?"

He walked over to the spear and wrenched it out of the tiles with a one-handed tug. He spun it around like a baton, then snapped it back. It vanished as if it had retracted into his hand. The false smile also vanished. "By the way, get it right. My name is Sammael."

He walked out. The dull click of his shoe heels echoed the length of the chamber until he was gone.

•　　　•　　　•

Benito Nomini walked straight through the main building of the Musées Royaux des Beaux-Arts de Belgique without stopping to admire the dozens of paintings and sculptures on display. He did notice how much had been moved around since his last visit. Several floors up, he found his objective. The locked door on the salon did not slow him down. He flicked open his straight razor and mentally transformed it into a key. "Glad I got you back," he said quietly.

He slipped in the key, opened the door, walked right through the throng of workmen and their forklift, and stepped up to Michel Draguet, the Curator of all the museums within the national galleries. The boldness of his approach was enough to interrupt the conversation Draguet was having with the workmen.

"Benito? My God man, what's it been, ten years?" he asked incredulously in French. "You haven't changed a day."

Benito shook his outstretched hand and responded in the same language. "You are also every bit as handsome and vibrant, my friend."

"What brings you here today?"

He pointed at the back of the winged statue the workmen were moving. "I heard a rumor you were moving my favorite piece. I wanted to make sure you didn't hide it behind anything trendy."

Draguet slapped is hand over his heart. "Mon ami, you wound me with your cynicism. You know I love *L'ange du Mal* every bit as much as you do. No, no, I'm moving it around the corner to the bigger hall where I can finally show it next to Joseph Geffs's *Adonis Allant à la Chasse avec son chien*."

Benito raised an eyebrow. "The Light Adonis next to the Dark Adonis? I like it."

Draguet grinned. "I'm so pleased. Of course, the ultimate pairing would be to reproduce Pierre Langlet's *Salle de Sculpture du Musée de Bruxelles* and put it alongside brother Jean's *Love and Malice*."

"Ah, but that painting is a fiction," Benito chuckled. "*Love and Malice* in in Buckingham Palace."

"Exactly! So how have you been? It has been far too long."

"It has. I was detained with boring obligations, no fun at all, but now I'm back. How about you? Are you still giving your politicians hell?"

"Oh, absolutely. The arts councils do nothing but complain about humidity and preservation, like I know nothing of how to care for fine art. They want me to spend all the money on rebuilding and upgrading everything. They have no vision."

"What do critics know? If Bishop Von Bommel hadn't deemed it too sensual and removed it from St. Paul's Cathedral in Liège, we wouldn't have this beauty with us today."

"Oh, you must not have heard," the museum director touched his arm for emphasis. "Over the last several years I amassed the definitive collection of Magritte works, I built a new showcase museum, and I'm opening it this winter. You must come."

"I wouldn't miss it for the world. Sounds like you've got the tiger by the tail."

"There were times when I wasn't so sure. Now that you're back, I feel the world is once again my oyster. You've given me brilliant counsel many times. I'll be counting on you to help me with my projects going forward."

Benito walked around the front of the sculpture and admired the languid, sensual figure of himself. He fondly remembered young Joseph Geffs and the posing sessions, in spite of having to shave his entire body. "You can count on it."

26

A HALF HOUR BEFORE THE GATE OPENED, Renpo walked the fairgrounds learning potential crowding points and escape routes if the battle went public. He also got to see all the craft merchant booths, the beer and wine alley, the small players stage, and the main event stage. The merchants and the players were all busy getting ready, but they were also chatting with each other in good spirits. They all clearly had done fairs like this before.

He kept up a cheery demeanor when he got a lot of smiles and a few curious frowns as he walked by with his bald head, saffron robes, and sandals. He did his best not to let his worry show. These good folks had no idea what might happen today. He sincerely hoped to keep it that way.

It had rained the night before, and the sky looked like it was going to rain again. The gravel covering the ground kept the mud in check. Grass grew where gravel didn't cover.

He had asked Desiree to join him on his tour, but she said she already knew the map and had to help Sanantha and her staff in the office trailer behind the mainstage.

He made his way around to the front entrance and was surprised to see protestors. They were carrying signs accusing Alec of devil worship. Renpo frowned at the ironic mistake. The devil was trying to ruin the Celtic gods. A couple of them had signs identifying them as Westboro Baptist Church. There were police outside the gate too, keeping the protestors away from the line of folks waiting to come in. Renpo checked the cell phone Desiree had given him. Saturday, October 31, 2009, 9:50AM. *Ten minutes to opening.* He walked back to the trailer office.

A shiny black tour bus pulled up from the back entrance road and parked behind the main stage. The sign over the windshield said, "Garbage". He shook his head. He still had a lot to learn about Western culture.

Renpo walked into the office and watched Sanantha, Desiree, and two other ladies going through papers and making phone calls. He was distracted by Sanantha, as if something was wrong. He checked his breathing and realized he didn't trust her.

Desiree hung up the phone and saw Renpo.

"How's it look out there?"

"Everyone appears ready. It stopped raining. The vendors and the crowds are both looking forward to today. We have religious protestors, but the police are keeping them at bay."

"Yeah, Benito arranged for police protection."

"Also, your band Garbage just arrived in their bus."

Desiree jumped up. "How exciting! I should go welcome them. She started shaking her hips dancing toward the door singing, "Stupid girl ..."

Renpo still did not understand. "I'm not sure I see the connection of the fair to a rock band."

Sanantha looked up and cut in. "Benito says the twenty-something demographic that likes their music is very likely open to reviving their old Celtic heritage. They're also a huge draw."

"Man, I wish my father could come meet them," Desiree said. "He's a huge rock fan."

Renpo couldn't shake this feeling. Every word made him worry more.

Desiree added. "She's Scottish, but they have Celtic roots too." Desiree paused and turned to Sanantha. "I meant to ask you about that. Didn't Shirley Manson say earlier this year that she quit the music business?"

"True, but she is really supportive of cancer research for kids. Her payment to perform is our agreement to donate a third of the gate to her favorite charity the Pablove Foundation."

Renpo realized this meant they weren't looking at hundreds of people at risk, but thousands.

•   •   •

The Archangel Michael strained against his chain to see further down the cavern. He smelled water but could not see its source. Sammael said he escaped by taking Osiris to his underworld. That underworld is built around the subterranean Nile. Could that river be above him now? He could surely find their escape route and follow it, if he could just get free of this rock.

Maybe he could take the rock with him. Sammael wouldn't have thought of that since he wasn't physically strong enough. He materialized his flaming sword and hacked at the ground around he stone, carving away great rooster tails of soil and rock. He was pleased only the anchor stone itself appeared to be magically protected.

He was too busy wailing away to notice he was no longer alone.

"Excuse me," came a quiet woman's voice.

He spun around and watched a frail woman in a white dress float down through the granite ceiling. She wore a wimple shawl and held a bunch of lilies in one hand at her breast. "Well, a saint come to visit me. To whom do I have the pleasure?"

"I am Catherine of Siena," she said as she landed softly.

He bowed slightly. "Of course, how rude of me. Thank you for your work defending Gregory the Eleventh from demons on his return to Rome."

She smiled sweetly. "That wasn't a test, but you passed. I'm not here to visit, although you are as charming as I was told. No, I have something you need. I lucked upon it several days ago. I apologize for taking so long to find you. This place is very secluded."

"It was designed as a prison. I am grateful you came, but how did you get involved with my quest?"

"Alec Doogan asked for my help some time ago."

"Good Catholic boy. And how did you find me?"

"The souls in the Egyptian Land of the Dead above us were dancing to your singing. It was my only clue. You may have added to their legends."

"I sing to clear my head to think. I was singing pretty loudly for the last few days in hopes that someone would hear. So the underworld Nile is up there?"

"Yes, but you will need this to get there." She handed him Osiris' key.

His face lit up. "Saint Catherine, I will see to it that your name is praised in song throughout Heaven." He slipped the key into his shackle and it opened. "Thank you, dear lady!"

•   •   •

Renpo found himself tapping his toe to the catchy tunes Garbage played while he watched the crowd from behind the wing curtains. The crowd knew all the words and sang along to "Stupid Girl", which told the story of a woman who squandered her blessings for attention. Renpo was saddened by the story, but the audience loved it. Ms. Manson's enthusiasm and her band's seamless accompaniment was a joy to watch even apart from the music. Such great teamwork.

He wished he had a team. With Joseph and Michael gone, and Sanantha, Benito, and Alec providing the bait, he and Desiree were on their own. Renpo clutched the cell phone, keeping it ready to call her at the first sign of trouble.

She had trained like a champion this week. With Isis configuring her brain, Desiree could hold onto *satori* for twenty minutes. That was longer than he had ever held it. On the other hand, she could hold *satori* for only twenty minutes.

Ms. Manson thanked the audience for staying even when it started to rain. The weather did not diminish their joy. The band then finished their set with an ironic celebratory rendition of, "I'm Only Happy When It Rains". The crowd cheered wildly. Still no sign of Sammael attacking.

Renpo had also watched carefully earlier in the afternoon when he followed Alec around the fair. He would stop occasionally and perform some small bit of magic, like refilling everyone's drink or erecting an ice sculpture out of the water on the ground. Alec would then answer questions about the Celtic religion and which gods he contacted to do which magic. People in earth-colored robes followed behind and handed out literature promoting their own pagan churches. Everyone seemed to have a great time. Renpo had been sure such a positive conversion would bring Sammael out. It had not.

As the band's stage crew started clearing off their equipment, Renpo realized he was both in their way and on the wrong side of the stage to cover Alec's entrance. He ducked behind the main black backdrop curtain to walk behind.

A man with wavy black hair wearing a brown tweed overcoat crouched down working in an uplifted panel in the stage. Renpo took a step closer and saw he was handling electrical cables. He did not look like one of the stage crew, since they were all wearing black tee shirts. He didn't want to accuse anyone of anything, but this was suspicious. He slipped his hand into the inside pocket of his robe and touched the Pearl.

Recognition hit. "Oh, hello. You must be Mr. Nomini." He stepped closer. "We haven't met. I am Brother Renpo."

Benito stood up and pushed the panel back down with his foot. "Of course you are. So nice to finally meet you."

Benito reached up to shake his hand, when Renpo watched his appearance change. His nose grew longer, his brows grew thicker, his skin grew darker, and his hair grew longer and curlier. "Mara," escaped his astonished lips. He took a step back. "No, Benen the acolyte. No!" he gasped. "Sammael! You were here all along?"

"All of the above," he said with chilling cheeriness. "I'll bet you figured it out with that Pearl thing. I can't very well have you sharing your discovery."

Benito took a step toward him and Renpo drew on his training. He also took two steps back. "I walk in the Buddha's footsteps. You cannot tempt me or sway me from my path."

Benito shook his head and took another step. "I didn't kill Prince Siddhartha, because he would have become a martyr. That hardly applies to you." He twisted his fingers and nothing happened. He looked intently at Renpo and slowly grinned. "That little bitch disarmed it. That's fine, I like the hands-on approach."

Sammael stepped up to him and Renpo leapt back, whirling his arms around to pull his *chi* up defensively. Sammael's body contorted inhumanly, leaving Renpo unsure what he was seeing. When Sammael stood back up, he had transformed into a monstrous, coiled, black snake.

Renpo's heart skipped a beat. He fought frantically to stay focused. Sammael sprung at him and he flinched to one side, but, gripped in fear, he hesitated and couldn't move as fast as he wanted. Renpo moved his *chi* away from where he thought the snake would hit him, but it didn't make contact. It raked its fangs across the space in front of the monk. Renpo thought it had missed, until he felt all the warmth in his chest pulled from him like a robe slipping off. Cold, unbelievable cold. He had not anticipated cold. Sammael landed in human form. Renpo looked up at the archangel in disbelief. It was the last thing he saw before he fell dead.

Sanantha walked up the backstage stairs and saw Benito knelt over Renpo's body. Before she could ask what happened, he pulled his hand away as if something had bitten him.

"What's going on?"

Benito had a panicked look Sanantha had never seen on him. "I think he had a heart attack. I found him back here clutching his chest and then he stopped breathing. I don't know CPR. I didn't know what to do."

She knelt at his other side. "He just now stopped breathing? That's good. Step back." She rolled the monk onto his back and started chest compressions. "Call for help. There's a medic at the office. Tell him what happened, and he can bring a defibrillator."

Benito got up and ran toward the trailer.

"Just call the office!" she yelled, but he kept running.

After two minutes, Renpo was not responding and neither Benito nor the medic came back. "Hey, I could use some help back here!" The heavy curtains absorbed her voice, just as they were designed to do. She considered stopping compressions long enough to pull out her phone and call. "Help!" she tried again. "Can anyone hear me!"

Desiree peaked her head through the curtains from the stage side. "Oh my god, what happened?"

"He had a heart attack. Benito found him and went for help."

Desiree reached into his robes while Sanantha continued her forceful pushing.

"What are you doing?"

"Seeing if that's going to work or not." She pulled out the Pearl. "Ah, Sanantha. You can stop."

"What? He was only out for a minute before I got here."

"I don't know why, but I can tell you his life force is not even here anymore. It's like he's been dead for a while."

"You have an awful lot of faith in that thing," she said disdainfully without stopping.

"Okay, if you think he's retrievable, let me try."

Sanantha did not know what she meant.

Desiree looked at her with raised eyebrows. "Like you did with me in Malaysia when the medic said I was dead."

Sanantha frowned and slowed her rhythm.

"Because I was."

She lifted her hands off, and Desiree put her hands on. "Do you need me to guide you in how to get Erzulie to mount you?"

Desiree smiled at her and her eyes turned a darker shade of blue. Sanantha was shocked.

"Thanks but that won't be necessary."

Sanantha watched with some wonder as Desiree shook her head, then sat up, whirled her arms around and put her hands back on his chest.

"I can feel him there. I just can't get a grip."

She stood up and did a whole body set of moves that ended with her back down over him laying her hands.

"Come on, calmly. Focus. You can do this," Desiree told herself.

Heavy footsteps interrupted them. They turned and saw Michael walking the stage width behind the curtain. His black trousers were intact, but he was wearing a shredded white shirt and only the top half of a gray trench coat. "Nice try," he said with no sarcasm. "Or at least a nice start, but we don't have time for this." He looked down at Renpo and commanded, "*Talya koum!*"

Renpo's body spasmed and his eyes jerked opened.

Sanantha couldn't even find words, and just blinked her astonishment.

Renpo propped himself up on his elbows and looked at everyone fearfully. "Benito is Sammael! The Pearl revealed him to me and he took my life as easily as pulling a scarf off my shoulders." He looked up. "Angel Michael, you're back. Did you raise me? Thank you!"

The tall man nodded. "You're welcome. Yes, Benito is Sammael. He got the drop on me and imprisoned me, but I escaped."

All these words flowed past Sanantha as she started breathing hard and tried to make sense of this. She wanted to refute it, loudly, forcefully. Now both Renpo and Michael said they saw it first-hand. How could this be true? Benito had done nothing but help them. It made no sense.

She noticed Desiree looked panicky too. "Of course. What better way to discredit the Celtic gods than to draw them out into the open yourself?"

Sanantha grabbed her arm. "Why would he do that?"

"The Celtic gods are another remnant of the Egyptian gods, just like the gods of Voodou. In fact, these Celtic pagans are the last big group of people on Earth who believe in what is left of the Egyptians. This is his final play to snuff out the pantheon."

Sanantha took an involuntary step back as she digested this news. She didn't doubt it, but it was all too much to take in. She had slept with the Devil. "No, no, no," she said quietly to herself.

"Oh shit," Desiree sighed. "That means he knows everything about this event — he designed it. He's going to make his move during Alec's big final show. Where is Alec now?"

No one spoke up.

"Does anyone know where Alec is right now?" Her voice scratched with tension.

Renpo stood up. "Desiree, you're letting fear drive you. We need you to reject the fear. We need you right now to focus. This is what you trained for. I can see Isis is active in you already. We need Desiree's focus to use all that power."

She took a couple of breaths and looked him in the eyes.

"You can do this," he stated with no waiver.

"I can do this," she repeated back.

"Go ahead. Take a moment. We can afford a moment while you get ready."

She sat down on her knees and closed her eyes.

Sanantha looked around in case Benito came back. She noticed Michael did he same.

Desiree's breathing slowed. She put her head down. Her breathing slowed further. Sanantha looked closely. It had stopped.

Suddenly she took a breath, lifted her head, and opened her eyes. As she stood up, Sanantha caught a glimpse of her nearly black eyes. She moved rapidly and fluidly, yet she projected an air of complete calm. She picked up the Pearl and turned to Michael. "Battle stations."

27

DESIREE AND MICHAEL RAN TO OPPOSITE WINGS. She heard an announcer's voice, muffled by the heavy draperies, followed by entrance music. She rounded the corner and watched Alec take center stage. The rain had stopped. She surveyed the lights above, the speaker towers, the follow spot booth out in the middle of the crowd. She looked out over the wet crowd and estimated four thousand. No sign of Benito. She caught Michael's eye on the other side of the stage. He shook his head.

"Good evening, fellow Celts and Celtic at heart!" Alec yelled into the standing mic. "Have you had a good time here today?"

The crowd cheered.

"This was fun, right? Great music, great food, and maybe you learned some things about our heritage. Our ancestors worshipped gods and knew nature in ways we have forgotten. Those gods are not dead. They have been waiting patiently for us to rediscover them. I have been lucky enough to bridge that gap, to confer with them, and I am here to tell you they are thrilled to have you back!"

The crowd cheered.

"To show you how glad they are, they have agreed to let me show you some of their power. Now when I perform these incantations, and contact the gods, and they agree to use their power to break the laws of physics, it is only to show you their benevolence. They want you to see how they are here for you.

"Tonight I will call upon the god Ambisagrus, who can control the weather. This spell will include you. You've shown your support by coming out in the rain. Now I'm going to thank you with a gift of comfort."

He set the mic aside and started the dance Desiree had watched via satellite from the Sudanese desert. He made big sweeping arcs with his arms, grasping at the air below and gesturing to the sky above. He muttered incantations while he moved. Desiree could pick them out but wasn't interested in what he was saying.

She heard Renpo and Sanantha step up behind her. In her heightened mindfulness, she heard every footstep of every crew member backstage. She added footfalls to the list of places she checked for signs of Benito. Many of the audience were wearing event tee shirts with Celtic knot work designs. From what Sanantha had told her of Benito's love of fashion, there was no way he would hide in the crowd wearing one of those.

Alec finished with a flourish. The crowd waited quietly to see if he was done. He took the microphone. "This spell takes a moment to build. When I practiced it in the desert, we were really happy with how quickly it takes effect. While we are waiting, I will reproduce a spell you have probably seen on YouTube." A section of the stage slid away and hydraulics lifted a three-foot-high, fifteen-foot-diameter, clear plastic pool of water up to stage level. Desiree could hear the mechanism strain against the weight of the water.

Alec walked over to it carrying the microphone and its stand. "For this spell I call upon the river goddess, Boann." He set the stand aside and began the spinning, hopping dance. Again, he recited an incantation while moving. The water in the pool started sloshing

Jay Hartlove

around in a whirl that lapped over the edge. Alec gestured at the water each time he turned around, and it responded by swirling in a neater, tighter pattern. The center of the water lifted up and the rest of the volume followed. It climbed into a spinning column eight feet high and three feet thick. Alec yelled one last command and thrust his hands out at the water. It froze solid in one second, complete with the cracking sound of the strain of coming to a halt.

The crowd cheered with abandon.

Desiree felt the air pressure change. The air smelled warmer and wetter than it should. She saw something, moisture, rising above the crowd. A moment later, the audience started laughing and cheering as the water in their clothes evaporated and drifted upward.

"Ah, you like that, eh?" Alec said. "That's the storm god taking over."

The moisture accelerated its ascent and in minutes the crowd was nearly dry.

Desiree walked out to him and pulled him aside. "Alec, I need to tell you, Benito is out to sabotage your event. I know that doesn't make much sense, but it's the honest truth. He's going to pull something bad, and it's going to happen any second."

"You're right, that doesn't make sense. The spells are working perfectly. If he was going to sabotage it, he missed his chance."

He turned back to the microphone. "This water is going to float up and away, and harmlessly fall over those far hills."

Desiree felt like her skin was pulling, and her hair was lifting. It wasn't the moisture leaving, it was something more, something she didn't understand at first.

"Alec," she said grabbing his arm. "Electricity."

A bolt of lightning flashed out of the clouds and danced across a section of the audience. Several bodies flew back from the impact and everyone screamed. Two more bolts crackled to the ground, one strafing the audience and the other striking a tall metal lighting standard near the stage. It fell into the crowd, creating a shower of sparks when it hit the ground.

"Oh my God!" Alec yelled. "What can I do?" He repeated a set of moves from the spell while calling out, "Mighty Ambisagrus, hear my

263

plea! Spare these people. They are your loyal followers. They are here to worship you. Do them no harm!"

Another bolt exploded across the backs of several fleeing people.

"What? No!" Alec screamed. "I call on you, Boann, my most trusted guide. Please bring the water back to stop the lightning. Please save your faithful!"

The water continued to rise and Desiree felt the electrical discharge growing again. She could not stand by and watch. "Screw it. This is Samhain, the barriers will be thin."

"What?" he asked in full panic.

"I'll be right back." She opened her right arm and whirled the god *chi* into her hand while pouncing sideways. She brought her hand down and cleaved open a gap while stepping through in one motion.

She stepped out onto a grassy meadow surrounded by low hills. The sky glowed the most beautiful sunset pink she had ever seen. The air smelled of flowers and water and mud and life. Every blade of grass, every leaf on every bush was verdant green.

She knew time flowed much slower here, but she did not have time to waste. "Do not hide from me. I will not be distracted by this idyllic scene you've created. I know you're here. Come out and talk to me."

Bushes and rocks stood up and the trees stretched their limbs. When the leaves fell away, she expected loincloths and beaded necklaces, but they wore furs, tartans and horned headdresses.

"I understand this is how you are now worshipped, but I know who you are. Your worshippers are being killed right now by our ancient enemy. You have abandoned the young magician you empowered. You must show him mercy. Frail men can't be expected to handle such power without guidance and patience. You are wrong to punish him for not being able to handle it with grace. His only fault is hubris. He was seduced by Sammael into sharing your magic with the world. I know you value your secrecy, but you must save the fans who are being killed."

A tall god in a fur stole and a huge sword stepped up to her and peeled off his Celtic visage to reveal his true falcon head. Horus said, "Dear mother, we never aided Alec Doogan."

"What?"

"All the magic he used was given to him by Sammael who crafted it to look like our magic."

Desiree nearly lost her *satori* focus. In her heightened state she made quick work of assimilating this news, but it was still shocking. She realized this was exactly what Sammael had done to the Egyptians 3,200 years ago at the start of her quest.

"We pity your magician friend, but we will not come forward to help him. Over the eons, we have come to see our role is to help or hinder mankind only enough to make sure mankind can exercise free will. Free will is the only thing that keeps chaos and evil at bay. We live by the fourth pillar of discretion."

"Your followers need the other three pillars of strength, assertiveness, and intelligence. Right now, Sammael is blaming us for a catastrophe that will drive people away from us once and for all. We will vanish into history with no followers and no hope of ever returning. If you will not help me stop him, at least give me Joseph back so he can help me."

An extremely broad-shouldered god with a pointed beard and goat's ears walked up. He grew taller and thinner, his beard pulled out into a long snout, and his ears elongated and became squared. She felt Isis hold back a long-standing revulsion at her brother-in-law, the murderer of her husband.

"Set! Your Celtic incarnation Ambisagrus is who they are blaming for the fiasco. You're in this whether you like it or not. You must let me have Joseph so I can make this right."

"Joseph is mine. He never finished his sentence after your champion stole him from his duly assigned incarceration."

At this point Desiree was letting Isis run the show. Left to her own, Desiree imagined she would not stand up to these gods so forcefully. "His transgression was exceeding his position as a servant of the gods. His servitude to me is fulfilling his position."

The tall god tilted his mule-like head in clear distain. "You are using him to further your revenge plans that we do not condone."

"Hold that against me, if you will. I am saving you from oblivion. Don't hold my tasks against Joseph."

"You can have him if he remains your servant. If he really is your servant, then you must know his true name. What is it?"

"Bring him forward and I will name him."

Set gestured and one of the rocks stood up and became Joseph. Joseph brightened when he saw Desiree, but then kept his eyes down when he stepped up.

Desiree slipped her hand into her jacket pocket and held the Pearl while looking at him. She nearly gasped when the totality of Joseph's life suddenly became known to her. Thousands of years of servitude, often trying to do the right thing without having enough information, being bound in utter darkness where his sight could do him no good, she had no idea what a tragic figure he was.

"Tancellus the Unblind."

Joseph's smile crept back into the corners of his mouth while he continued to look down.

Set snorted. "Good enough. Finish your quest so we can all return to living in peace."

She met his gaze with an honest, "Thank you." She took Joseph's hand and cleaved her way back into the real world.

As she had hoped, they stepped onto the stage only seconds after she left.

Alec jumped back at their appearance. "Whoa. Can he help?"

"He can help stop the source." Then to Joseph, she said, "Benito is Sammael. He was hiding right under our noses."

"What?" Alec gasped.

"That would explain why he avoided crossing my path," Joseph said. "I would have recognized him. Do we know where he is right now?"

"No. I've got Michael looking for him too."

The ice column cracked loudly, then all at once turned back into water. The water fell into the clear plastic pool and split it open.

Desiree calculated the water's path and saw it was going to run across the fallen light standard and electrocute a hundred people standing in front of the stage. "Joseph, stop the water."

She saw him look at the light pole and make the same calculation. He vanished in a black cloud of smoke, only to reappear the same instant fifty feet out in the audience off to one side. He whipped off his sunglasses and fired an arc of brilliant white light from his eyes across the bouncing wave of water, lifting it back and shattering it loudly with the sound of surf pounding, spraying it across the stage and into the audience away from the fallen pole.

The crowd was horrified and amazed at the same time. Some ran while others were frozen in indecision. Desiree grabbed Alec to hustle him off stage.

A huge cloud of black smoke erupted from beneath the stage. It quickly formed into a figure with a beard and goat's ears, thirty feet tall. It raised its arms out menacingly. "I am Ambisagrus, your God of Thunder, and I have taken my tribute sacrifice." The voice that boomed out of the stage speakers was just as terrifying as the smoke figure itself. "But I am always hungry for more! Come to me and I will deliver you too from this earthly hell into heavenly paradise!" The crowd turned and ran screaming in panic.

Joseph teleported to Desiree's side. "I can't see into the system to find where he has a microphone," Joseph said frustrated.

"I can hear him," Desiree said closing her eyes. Now she understood. This was *ting jing* — the listening energy Renpo had told her about.

The voice burst into maniacal laughter.

Desiree opened her eyes and pointed behind them. "He's behind the stage by the tour bus."

Joseph vanished in a sulfurous cloud of black smoke.

He materialized where he sensed there was a clear space. He did not know where anything was behind the stage, so he made his best guess. He landed near a couple of trailers and saw a black tour bus fifty yards away. Sammael was alongside the bus standing among stacks of speakers and musical instruments, holding a microphone. He looked up and saw Joseph. Joseph did not have a clear shot, so he teleported to get closer.

He started to materialize next to the demon, but his landing space was suddenly filled with an explosive fire. He looked at where he knew Sammael would be, and watched him take a step to the side and vanish. Joseph couldn't pull himself together in the explosion and had to abandon the teleport. He returned to where he had been.

Sammael didn't go far. Joseph spotted him beside the office trailer. Sammael met his gaze. He took his glasses off to take the shot, and Sammael spun his arm around gathering a counterattacking spell. Joseph fired. The bolt lanced straight at him, but he couldn't see if it hit because the entire field between them burst into flames, ten feet high. He could see through ordinary fire, but not this hell-borne inferno.

Joseph saw the door on the tour bus start to open above the tops of the flames and he slammed it shut with another bolt. He still could not see Sammael.

The powerful stench of sulfur didn't bother Joseph, his teleportation created the same smell. The roar of the flames, on the other hand, masked Sammael's movements further.

A massive scimitar swung out of the fire, it's whistling sound buried in the roar. His vision saved him though, as he saw the air change direction as it approached. He deflected it with his arm and the blade shredded the length of his gray suit coat, leaving a long bloody slice. He fired where he had to be and Sammael jumped, tumbling out of the wall of flames.

He came up swinging the sword again. He held a silver cape or net in his other hand. Joseph ducked the sword arc and fired again. Sammael swung the net around and the silver material dispersed his bolt harmlessly into a hundred white lines.

Joseph glanced at his bleeding arm and saw it was not a magical wound. He also saw the truth of Sammael's wounds under his clothes, a slash across his chest and a bullet hole in his shoulder. The slash looked supernatural in origin, but it was an ordinary bullet hole. He had not healed it.

Sammael swung the sword around again, Joseph raised his left arm and let the sword cleave into his rib cage before he clamped down on it with his left arm. It hurt, but he had recovered from worse. As Sammael watched in surprise, Joseph stepped into him and grabbed the net with his free hand. He fired.

The point-blank full-face blast sent Sammael flying back tumbling over the flames twenty feet in the air, his clothes shattered away from him in a spray of fabric.

Joseph had to take a moment to draw the sword out of his own chest. His gambit had worked, but he couldn't continue the fight until he took a moment to force his body to heal. *Just a few seconds*, he thought.

The flames parted away from him as Michael walked up behind and passed him. The fire peeled back like a parting of waves as the tall blonde angel marched after their adversary. Michael waved his hands from side to side and more of the flames went out. Joseph watched closely for any signs, ready to back Michael up.

A writhing mass leapt out of the last of the flames and wrapped itself instantly around Michael. A dozen giant snakes held his arms pinned and tried to topple him from his feet. Joseph didn't have the energy to teleport to his aid, so he started to run, holding his chest shut with both arms while he mentally knitted it back together.

The fire finally receded back, and with it the deafening roar, to expose Sammael laughing. He looked wounded from Joseph's blast, wearing only shreds of his shirt, but undeterred in his joy at having immobilized his greatest enemy.

In that distracted instant, a woman ran up behind Sammael.

She was dressed in a blue business skirt suit and had a blonde ponytail. To Joseph's surprise, and Sammael's too, she tackled him, flipped him onto his face in the mud, and handcuffed him all in one motion. "Gotcha, ya varmint!" she cursed under her breath.

Joseph ran over while she arrested him. "Benito Nomini, you are under arrest for terrorism and murder, both today here in Ireland and in Washington D.C. in 2001."

"You can't possibly hold me with those!" Sammael spat. She had him pinned with a knee in his back, so he yanked on the cuffs where he lay. They held.

Sammael was shocked; Joseph was impressed. Michael, behind Joseph, started laughing. Joseph looked back and saw him cleaving and shrugging off the snakes with his invisible shield wings.

Jill yanked him up onto his feet. Sammael looked to Michael who approached. "These can't hold me!" he seethed. "She isn't even a believer!"

Michael stepped in with a pair of heavy gold cuffs. "They can for long enough. Agent Bitterman's faith in her principals is what is holding you. Excuse me Agent, these will work much better."

She stepped aside and Michael clamped his bands on Sammael's arms.

"There's no keyhole," she commented.

Michael winked. "Custom made."

Joseph saw her look over Michael's now bare, heavily muscled torso. "Nice six pack, Agent."

"Thank you for making the arrest. I think you will agree that Interpol should take him into custody, since he has now committed crimes on two continents, and we have facilities here."

She twisted her face around at him in curious doubt. Clearly she knew there was more going on here. Joseph expected her to object or ask questions, but she just looked from Michael to Sammael to Joseph.

28

DESIREE STORMED DOWN THE BACKSTAGE STAIRS and walked right up to Sammael while Michael held him by his arms behind him. Sanantha followed three paces behind her.

"Nice eye color, Your Highness," Sammael said sarcastically.

She handed the Pearl to Sanantha and got up in his face. "Nebwenenef!" she hissed.

Benito laughed out loud, a great belly laugh, for a long time. "I haven't heard that name in a long time!"

"That isn't really your name, 'He who shall not be named.' I know your real name. My champion found it for me eight years ago."

"Your Highness," Joseph cut in.

"Yes, I know better than to utter it and give him power. I've waited thirty two hundred years for this moment. I reincarnated Royarna because I thought he could catch you, and he did! But you were too slick to stay caught. So I manifested. I thought it only appropriate that I take over the body of one of your victims of evil.

"I knew you couldn't resist the chance to discredit my pantheon once and for all. By stepping into the light, you revealed yourself to be the true murderer of the Druids six hundred years ago — something you managed to keep hidden even from Heaven. I had to pull in help from faiths all over the world, go up against my own kind, risk using our true identities as bait. I had to deceive my friends, but today I have justice. Your reign of terror ends now. Your God threw you out of Heaven. I can't wait to see what He's going to do to you this time."

"Are you done?" he said calmly. "Now that mankind no longer trusts your remaining Celtic shadow selves, your entire pantheon is about to run out of power and dissipate. I have already won.

"That furious, terrified crowd you hear out there is about to tear your fair to the ground and tell the whole world to abandon you. Your fellow gods won't help you. They've given up. They're already as good as dead. You always were the naïve trusting one."

Desiree saw what he was doing and chose to not let herself get upset. She was glad she was still in *satori* and had such self-control. "You don't get to claim this was all according to your plan. You got caught because you were so petty you couldn't resist trying to wipe out my family. I set this trap and you took the bait."

Desiree saw a cold force coalesce in his chest as he spoke. He was up to something.

"Tell me," Sammael said calmly. "Is there any part of your original human self still alive, or did you entirely die in Malaysia?"

She watched the cold roll up into his second chakra, his voice. She tapped her own *chi* and let it roll down into her arms.

"To that scrap of humanity still within you, I have only one thing to say."

She didn't know what he was going to do, but she could not afford to wait and find out. If he was going to throw *chi*, then she had to neutralize it. Renpo showed her this — this *hua jing*. She spun her hands around as fast as she could and flung her energy out.

It was not a moment too soon. The burst of *chi* left her palms just as the words left his mouth. "Drop dead."

Her wave of heat crashed into the freezing blast of his words and audibly shattered them. Everyone watching gasped, even Michael.

272

Sammael squinted down over flared nostrils and said nothing.

"Been there, done that, got the tee shirt."

Sanantha had been breathing harder and harder, working up her anger. Desiree also saw fear in Sanantha's unsure, darting eyes. She stepped up and struggled to put it into words, but could only manage, "You!"

Benito looked at her dubiously. "Am I the first man to break your heart by not telling you his whole agenda?"

Sanantha was left speechless as his barb hit home. She glared at him and said nothing more.

Desiree wasn't sure what, if anything, she could say to help her friend. She wanted to assure her that at least the danger had passed with his capture, but realized she was going to have to live with this for a long time.

"Spite is my garden," he said softly to her.

Desiree, with her eyes still nearly black, tilted her head and regarded him. "It is, isn't it? You feed on people's hate and their need for revenge." She reached up and carved the air with her fingers and left a bright glowing golden line, curved and jagged, hanging in the air in front of Benito.

"No, you can't," he seethed and pulled at his bindings.

When she completed the symbol, she wrapped her hands around it and held it.

"You can't!" he pleaded.

She smiled when she realized this is what Osiris meant when he said she could change fate. She pulled the symbol to her breast, embraced it, and it dissolved. "I am a god."

"After all I've done to you, you cannot forgive me!"

"I already have."

Benito slumped in Michael's grasp, the fight visibly gone out of him.

Michael grinned his most disturbing smile and spoke softly into Sammael's ear. "That means He doesn't have to."

The crowd out in front of the stage roared anew.

"I've got to convince them this was your doing and not Alec contacting the Celtic gods," Desiree said.

Michael flashed that disconcerting smile Desiree did not like. "You're on your own trying to prove anything to an angry mob." He turned to Jill. "I apologize for the deception."

"Did I just collar the Devil?"

"You did. Congratulations. I assure you, he will receive judgment and justice, just not here on Earth. Thank you very much for all your help."

Michael reached into his pants pocket and produced a set of car keys. "Joseph, you said you liked the car." He tossed them to him.

"Now if you will all excuse me, I have an appointment."

He materialized his enormous white feathered wings, spread them to their full width, looked to the heavens, and vanished with Sammael in a rainbow flash of light.

29

A S SHE RAN FOR THE STAGE, Desiree felt Isis fade away from her. She could not hold *satori* by herself and she slipped out of her heightened state. The world suddenly grew beyond her grasp and her senses seemed to dull almost to the point of failure. It was like she was suddenly in a fog covered in thick wool. She was sorry to see the goddess go, but realized with Sammael forgiven and sent to God for punishment, Isis's quest was over.

Desiree's work was not. She was not going to let Sammael's deception destroy the old gods. She was not going to let him win his last gambit.

Alec had stayed behind on the stage, too shocked by the destruction, wondering what he could do. She flung through the multiple curtains, looking for him. She got all the way through to the stage, just in time to watch him collapse. Fair security was holding the crowd back from climbing up onto the stage. She ran to him and scooped up his head.

"The paper seal," he said weakly. "He cursed me with the Lazarus Gospel."

"Where does it hurt? What can I do?"

His eyes rolled up.

"Alec! Stay with me." She fumbled for the Pearl and remembered she had handed it to Sanantha. She laid her hands on his chest, took a breath to calm herself, and opened her mind to feel what was wrong. She only felt cold. Dead cold.

She reached deep to find whatever god *chi* she might still have. She felt the familiar warmth in her heart, even if a lot less than she had moments ago. She opened her arms, spun them around and smacked down on his chest.

"Holy Isis, please do not leave me now. Please do not abandon this poor soul you and I tricked into drawing Sammael out. He did his part. Please don't let him die at your enemy's hand."

She felt the heat reignite in her chest. "Yes!" She let it all flow through her hands into his chest. "Come on, Alec! What was Michael's command? *Talya koum!*"

Nothing.

Joseph materialized behind her. "He's not just dead. He's cursed."

"How do we break the curse?"

"It's a death spell. Your power should be enough to break it," he said pointing at Alec's neck.

"Break what? I don't see anything!"

"Oh, that's a problem. I can see it but I can't break it."

Sanantha ran up, breathing hard.

Joseph told her, "Press the Pearl up against her back while she works on reviving him."

Sanantha did so. She grinned at Joseph. "Just like old times, eh?"

"Oh my God, it's hideous!" Desiree grabbed at the black snake that coiled around Alec's neck and chest, but her hands passed harmlessly through it. It turned up at her and hissed viciously. She summoned a huge dose of her *chi* into her hands and tried again. "I can't touch the damn thing!"

Renpo, whom Desiree had not even noticed, quietly walked up and reached into Alec's pants pocket. "He covers his hands with the fluid when he does his magic." He pulled out a glass vial, opened it, and spilled the yellow, pungently flowery liquid all over her hands.

She grabbed again and got a grip. She pried up its head, fighting against its muscular writhing.

It coiled its body tighter around Alec's torso.

"No you don't!" She got both hands around its neck and twisted with all her might. It snapped and dissolved into black smoke. She immediately drew on her *chi* again.

Before she could slam her hands down, white shafts of light shot out of her palms, five from each hand. A crown of twelve more rays erupted from around her head. She looked up at her friends' astonished expressions. "Can you guys see this?"

Joseph smiled widely. It wasn't a good look for him. "It is your true self."

Sanantha dropped to her knees. "Holy Matrisse," she said in awe.

"Wow," is all Desiree could say. She pressed her hands down on Alec's chest.

He coughed and drew in a sudden loud deep breath.

The crowd watching from in front of the stage also drew in a loud breath, of amazement.

Sanantha helped Alec sit up. "How are you doing?"

He coughed a few times, then looked around. "I thought I was gone."

"I think you were."

Desiree stood up and noticed the audience pushed up to the stage, watching her with wide-eyed wonder. She looked passed them at the bodies strewn on the lawn and the loved ones grieving over them. A wave of sadness and compassion washed over her. She looked down at her illuminated hands. She remembered how Isis had given the High Priestess in ancient Giza these same rays. She also remembered how Isis had looked back up at her from the pond reflection with a look of infinite love. She thanked the goddess with all her heart. She walked to the stairs at one end of the stage and stepped down into the mosh pit. The security crew hesitated to let her pass. The onlookers were astonished, not hostile. The guards made her a path, and the crowd parted for her as she walked to the nearest fallen patron.

She knelt over the young man. She studied his still features and imaged what he looked like alive and happy. She touched her fingers in the mud, and then placed them on his forehead. "Into water you perished, and from water you are reborn."

He gasped back to life. His girlfriend squealed her overwhelmed surprise and joy. The girl lifted his shoulders and hugged him while he looked around dazed. The kneeling young woman looked up at Desiree with tears streaming down her face.

"Thank you."

Desiree moved to the next victim, a young woman in a faire tee shirt. Her boyfriend stood up and blocked Desiree.

"I vanquished the evil one who caused this," she told him. "He tricked us all. He is now gone, and you are safe again. Let me set this right."

"How do we know you aren't down here to finish the job and turn these people into your zombies?"

A crew of emergency medics ran up and examined the man Desiree had revived.

She pointed. "Ask them. I am only putting right what my enemy made wrong."

The medics nodded. "He's in good shape," one of them said. "He'll have a scar where the lightning hit him, but he looks fine otherwise."

The defensive young man waivered.

Desiree took his hand. "I love her too. Let me help."

He stepped aside and she repeated her prayer and revival.

He helped his girlfriend up and hugged her. The revived woman looked at Desiree with a love that reminded Desiree of the love she felt when she was tumbling in the river of her mind. A deep, pure love. Desiree returned the look.

The medics came over and checked out the woman.

After the fifth or sixth person she revived, the victim's loved ones started calling her over so she didn't miss their fallen. The revived started following her and the medics, watching in amazement.

Sanantha, Joseph, Alec, and Renpo watched this spectacle from the stage. The joy of the following crowd grew with its size.

"You know," observed Sanantha, "if our religion is to have a revival, it is better to have a savior than another martyr."

Alec laughed, "I'll second that, considering I was almost the martyr."

Joseph agreed. "Winning over hearts is a better way to bring back the glory of the Neters than by superior might, which was my old master's plan."

"I hope the Neters welcome the attention this revival will bring," Alec said. "The gods did not want Isis to do this and they have grown to like being in the background."

Renpo spoke up. "Ms. Desiree's ministry is based on revealing the truth, which was the Buddha's mission." He folded his arms and nodded. "Maitreya turned out to be a woman." He looked down the line of them standing together. "You realize we only defeated the Devil by working together. Isis brought us here from the corners of the Earth, but it was us setting aside our differences that let us succeed. Maybe this is what is takes to defeat evil in the world."

30

S ANANTHA FELT WEAK AND NAUSEATED as Renpo's comment reminded her of her part in this drama. She had been seduced by the Devil. She still found it hard to believe. Holding back tears, she leaned closer to Joseph next to her and whispered, "Can you please tell me if I am pregnant?"

He gave her a mildly shocked look. He looked her up and down, then shook his head no.

She let out a relieved breath. It was still all too much. She sat down and started to quietly cry.

Could she ever trust her own judgment again? How could she have not seen what Sammael was doing? Her shield against adversity had always been to be the most informed, most sane voice in the room. Not anymore. How could she ever ask Desiree to forgive her? Desiree had tried to warn her, and she had dismissed her out of hand. She feared she had broken their friendship.

Joseph and Alec on either side of her knelt down and put a hand on her shoulder. Neither of them said anything. She was further embarrassed when she saw in their eyes they knew exactly why she was crying.

Sanantha noticed the rays of light out in the crowd had gone out. She guessed Desiree finished bringing all the lightning victims back to life. She made her way across the field back to the stage. Her adoring fans followed closely.

As Desiree approached, Sanantha saw she was walking with someone, holding his hand. When Desiree climbed the stair, Sanantha saw it was Simon Herrera.

Her anger welled up right where it had left off. She stopped herself. A lot had happened since then. Sammael's words still rang in her ears. 'Spite is my garden.' Could she afford to be spiteful after hearing that?

"Look who I found in the audience," Desiree announced. "He wasn't going to come up because he wasn't sure he would be welcome."

He walked straight to Sanantha, ignoring the others standing by, and squatted down in front of her. "Are you all right? I was really afraid for you up here."

Sanantha was feeling too weak to get up. "Afraid for me? You were in the lightning strike field. You could have been killed."

"No big deal," he chuckled. "Desiree would have brought me back." He looked her in the eyes. "I owe you an apology. I am sorry I did not ask you to marry me the very first time it came up. I never stopped loving you. My love for you was such a given for me, I took your love for granted. That was a terrible mistake."

"Thank you for saying so." She took a long, slow breath. "I owe you an apology too. I was not faithful to you. I let myself be seduced. I welcomed it. I'm sorry I did not listen to you when you came to warn me. I can't imagine how you would want me. I've been tarnished by the Devil. I feel violated and guilty."

He took her hands in his. "Sanantha, how could you not be seduced? He was the Devil. You're human. You didn't stand a chance. If you must feel forgiven, I forgive you, utterly and completely. I love you no less for it."

Sanantha looked down. As good as this was to hear, it would take a long time before she could forgive herself.

He stood up and tugged her hands to stand. He reached into his pants pocket and handed her a small velvet box. "If it's not too late, can you forgive me?"

She took the box but did not open it. She sniffled and wiped her tears. "Um, you're still married."

"No, I am not. I filed the papers and the divorce is final."

"You didn't know I would say yes."

"I had faith."

She opened the box. The diamond ring was perfect.

"Will you marry me?"

This was all too much, but knowing Simon would be there for her made it seem possible. She fell into his arms. "Absolutely."

Desiree watched with a face-stretching smile. She turned to Alec. "Who is Ashera?"

He blinked. "The ancient Hebrews, long before Exodus, believed Yahweh had a wife who was the feminine god. With the rise of monotheism, Yahweh became God, and Ashera was dismissed as a bad foreign influence." Alec looked at her as if he expected her to explain why she had asked.

She mulled over his answer. "I still don't know what I have opened myself for. Am I Isis, Erzulie, Airmid, Guanyin, Maitreya, or Ashera? And what happened to Desiree?"

Desiree heard a woman's footsteps walk up behind them. "Oh, hello, Agent Bitterman. Have you been watching this whole affair?"

"Oh yes. I figured if I watched quietly for long enough, I would be able to make sense of it. Sounds like y'all are in the same pickle."

"I know I'll be replaying it in my head, trying to make sense of it," Alec added.

"I just got an email from my boss congratulating me on the arrest. It seems Agent Archibald," she paused for emphasis, "took the liberty of filing an Interpol booking report for Benito Nomini.

"That leaves me in an interesting position." Jill pulled her ponytail hairband out and let her shoulder length blonde hair fall loose. "Just the other day I was reading the part of the Bible that talks about how Herod told the Magi to report back to him after they found the baby Jesus. They didn't. If they had, the whole story would have turned out very differently."

Desiree got a little worried about where the member of law enforcement was going with this story.

"When I read that, I asked myself how I would have handled it if I had been in their sandals. Would I disobey the king and refuse to report if I thought it would give a good start a chance to succeed? I guess I get to answer that question for myself after all."

The cloud above them started to drizzle its water back down. Desiree recalled how Sanantha had said it rained when Charles Redmond died in her arms. That was an ending. This was a beginning, one Agent Bitterman was apparently willing to let succeed.

Desiree was grateful the soul Isis had given her came with a connection to the goddess. She was happy Isis could rest now that her long quest was done. She was happy to use her gift to make sure people never forgot the gods.

She walked to the front of the stage, oblivious to the rain, and sat down with her legs over the edge. Some of the victims and their families peppered her with questions, while others stood by looking at her adoringly. She might not understand the details of who she was, but she knew why she was here. She was here for them.

ABOUT THE AUTHOR

Jay Hartlove is the award-winning author of the urban fantasy "Goddess Rising" trilogy (*Goddess Chosen, Goddess Daughter,* and *Goddess Rising*) and the fantasy romance *Mermaid Steel*. He is also the playwright, director and producer of *The Mirror's Revenge*, the musical sequel to the "Snow White" fable, which had its theatrical run in the San Francisco Bay Area in August 2018 to rave reviews.

His stories are filled with conspiracies and the supernatural, gods, dreams, angels, and hidden connections. His creative motto is "Dark Secrets Revealed". He loves to take stories where the reader does not expect, with sympathetic villains, heroes with very dark pasts, and lots of plot twists. He was selected as one of the "50 Authors You Should Be Reading" by *The Authors Show*.

Jay is a former competitive costumer, having won Best in Show at both San Diego ComicCon and WorldCon. You can read more about Jay's creative adventures, including much of the research he put into his books, at *jaywrites.com*.

YOU MIGHT ALSO ENJOY

GODDESS CHOSEN

Book One of the *Goddess Rising* Series

by Jay Hartlove

The man who would beat the devil isn't a hero,
but a ruthless madman.

GODDESS DAUGHTER

Book Two of the *Goddess Rising* Series

by Jay Hartlove

How far can you genetically alter someone before she
becomes someone else ... before she loses her soul?

THE STORK

A Shelby McDougall Mystery

by Nancy Wood

Shelby McDougall's past is behind her.
Almost.

Available from Paper Angel Press in
hardcover, trade paperback, digital, and audio editions
paperangelpress.com